Doing It
the
Hard
Way

BEDTIME, PLAYTIME by Jaid Black, Sherri L. King, & Ruth D. Kerce

HURTS SO GOOD by Gail Faulkner, Lisa Renee Jones, & Sahara Kelly

LOVER FROM ANOTHER WORLD by Rachel Carrington,
Elizabeth Jewell, & Shiloh Walker

FEVER-HOT DREAMS by Sherri L. King, Jaci Burton,
& Samantha Winston

TAMING HIM by Kimberly Dean, Summer Devon, & Michelle M. Pillow

ALL SHE WANTS by Jaid Black, Dominique Adair, & Shiloh Walker

Doing It
the
Hard
Way

T. J. MICHAELS

SHILOH WALKER

MADISON HAYES

POCKET BOOKS
New York   London   Toronto   Sydney

Pocket Books
A Division of Simon & Schuster, Inc.
1230 Avenue of the Americas
New York, NY 10020

Copyright © 2009 by Ellora's Cave Publishing, Inc.
Jaguar's Rule copyright © 2006 by T. J. Michaels
One Night with You copyright © 2007 by Shiloh Walker
Miss October copyright © 2006 by Madison Hayes

First Pocket Books trade paperback edition February 2009

POCKET and colophon are registered trademarks of Simon & Schuster, Inc.

For information about special discounts for bulk purchases, please contact Simon & Schuster Special Sales at 1-800-456-6798 or business@simonandschuster.com

Manufactured in the United States of America

10   9   8   7   6   5   4   3   2   1

Library of Congress Cataloging-in-Publication Data

Doing it the hard way / T. J. Michaels, Shiloh Walker, Madison Hayes.—1st Pocket Books trade pbk. ed.
    p. cm.—(Ellora's Cave anthologies)
1. Erotic stories, American. I. Michaels, T. J. Jaguar's rule. II. Walker, Shiloh. One night with you. III. Hayes, Madison. Miss October.
  PS648.E7D656 2009
  813'.60803538—dc222008024072

ISBN-13: 978-1-4165-7826-0
ISBN-10:   1-4165-7826-9

Contents

Jaguar's Rule

T. J. MICHAELS

To Tam and Mike, thank you for your wonderful ideas and such marvelous experiments with dinner so I could write. My mom, Loretha, who encouraged Reya to take a chance. My critique partner, Diana Rubino, for not blowing my hair back when I forgot to spellcheck! And last, but definitely not least, my editor, Lesia, who graciously gave me the last three hairs on her head in exchange for a wooden spoon and the metal bucket over my head!

Prologue

ayday, Mayday, Mayday! This is Gulfwing Foxtrot X-Ray Miami Miami. Position approximately one hundred miles west of Belize City. Dropping altitude from thirty thousand to eight thousand feet. Speed, four hundred twenty-nine miles per hour. Throttling back. Heading unknown. Struck by lightning, fire on left engine. Some instruments offline. Ditching aircraft. One person on board. Gulfwing Foxtrot X-Ray Miami Miami, over!"

"Mayday, Gulfwing Foxtrot X-Ray Miami Miami. This is air traffic control at BZE Goldson International in Belize City. Your position is approximately forty-two miles west of Dangriga Airstrip. Will alert them of your emergency."

"Roger that, BZE, but I don't think I'm going to make it. I . . ."

Static.

"Come in, Gulfwing Foxtrot X-Ray Miami Miami. Mayday, Gulfwing Foxtrot X-Ray Miami Miami, please respond."

Silence.

One

The big male swatted at the female's head but missed. She'd eluded his huge paw, jumped to the side of the unconscious human lying facedown on the ground, his blood mingling with the wet grass. The female crouched again, ready to spring and prepared to fight for the human. He didn't doubt he could take her, but the set of her powerful shoulders and the gleam of the moonlight off her bared canines made him think twice. He'd seen this particular female before, often out in the jungle. None of the other males ever approached her. Perhaps she was a formidable foe?

But he wasn't just another male. He was a prime of his species, a jaguar, a fully grown *panthera onca* who always got what he wanted. He decided he wanted her.

She thought he was after the body she guarded. Good, let her. He would back off for now, taking the opportunity she'd unknowingly given him to watch her closely and see just what kind of female he was dealing with. But he had no doubt that in the end, she would find herself underneath him while he thrust with powerful strokes into her body. Oh yes, she would yield. He would see to it. And perhaps afterward, he would keep her.

∞

Uhhnnn, owww. Aaron was sure someone had split his head open
and used a metal baseball bat to work sand into the wound. And
those voices! God, why wouldn't they just shut up? The buzz over-
laying the words of whoever needed to shut up drilled through
his brain.

Each breath sucked into his lungs felt shallow, as if he couldn't
drag in enough air, and every breath out left behind a tight burning sensation. Why couldn't he take a deep breath and hold it?
Pain this intense could only mean one thing—he was dying.

The voices were louder now. Damn it. Ready to glare at the
people talking when his head pounded like a drum at a rock con-
cert, he was somewhat surprised at the gritty feel behind his lids
as he forced them open. He blinked then blinked again, but the
blurry images wouldn't clear. They just moved back and forth in
the dimly lit room. The sound of a million cawing birds filled his
ears, and the sweet scent of wet grass floated on a cooling breeze
across his skin. His *bare* skin. Did they have bare skin in the hereafter?

He blinked a few more times, wincing as the side of his head
exploded with a new round of pain. And who was the bearded old
man leaning close to his face? He wanted to lift his hand to smack
the man and tell him to back up a bit. The garlic on his breath
made Aaron's stomach lurch but the pounding in his head was so
fierce, just the thought of blowing chunks made him grit his teeth
to hold back the bile while the vein in his forehead threatened to
burst. The old man was speaking. What? Sounded something like
mud, or blood, or . . . he just couldn't make it out, his thoughts

were too scrambled. Oblivion had been pretty sweet compared to this. Perhaps he could slip back into it?

But not before he caught a glimpse of the angel standing just behind the garlicky old man. Now he remembered, sort of. Lightning. His plane had gone down in the jungle after the engine under the left wing caught fire. The image was blurry but he knew an angel when he saw one. Was she here to take him to heaven? He was sure he'd done at least a few good deeds to warrant making it through the pearly gates.

This angel had milk chocolate skin and a set of piercing, almond-shaped, light gray eyes that made his pulse skip a beat or two. And her hair, a shoulder-length mane any woman would kill for. Thick and curly, it hit her shoulders at the perfect length and made his fingers want to reach out and touch the silky black-assin tresses before he floated away to the hereafter. The image of his angel wavered.

"Wait! Come back, beautiful! Can't we spend some time? Maybe talk awhile before I leave this plane?" Could she hear his urgent whispers? Of course she could, all supernatural beings had great hearing. So why didn't she respond? Instead, she just looked at him with a strange mix of pity and irritation. What the hell kind of angel was she anyway? She was supposed to be smiling at him, preparing him for his journey. Well, she obviously wasn't interested in doing her job. Maybe if he lodged a formal complaint with God, she'd get fired.

The garlic master was back. His stomach lurched. *Damn it, old man*, he shouted in his head, and immediately regretted the ferocity of his thoughts. Now his neck, shoulders and ribs joined his head, pounding relentlessly against his skin from the inside out.

The older man stuck him on the top of his hand with something and the beauty faded away fast, but not before he got a
good glimpse of the swell of the angel's breasts and the curve of
her shoulders. Since when did cherubs wear tank tops? It sure
looked good on her. And how could he be in so much pain and
still manage to achieve a hard-on? *Damn, she's sexy*, he smirked at
himself as his eyelids fluttered closed. Hell, even in his state of
impending death, he was thinking with his cock instead of his
brain.

I'm no better than the half-assed angel, he thought as sleep claimed
him.

Reya followed Dr. Matons out of her bedroom and closed the
door with a quiet snap. After brewing herself a cup of tea, she
joined her old friend out on the screened veranda and plopped
down in her favorite plastic patio chair. The smell of the passing
storm was heavy in the air, along with the scent of charred wood
and jet fuel. In spite of the evening's hair-raising events, she was
calm and determined.

Vanilla and clove scented smoke floated up from Dr. Matons's
pipe. She should have never asked her aunt Sulu to send the stuff.
Now the old curmudgeon would never again settle for the local
tobaccos.

"Well, our little patient was lucky tonight," Dr. Matons drawled
around his pipe.

"*Little* patient?" Reya queried with amusement. She was sure
she'd never met a man so long his feet practically hung off the
edge of her bed, or a more muscularly perfect specimen as the

one lying in her bedroom. She and Dr. Matons had spent the past several hours removing glass and plastic from various patches of skin. They'd stitched the deeper cuts across his back, wrapped his chest tightly and cleaned off all the blood. She'd seen every inch of his magnificent body and there was nothing, and she meant *nothing*, little about him.

"It's a good thing you were out on patrol when his plane went down. I don't know if he would have made it otherwise," the doctor said, blowing out a ring of thick smoke. "He is certainly handsome, as men go." His eyes crinkled at the sides as he watched her. The old matchmaker. Always looking for someone to pair her up with. Even an unconscious man in serious condition.

When she didn't answer but stared out into the night, he continued. "I gave him a strong painkiller, but he's not out of the woods. Do you mind if I sleep here so I can check on him during the night?"

"No, I don't mind at all. Why don't you take the office? The futon in there is pretty comfy. I'll take the couch." Her eyes hadn't strayed from the tangle of ferns and vines leading into the dark canopy of jungle no more than a hundred yards from her back stairs.

"You're not planning on going back out in this deluge, are you?"

"The storm is almost past. I'll be fine. Besides, something weird happened out there tonight. If you're still awake when I get back, I'll tell you about it."

The moon, pale and obscured by dark thunderheads, was the only light shining onto her second-story veranda. Reya unlaced her boots, toed them off and set them beside the screen door that led down the back stairs. Dr. Matons continued to puff on his pipe while she peeled off her tank top and blood-spattered pants, tossed them in a pile and loosely tied a small bundle around her neck.

"Be careful, my dear. Wake me when you return," Dr. Matons called quietly. Extinguishing his pipe, he rose and slipped through the sliding-glass door and into her living room.

Reya watched his retreating back until the subtle snap of the office door told her she was alone. Shirt, pants and shoes in a neat pile on the floor, she dropped to her knees. Muscles rippled and bunched as raw power surged through her limbs—heady, thunderous power as her body shortened then stretched. Her tall frame shuddered as thick fur burst through her pores, replacing smooth skin. The cooling breeze ruffled the sleek fur on the tufts of the ears of a black jaguar as she stalked down the stairs and loped into the surrounding jungle.

Two

Aaron was immediately aware that he lay on his back at a perfect forty-five-degree angle in a firm but comfortable bed, but the rest of his thoughts were fuzzy, unclear. But not so unclear that he didn't realize someone was in the room with him.

A breeze wafted over his cheek, drying the light sheen of sweat covering his face. Opening his eyes just a crack revealed a wide, and equally tall, opened window. The shades were pulled up to reveal a cloudy pre-dawn sky. He could smell rain in the air, but whether it was coming or going, he couldn't tell. Relief coursed over him as he took in his surroundings. Okay, so he wasn't in heaven, unless the hereafter had IV drips and makeshift hospital accommodations. His too-dry tongue flicked out to lick even drier lips.

"Wh-Where am I?" his voice croaked like a half-dead frog.

"Cockscomb Basin Wildlife Sanctuary near Maya Center. About two and a half hours from Belize City. I found you just after you crashed in my jungle, and pulled you to safety," said a female voice, just above a whisper. That voice sent a very nice tingle down the inside of his thighs. He pushed the thought away. After all, it was ridiculous at a time like this.

"My plane . . ." He paused to pull a breath into his achy chest. His lungs burned on a long moan. God that hurt, both the breath and the moan. Wiggling his fingers, he was glad he could feel all of them, including the secure wrapping of bandages along his wrists. Slowly raising his hand, he gently pressed on the area of his chest that pulled and twinged with each breath. Great. Broken ribs.

"Did my plane go up?"

"In smoke you mean?" the female asked, somewhat brusquely. She didn't sound upset, but like she'd rather be doing something else. Finally she said, "I'm afraid so. The fire crew was able to get the flames out before too much damage was done to the sur-rounding fauna."

Was that a bit of snot in her tone? What was her problem? She was obviously more worried about the damned trees and grass while he was the one lying in a strange bed in a strange place, obviously injured. So, she'd rather be doing something else? Well, hell, he could think of a few things he'd rather be doing as well.

His eyes closed, refusing to keep up with the blur of her move-ments, to the bed, away from the bed, to a door and back. But at least he felt better than he had the last time he'd awakened and thought he was dead. That had been a whole new kind of pain right there.

"You're Aaron James, right?"

His eyes opened all the way now and would have popped wide in surprise if the headache from hell hadn't come rushing to the front of his forehead just then. His face felt tight and swollen. He slowly turned his head toward the sound while his mind began a slow whirl. Was he more intrigued with the fact that a female in the middle of nowhere knew who he was or with the sultry quality of the voice of the woman he'd thought was an angel? And she stood not three feet from him.

"Soooo," she drawled, "you're Aaron James, right?" Her expression somewhat amused at his befuddled state.

"Mm-hmm," he groaned. "How did you know?"

"I managed to salvage some of your belongings. Black duffel's in the closet. Is there someone I can call for you?"

"No." It came out a bit more forcefully than he'd intended, but he preferred to take care of contacting his family himself. He was the youngest sibling, and his brothers had expressed enough worry over him flying alone from their Miami offices to Belize. The last thing he needed was the deuce of them coming down on his head while he was healing. He was a successful architect, almost thirty -five years old, and held his own in their family business. Yet they still treated him as if he couldn't tie his shoes without their aid. He was well aware they'd promised their father on his deathbed that they would "take care" of their baby brother. Their need to protect him was understood but no less nauseating.

The woman moved closer and sat on the edge of the bed. The scent of apples and cinnamon floated to his sore nostrils as her long fingers held a small glass of clear liquid to his parched lips. Mmm, water had never tasted so good. Though it hurt to swallow, he forced himself to take a few sips, thankful when his throat was lubricated enough to comfortably drink a bit more. The glass was set with a thunk on what he assumed was a nightstand, but he couldn't turn his neck enough to look without his head doing the thrum-thrum to the beat of his heart.

"You know who I am, but who are you?"

"Reya. Reya Daines. Do you think you can sit up?"

He suddenly remembered the business he was supposed to be taking care of in Belize City before his plane went down. Sit up? A semi-unfuzzy mind yelled *yes, sit up and get moving*, but his body said forget it. He slowly shook his head and settled down farther into the soft sheets.

"How long have I been here, Reya?"

"A few days. Dr. Matons and I have been tending to you. He's been keeping you sedated so you're going to feel groggy and a bit nauseous for a while."

You don't say, he thought sarcastically. No wonder his brain was a weird mix of stuffed cotton and muted pain.

"With that said, it's time for your next dose. I'll be back shortly and we'll see about getting some food into you," she said quickly, leaning forward to fiddle with something over his head before settling down on the side of the bed again. The back of his eyes started to throb, forcing him to close them again on a ragged moan.

"Don't worry, Aaron. I'm medically trained," she said quietly, mistaking his discomfort for concern. He was in too much pain to be concerned about much of anything.

"Injuries?" he asked, trying to string as few words together as possible. Her answer was a relief.

"Your ribs are bruised." Oh thank God, bruised, not broken. Other than a concussion and a bruised kidney, the laundry list of injuries she rattled off was mostly cuts and bruises. "You were banged up pretty bad, minor internal injuries. Thankfully, the doc has equipment here to detect that kind of thing. A few of your issues required stitching, so don't scratch your neck or right above your right eye. The ribs and the knock on your skull are going to bother you for a few days yet."

She raised a needle, walked around to the other side of the bed near the window and inserted the sharp tip into the IV taped to his right forearm.

"What are you giving me?" his words quickly started to slur.

"You're on a glucose drip with antibiotics and a little something to control the inflammation and swelling. It's to prevent infection, but more importantly, dehydration, at least until you can eat and drink on your own. Right now I'm giving you some codeine to help control the pain."

"Bud whad-da-bou-da doctor?" Oh yeah, he was fading fast.

"Dr. Matons has hardly left your side so I'm administering this dose so he could get some breakfast downstairs."

What? The doctor was having breakfast downstairs? What the hell kind of backwater place had he crashed where a doctor's breakfast was more important than his patient? Six seconds later, he didn't give a rip as a cool feeling traveled from his wrist up to his forearm. He raised his arm enough to see the IV secured to a fat vein with white paper surgical tape. Reya withdrew the needle and moved away. He heard a quiet clink as she disposed of it. His breathing deepened as he drifted away, but not before his keen nose and ears caught the soft thud of her shoes as she made her way across the wood floor. And boy did she smell good.

∞

Dressed in her ranger's uniform of dark green camouflage pants with matching bandana, short-sleeved black shirt and hiking boots, she hurried downstairs, her mutinous mind on the man in her bed. She'd taken her time looking him over as she and Dr. Matons changed bandages and checked stitches. The man's wide, solid chest was sprinkled with dark downy hair as black as the hair on her own head. And even in sleep, his biceps were large and defined, the ridged lines of his stomach easily visible and his thighs large and muscular. His body was that of a bodybuilder crossed with a long-distance runner, built for strength and endurance.

And the long, thick rod nestled between powerful thighs looked built for endurance too. Even in slumber, the thing was formidable. She'd shuddered, but from longing or fear, she wasn't sure. He had to be a bad boy. Good guys just didn't come this handsome. A shadow of growth along his jawline enhanced his high cheekbones. His skin reminded her of French vanilla ice cream, the color of decadence and far from plain. She'd never wondered what a man tasted like. Until now.

Then those deep gray eyes of his drifted lazily open and she'd almost forgotten what she was doing.

She told herself it was the color of those eyes that snared her thoughts, not the beautiful ruggedness of his face or the strong lines of his body, which she'd seen gloriously naked while she and the doctor tended his wounds. Even with loads of bruises and swelling, he was gorgeous. Yep, it was the eyes—that was her story and damn it, she was sticking to it.

Other than her twin sister, Reya had never met another person with eyes exactly like hers. The shape was different but the color was dead-on. Not just a similar shade of silver, but so exact someone could have taken his eyeballs, stuck them in her head, and she wouldn't have been able to tell the difference.

Suddenly remembering the day she found Aaron. A jaguar had challenged her, or at least that's what she thought had occurred. Her brows snapped together over the unsettling circumstances of Mr. Aaron James landing practically in her backyard. But she didn't have time to think about that right now. From the hum of voices and clattering of dishes making its way up the staircase, she had a full house waiting for their breakfast.

The dining room was packed, her place being the only bed-and-breakfast that catered to the park rangers and the guests who visited the preserve. Other than her guests, most visitors stayed in the rustic cabins or dormitories, but they all seemed to make their way to her establishment for breakfast or to schedule a guided diving trip.

The sun had risen quickly into a clear blue sky, shining through the tall plate-glass windows of the dining hall. She signaled to one of the waitstaff to lower the shades on the eastern side of the large room, then made her way through the throng. Spotting Dr. Matons conversing with her housekeeper Bethsaida, she poured herself a cup of rich coffee and joined them at a table close to the kitchen doors.

The second her butt hit the chair, a bowl of peeled, sliced apples and a small dessert cup full of ground cinnamon was set in front of her. Thanking the young woman who served her, Reya scooped up a good helping of cinnamon with an apple slice and sighed with pleasure as the tart, spicy treat hit her tongue.

"So how's our patient?" Dr. Matons asked around a bite of fresh melon.

"Seems fine. I gave him a dose of pain meds. I told him I'd be back up to check on him, bring him something to eat, but he'll probably sleep for at least a few hours."

so he did wake?"

"Yes, woke up in a bit of pain, but he was coherent enough to ask where he was and what happened to his plane."

The worry lines at the corners of Bethsaida's mouth deepened before she asked, "Did you tell him what happened? I mean, does he understand how you rescued him? And what you rescued him from?"

Reya's face remained calm and clear while her mind raced to find a diplomatic and friendly way to say "hell no." Then again, she'd never been good at tact anyway.

"Hell no," she responded quietly, not wanting to draw the attention of the patrons or her fellow rangers. Bethsaida's eyebrows flew upward as a half grin graced her lovely features. An older woman with a striking head of salt-and-pepper hair that hung clear down to her waist, Bethsaida had given plenty of men a run for their money in her day. At sixty years old, she was stunning. All that hair graced a lovely, sun-browned face, and hard work kept her body strong and shapely.

Dr. Matons swallowed another piece of sweet melon and said, "It's probably best he doesn't know. Let him remember on his own. Besides, it would be better if he didn't recall the events of that night at all. Soon he'll be well enough to travel and hopefully your secrets will remain just that, *yours*."

"Sure, Doc," she murmured in response, but her mind only caught one of every three or four words, thinking back to her confrontation with the unfamiliar, very large cat. A big, beautiful male she'd never seen before, with large, distinct, black rosettes all over his perfect coat. The light of the fire from Aaron's plane had cast an eerie glow about his body, and when he challenged her for the man, Reya had been shocked. Jaguars didn't eat people. What the hell was that about? Maybe she'd try to find the male on her next patrol. Lord, she hoped he wasn't feral. The last thing she needed was a fight with a large, crazy cat.

She looked up at the doctor and the woman who helped her run the place. Their eyes were plastered on the front door, their faces drawn and taut while trying their best to look unconcerned.

"What is it?" Reya asked, glancing back and forth between her two best friends. When neither answered, she followed their eyes to a spot across the room.

"Damn it, not what I need right now," she grumbled into her mug. Maybe she could make a clean escape into the kitchen and help Cook cut up something, anything. She could have kicked herself for not moving fast enough when a slick, oily voice reached out to touch her from behind. Yuck.

"Good morning, Reya." The sound rolled over her skin. She almost cringed. Trefor Dionisio, *dimwit extraordinaire*, obviously thought just because he was the new director of the preserve and a meaty hunk that he'd move her. Hell, other than her need to survive and God, she'd never been moved by anyone or anything. And even God was pushing it.

But then again, there was the beautiful man in her bed . . .

"Hey, Trefor. What can I do for you?" she replied cordially, though she had yet to turn around to face him. She'd rather look at the bottom of her coffee cup. Yahoo, it was empty! Great reason to leave the table.

"I brought your schedule," Trefor replied, thrusting the paper out to her, effectively cutting off her escape. Damn.

She looked down at his hand and the paper it held as if they would come alive and eat her. Blowing out an exasperated breath, she snatched it from his hand and read it over quickly. It took next to nothing for the man to irritate her, but what was on the schedule was well *beyond* next to nothing.

"Trefor, this can't be right," she said firmly, with more than a little surprise in her voice. "I can't work this schedule. It's not even close to what I agreed to when I came on board here."

"I understand that, but that agreement was with the former director."

She let a clear challenge blaze in her eyes and he appeared to back down a bit before saying, "Look, Reya, we're two men short since the attacks started. You're the lowest on the totem pole. Unless, of course, there's something you'd like to trade . . ."

He let the word hang in the air, and so did she. Besides, it was pretty clear what he was trying to say, the bastard.

"Look, Trefor, I can't work this schedule. There's no way I can help Dr. Matons with patients, run my B&B, take my customers scuba diving and do patrol eight of the next ten shifts. If you don't like it, then fire me."

Her good friend Marc stepped up and laid a gentle hand on her shoulder. "Trefor, you know this is bullshit. I'll take some of her patrols. I'll even redo the schedule myself and have it back to you for approval by this afternoon."

A frosty smile plastered on her face, she handed the piece of paper back to Trefor then smiled warmly at Marc with a whispered thanks.

A deep growl rolled up from Trefor's chest, but Reya couldn't have cared less. She snatched her mug off the table and disappeared into the kitchen with Marc, Bethsaida and Dr. Matons all covering her back.

∽∾∽

The next morning, after her typical routine of rising early, helping Bethsaida with the guests and avoiding Trefor, Reya returned to her apartments. Dr. Matons hadn't been surprised that their patient slept through all of yesterday and clear through the night. But today, the doctor wanted him to try to eat something.

Easing her way into her bedroom, she stood next to the handsome man in the bed with a glass of fresh squeezed orange juice and a steaming bowl of escabeche-onion broth with stewed chicken. Her breath caught in her throat when his lids slid slowly open to reveal slate-gray, soul-stirring eyes. Damn, she couldn't get over how much they looked like hers though her pupils were larger because of her *panthera onca* genetics.

She mentally kicked herself in the ass, knowing if her brilliant mind didn't get her goofy thoughts in hand, she'd never get anything done. Her task list was full of all the things she loved, but strangely, she had no desire to do any of it. She'd rather stand next to her bed and gaze into Aaron's eyes. Jeez, what a wet noodle she was becoming.

Thankfully Bethsaida oversaw the cleaning and waitstaff of the B&B, but Reya still had to get down to the boat to meet her diving party. The trip down the Sittee River to the dive site and back would take hours. And she still had to be back home in time for tonight's patrol.

Last night she'd spotted the rogue that had challenged her for Aaron's prone body the night his plane went down. A sense of foreboding caused a shiver to slip up her spine. Oh yes, they'd meet again soon, her and the rogue. Face-to-face. Perhaps claw-to-claw.

She set the food on the nightstand and touched the pulse point on her patient's neck. A lazy smile spread across her lips at the feel of the strong beat under her fingers. Yes, he'd be up in no time. Damn. Though her back was tired of sleeping on the couch, she could really get used to seeing him in her bed. He'd occupied her personal haven the past four days and the man sure looked good in this particular spot.

"Good morning, Aaron. How are you feeling?"

"No more meds."

A single black brow winged upward at his answer. Actually, it was more of a demand. "Excuse me?"

He took a deep breath, winced and said a bit more forcefully, "I said no more meds."

"Really?" she asked, hiding a grin. Pale as a sheet and practically gasping with each breath, but he didn't need any meds? Oh yes, this was definitely a man's man, handsome, strong-willed and obviously used to being in charge. Kind of reminded her of a stubborn, freeborn mule.

"I mean it. I can't think straight or even stay awake long enough to take a pee," he growled weakly. When she didn't respond he added, "I can take the pain. Thanks to you and the good doctor, it's at least bearable now."

"Have it your way," she said cheerfully, not sure what she was so cheerful about. Couldn't possibly be this newly discovered stubborn streak in her new roommate, right? She moved to the closet, pulled out a rain slicker and her dive pack then set them at the bedroom door.

"What time is it?" he asked around a yawn. His eyes followed her every movement then squinted against the light flooding through the bedroom window. A quick glance at her bedside clock confirmed the time. Seven o'clock in the morning.

"Dr. Matons will be up to check on you in a couple of hours, all right?"

"You're leaving? Where are you going?"

Head cocked to the side with a scowl, she regarded her patient. Reya answered to no one, except her aunt when she happened to go home for a visit, but coming from him the questions seemed so normal and unobtrusive. Aaron sounded so worn out and genuinely concerned, she answered before she remembered to be offended.

"I'm scheduled to take a group on a guided tour of the barrier reef near South Water Caye. Maybe when you're better, I'll take you down there for a dive?"

"When will you be back?"

"Just after lunch. I have patrol tonight so I'll want to get a nap before then."

Reya helped Aaron pull his big body up to a sitting position and stuffed several pillows behind his back. Against her better judgment, she handed him the bowl of escabeche. Not like she had much of a choice when the blasted man refused to let her feed him. His fingers shook through the whole process, but he did, in fact, feed himself while she snuck a final round of pain meds into his IV.

When his eyes closed Reya headed to the bedroom door with the empty bowl in her hands. Fingers curled around the doorknob, she stood there a moment. Her gaze slid back toward the bed.

God, something about the man beckoned to her heart and soul. And especially her body. Since the night she'd brought him here, she hadn't been able to think of much of anything but him, the deep timbre of his voice and the allure of his physical presence. And those gorgeous gray eyes sheltered by thick, black lashes. But why was she so gone over him? Could he be a shifter, like her? She had no idea, and she sure as hell wasn't going to ask him.

The next thing Reya knew, her feet had carried her right back to the bed and she stood looking down at Mr. Aaron James. Her fingers strayed over the cool skin covering the firm ridges of his forearm and then up to the mound of his biceps, secretly glad the IV was in the other arm so she could play with this one.

Leaning forward, she gently rubbed her lips against his, taking in their firmness along with his unique scent. Even with the smell of the glucose drip and the mild sedative floating about his body, his scent was strong, virile. Like musk, man and hot cinnamon candy.

Pressing her lips more firmly against his, she was surprised when his fingers found their way into the hair at the nape of her neck. Her innocent little peck became a hot, ravenous kiss as his mouth opened under hers and he pulled her closer when she would have pulled away in shock. He moaned softly, the warmth of his tongue laving against hers. The hum against her lips traveled clear down to her womb with a feeling so exhilaratingly sweet her knees buckled.

The second her butt hit the mattress she was caught up in the sexy tidal wave that was Aaron. It poured over her, pulling her under until the arousal she always kept so tightly controlled washed up through her bones.

He broke the kiss and released her, but not before he delivered a sharp nip to her bottom lip then sucked it into the warmth of his mouth to soothe away the sting. The ferocity of her response caught her totally off guard. His next words took her surprise up a level, to the brink of pure shock.

"Play hooky today," he said softly against her parted lips.

"Play hooky? You mean skip work?"

"Join me under the covers and I promise you won't regret it, Reya."

Her womb clenched and hummed, but the intensity of his expression was so *male*, it actually startled her right out of her lust. Forcing herself to push gently against his chest, she put a little distance between them while carefully avoiding his bruises.

"Aaron, we've only shared a single kiss. We don't even know each other." Oh but didn't she wish that weren't the case?

"If you let me, I promise to change that, beautiful." Seconds later, he was out.

"Shit!" she growled, unable to decide whether to be grateful or upset when the pain meds chose that moment to kick in.

One glance at her watch had her scrambling to the door, picking up her gear. There was no time to change clothes, so she'd just have to deal with the wet now plastered to the inside of her thighs. And all from a single kiss? What was she, a jag in heat?

Looking back to the bed, her brows bunched together. Well, was she?

Three

Aaron sat up and rolled his shoulders and neck, stiff from sleeping so hard for so long. The moon shone like a muted bulb, hidden by thick storm clouds. He'd slept all day and half the night. Closing his eyes, he breathed deeply. Reya's scent lingered, invaded his lungs and seeped into his body clear down to his balls.

Everything smelled like her. The sheets and the pillows. Even the damned air. He felt hungry for the sight of her. Maybe she'd give him another kiss. Just the thought of her warm, full lips on his sent a rush of warmth across his skin. What the hell kind of weird reaction was he having to her?

And where was the woman anyway? He strained his ears for the soft, barely audible sound of her footfalls but all was quiet. Where had she gone?

Perhaps she was in the bathroom . . . which was where? Gritting his teeth against the soreness, he sat up, pleased he'd done it on his own. His forearm was a bit sore, but at least the IV had been removed. Dr. Matons must have come in and relieved him of it while he slept.

He wasn't sure what day it was. The days and nights were one big blur of blood, pain, Dr. Matons and his damned pain meds . . . and kissing Reya. Now *that* he wouldn't mind reliving.

Legs swung over the side of the bed and the soft sheets pooled between his very naked thighs. Slightly dizzy, Aaron took his time and pushed slowly to his feet. Even in this humidity, the skin around his stitches felt tight. He resisted the urge to stretch and concentrated instead on the watery feeling in his legs. It was disconcerting and uncomfortable but made sense. Having been an athlete all his life, he understood that his legs would protest his heavy weight after lying on his back for days.

But there was one sign of recovery he welcomed. He had to pee.

Taking it slowly, he breathed a sigh of relief when he made it to the door he prayed was the bathroom. The woven bamboo door opened noiselessly and Aaron stood in the threshold with an appreciative tilt raising the side of his mouth. Reya had taste.

Her bathroom was a sanctuary. Done in pale green and blue tiles, it was like looking at an artful rendition of the Caribbean Sea. With the exception of the double-basin sinks, the room looked like one huge shower. With a drain built into the floor on the far side of the facility, it was completely tiled—the walls, the floor, even the ceiling. Massaging jets stuck out of the walls in various positions and one could actually enjoy the water on the front and both sides of the body all at the same time.

The woman obviously loved windows. A tinted floor-to-ceiling, screened patio-style window stood right across from the showerheads. But considering there was a sheer twenty-foot drop instead of a balcony, the window opened from top-to-bottom, instead of side-to-side. He bet it was one hell of a sunset from in here. Whoever designed it was a genius.

Well, at least his dick was still in working order. The thing was lucky as last week's lottery winner. A slew of bruises healed from neck to knees, but his dick was unscathed. Not even a scratch, thank God. He couldn't recall ever being so relieved to go to the bathroom.

Tiring quickly, he washed up and headed back to bed. Coming to a dead stop in the middle of the large room, Aaron tilted his head. What was that sound? It sounded like rain, but he'd just looked out the bathroom window and for once in what felt like forever, the sky wasn't leaking.

He turned and his body seized. Even the hair on his arms and legs stood on end, unmoved by the breeze flowing in through the always-open window.

Sexy and beyond desirable, his personal angel stood out on a private veranda. She didn't look at him, but he caught the way her eyes glowed just like a cat's when the moonlight hit them.

Reya. Stark naked. His knees weren't sure if they wobbled from the force of lust that hit him square in the chest or from sheer exhaustion. Screw exhaustion. No, he'd rather screw her.

Taking advantage of her outdoor shower while everyone else was in bed, Reya shivered as her keen senses picked up an inviting, totally male scent wafting through the nearby bedroom window and out onto the veranda. The hairs on the back of her wet neck danced deliciously at the thought of being watched. Aaron stood not ten feet from her on the other side of the screen as she showered. She felt his eyes move over her naked flesh, and his gaze burned a path down her back as he looked his fill. She'd never let a man take such liberty, had never craved for one to do so. But something inside of her reveled in the knowledge that all her gloriously naked, wet, sleek skin was open to him.

Ducking her head under the gentle flow of warm water, her hair became a dripping riot of curls and waves obscuring her face. Turning her head just enough to peer at him with a single gray eye, she looked at the man staring at her from her bedroom. Her hand wrapped around a bar of glycerin soap with the scent of Jamaican punch, spicy and sweet. Lathering up her hands, she spread the scented suds over her body, keeping her single-eyed gaze locked with his.

Bubbles covered her neck, her shoulder and her arms. She caught his swift intake of breath as her fingers slowly made their way toward her moist nipples that were now dark stabbing points. Encircling them slowly, the fragrance of the soap a mild aphrodisiac, Reya's eyes closed all on their own. Her head fell back when her hands came up underneath, then encircled her swelling breasts. When had a shower become such an erotic undertaking? Of course, it had nothing to do with the stranger who gazed at her as if she were his after-dinner dessert. The stranger she could see clearly through the screen over the pane of reinforced glass. The stranger whose large hand was wrapped around a bone-stiff cock as he took in the gleaming length of her body.

He was so beautiful to look at. Even with the fading yellow and blue patches on his arms, chest and face, he was the most handsome man she'd ever gotten this close to.

The muscles of her stomach chose that exact second to ripple and clench in response to the way he was looking at her. She took a deep breath and lowered her lashes.

"I apologize but while you were asleep, I went through your things," she said with a purr, running her hand through the silky cropped curls at the juncture of her thighs as she stressed the word "things."

"But I figured someone would probably be worried about you." She turned away from him to rinse the soap from her breasts and reveled in the stream of bubbles that rinsed down her stomach and flowed across her labia. Mmm, that felt good. Outrageously good.

"And?" he asked quietly, with just a hint of lustful menace as he stepped closer to the thin mesh screen separating them.

"And I took the liberty of calling your brothers."

"You what? Aw, shit!"

His bellow filled her bungalow and spilled out into the surrounding jungle. A few birds took flight into the night sky and her pulse flew up into her neck to join them. He tore himself away from the window, the slap of his bare footfalls loud on the hardwood floors. But not as loud as the stream of expletives following him out of her bedroom.

Not quite what she was expecting from a man with a raging hard-on.

∞

Reya was out of the shower in a flash and heading into the living room, a trail of water behind her. And Aaron was right there to meet her. He was pissed she'd called the James clan down on him, but one look at that bare, beautiful chocolate skin and the pearls of water glowing in the moonlight all over her body, and she could have called in an army and he wouldn't have cared.

She took three steps into the room and right into his arms. He gasped when his hard cock rode the ridge of the well-defined muscles of her stomach, scalding both of them. His arms automatically enclosed her body and wrapped tight as his head dipped to lick a few drops off her collarbone.

"What are you doing?" she squeaked.

"Making up for the time I was unconscious," he drawled, holding still, waiting for her to object. Her expression was both puzzled and hot. Needy but oddly confused, as if she couldn't understand how she'd ended up naked in his arms but wanted to be exactly where she was.

Dipping his head—and he didn't have far to go given her height—he gently nipped her bottom lip then laved away the sting. He'd never heard a woman growl like that before, but it was damned sexy, so he nipped her again. This time she opened for him, following the movement of his mouth with her own, trying to capture him with her lips.

His mouth crashed down over hers as something primal rose up in him. The need to brand her as his, even though she wasn't. To sear himself into her brain so she would never want another. He knew his thoughts were ridiculous, but his cock didn't care.

He broke the kiss, turned her away from him and slammed her back against his chest. She let out a whimper and arched into his hands as they came around to caress her breasts. Her growl became a loud wail when he squeezed her sweet nipples between his thumb and forefinger while his tongue toyed with an extremely sensitive spot on her neck.

She reached back, one strong hand holding his head as her body squirmed, trying to get closer. When his teeth clamped down on the muscle between her neck and shoulder she let out a wild yell, arched her back and pressed her ass flush against his cock. The fingers of her free hand dug into the cheeks of his butt, holding him hard against her as she writhed.

He put his whole body in motion now—his hands roamed over her breasts, stomach and thighs, his mouth was hot against her neck, her shoulders, nose buried in her wet tresses while his cock ground against the inviting crease of her lushly perfect ass.

But his body had more sense than his head or his cock. He wasn't up to this and when his knees started to buckle he reluctantly eased away from her lovely body, breathing like he'd run up the side of a mountain and down the other side.

"Oh, God, I'm so sorry," she said, her hand flying up to cover her mouth.

"Sorry for what, beautiful?" he asked quietly, unable to stop himself from reaching for her again. She took a step back, so he just followed her until she'd backed up against the door that led out onto the veranda.

"You just survived a plane crash. There's no way I should be coming on to you like this."

"So you only want my kisses and nothing else?" he teased. "Why? Don't you like me?" Tangling his fingers in her hair, he loved how thick and soft it was, even wet he was tempted to play in it. She was such a beautiful woman. Tall and lushly curved. Her body was strong, well defined and perfect for the kind of loving he enjoyed—hard, rough and long.

Her mouth opened and closed a couple of times at his ques-

tion. "It's just that, uh, well, you're a . . . and I'm not a . . . and see?
Well, shit!"

He laughed and his stomach muscles pulled. It hurt like hell,
but he just couldn't help it. Obviously her brain wasn't working any better than his so he decided to stop trying to make her
think. Instead a slow, sliding seduction of lips began, this time
gently and unhurried until she pressed closer and moaned softly
into the kiss. Damn, a naked woman sure did a lot for a man's
waning strength! Grunting, he leaned into her strong, warm body
and corralled her into the bedroom.

Aaron settled her into her own bed and slid in next to her, his
big body crowding hers. What the hell was she thinking? She
couldn't make love to a man she didn't know—even if his mere
presence made her forgetful, scatterbrained and so hot she could
barely stand to transition into her fur.

Yes, that was it. She needed to get out of this bed, transition
and head for the dense, lush sanctuary of the jungle and chase
rabbits until she collapsed, too drained to feel any arousal whatsoever.

But when the man pulled her up onto his chest, it was clear
he wasn't inclined to let her go anywhere just yet. She had to get
ahold of this madness consuming not only her but obviously him
as well.

"Aaron, we shouldn't be doing this," she said in hushed tones,
even as he arranged her legs on either side of his hips.

"Don't you like . . ."

"Don't you dare ask me if I like you," she said on a whoosh of breath as his fingers slid between the moist lips between her legs. "You're injured, and . . ."

"Not so injured I can't take a little taste."

Taste? Taste of what? Then she understood exactly what he meant when, in spite of the cuts and bruises on his arms and chest, he lifted her over his head, settled her soaked pussy right over his face and feasted.

His talented tongue lapped and licked until she shivered like a leaf caught in a gusty breeze in the fall. Every limb quaked and shook as her muscles bunched and released with the pleasure he stirred in her.

Looking down, she saw he was really into what he was doing. Gray eyes closed, his head moved around, back and forth, as he devoured her throbbing pussy. His tongue glided up through her moist folds. A talented tongue dipped into her eager hole while his mouth clamped down on her entire mound, humming his pleasure.

The sound blazed through every nerve, every cell until she thought her skin would combust.

It felt sooooo good! He drove her mad as she hovered on the brink of climax. If he didn't finish her soon she would just die. Riding his face like it was his cock, she panted as her stomach tightened and spasmed against the pleasure. Oh yes, she was so close.

One hand reached up and spread her lips, revealing the swollen nub of her clit. She held her breath as he inhaled her scent, murmuring against her pussy, then dove for the bundle of nerves peeking out from its little hood.

His lips wrapped around her clitoris and clamped down tightly as he suckled her, pulling her deep into his hot mouth, still humming his appreciation.

She lost it.

Her orgasm tore through her but he didn't let up. He kept laving her little bud, circling his tongue around and around until the fusion bomb in her cunt detonated, and she melted into a puddle of warm candle wax. The third time, the pleasure was so intense, she slipped into blessed oblivion where her mind could accept the delicious torture her body endured.

Four

Tonight he watched her in her pelt and wondered if she was aware he knew who she was. All this time he'd thought she was just another jag female, but an accidental glimpse of her showering on her screened veranda several nights back had revealed more than he'd ever expected.

He'd stayed perfectly still, perched in a tree, and watched the back of the building he'd tracked her to. After a while, his patience had paid off. She'd stalked from the cover of the jungle and stopped to look around. He hadn't been seen perched up on the thick branches and was glad for the broad leaves surrounding him. The female melanistic jaguar with her black, smooth coat glistening in the darkness walked up the back stairs of the building. A few seconds later, a beautiful woman with perfect milk chocolate skin and the body of a goddess stood up just outside the door leading into the covered shelter then ducked inside. The warm spray of water left a million sparkling droplets that shined like little diamonds all over her ebon skin.

The spicy rich scent of the soap she slathered on her body floated out and away from her little haven. But the soap couldn't conceal the sweet nectar gathering between her silken thighs, nor could it hide the unusually spicy scent of her womanly dew. He could smell it from here—she was in heat.

∽∽

She'd been on patrol since midnight and still hadn't spotted a single jaguar. Not even a female. While her senses weren't as sharp when in her two-legged form, Reya still smelled a strong wrongness on the air that enveloped her like a cold, wet blanket. The skin on her bare forearms began to prickle, making her wish she'd worn a long-sleeved jacket rather than her short-sleeved, light zip-up jacket. But whatever was out here, she knew no garment would protect her or anyone else from it.

The fact that another female jag had been found dead just yesterday only made her more uncomfortable. A band of spastic fireflies twitted around in her stomach as she moved deeper into the jungle along well-worn paths she'd traveled for years. Unnerved, she wished she'd come out in her pelt tonight instead of armed with a damned tranquilizer gun.

"Hey, Reya. How's it going?"

Reya didn't bother to turn around, having smelled the man long before he appeared. What was it about humans that made them forget they were in a jungle full of wild animals at night and walking downwind?

"Hi, Marc," she called with a smile and a wave. She sniffed the air again. He must have been around the jaguars tonight. She wondered if he'd sighted the jag that'd challenged her over her new roommate.

Sigh. Speaking of roommates.

Damned man. After a decadent night of hot sex, she woke with him glaring down at her. He proceeded to remind her of how she'd meddled where she wasn't wanted. Jeez, all she'd done was call his brothers and he'd hit the roof. It just wasn't right. If she'd had an accident or turned up missing, her aunt would worry. Wouldn't his brothers worry too? Why in the world did the man insist on "waiting until he could handle them," as he put it? From what he'd told her, his brothers were some pretty nice guys, if a bit overprotective, considering he was the youngest.

Too bad, she'd already made the call. So after the little confrontation early this morning, she decided to avoid him. Besides, her mind was supposed to be on her work, not that irritating, stubborn, perfectly gorgeous specimen in her apartments.

"So what's going on?"

Oh Lord, she'd almost forgotten Marc was walking with her. Glad the night-vision goggles perched on top of his head couldn't pick up heat signatures, she blushed furiously, took in a deep breath and pushed Aaron from her mind. Almost.

"I'm fine, Marc."

"I didn't ask how you were doing. I asked what's going on. You've seemed a bit preoccupied lately."

Reya was once again amazed at how perceptive her good friend was. Trusting him more than anyone else, with the exception of Dr. Matons and Bethsaida, she opened her mouth and all her concerns tumbled right out.

"That damn Trefor's been stalking me, Marc. He's really starting to get on my nerves," she snapped. "Besides his goofy idea that the attacks on the female jags are being carried out by poachers, his insistence that he and I were meant to be is just,

just . . ." She snorted, unable to even finish the sentence, it was so absurd.

"Well, you're a beautiful woman, Reya. Who wouldn't want your time?"

Marc had told her many times he thought she was attractive but it always came across as a compliment by a brother or something. Tonight, even under the dark sky, she sensed something different in his words and body language that made her uncomfortable. She just didn't like Marc "like that." A short rant about Trefor erupted past her lips as she brushed away Marc's words and what they might imply.

"He's always messing with my schedule. Always trying to insinuate himself on my time. There are other women out here who would love to hang with him. Why doesn't he just leave me the hell alone? I swear the man gives me the creepies."

By the time the last of the words were out of her mouth, she was practically yelling at the top of her lungs. But she just didn't feel better yet because there was something else she just had to get off her chest.

"And you know the man who survived the plane crash is recovering at my B&B? Well, he's getting on my damned nerves too!" And making her hot, bothered and all-around freaky.

"Who hasn't heard about him?" he replied, his voice sounding a bit tight as he warmed to the subject. "Everyone's been talking about how you and the doc are heroes. It's a good thing you had the foresight to have a couple of hospital rooms built into the top floors of the B&B when you designed the place."

"Well, I don't know about the hero stuff. Dr. Matons and I were just doing what anyone would have done. And the idea about the medical rooms was my aunt Sulu's, not mine."

"True," he grinned and said, "your aunt Sulu saw you through medical school. I bet she flipped when you told her you wanted to research big cats and scuba dive in Belize," he said with a chuckle, ducking when Reya pretended to whack him on the back of the neck. Reya could almost feel the cheeky grin on his face. But the man was right. Her aunt Sulu had completely wigged out at her grand idea to trek through the jungles of Belize. After the initial yelling and pulling of hair, her aunt had supported her in the decision, down to every detail of the B&B.

"So when does he get to leave the hospital rooms?" Marc asked in a casual tone. Reya didn't bother to tell him Aaron wasn't in a hospital room, but in hers.

"Actually, I'm just overworked and stressed out. Aaron isn't . . ."

"Oh his name is Aaron?"

"Yes, Aaron James. He's actually a neat guy. If my choices were between him and Trefor, I'd pick Aaron in a heartbeat. Actually, I'd pick Aaron under any circumstance. He's just testy because Dr. Matons won't clear him to get out of bed yet, and being waited on by a woman isn't something he's used to."

"Being waited on? Is that what he calls it? Being fed, taken care of by a medically capable woman? And he calls it being waited on? What a son of a bitch!"

Reya was taken aback. She'd never heard Marc speak strongly about anyone, even Trefor-the-asshole. But suddenly, her friend's body was tense and strained while he talked about a man he didn't even know as if he were the world's lowest dog.

"Marc, you need to relax," she said angrily, practically growling. "You don't even know Aaron. He happens to appreciate what I've done, what Dr. Matons and I continue to do. He just doesn't like that I *have* to do it, that I don't have a choice. He mostly hates the fact that he can't take care of himself right now. What real man wouldn't feel that way?"

"Sounds like you're sweet on him to me," Marc snapped back, moving to stand much too close and much too aggressive. She felt the muscles shift under her skin as her hands clenched and unclenched at her sides. Her anger and need to protect Aaron pushed the urge to shift up to the surface. What the hell was wrong with both her and Marc? He was acting like Aaron was taking advantage of her, while she was ready to shift and tear his head off for talking about the very man she'd just said was getting on her nerves.

Good Lord she needed a drink. Or better yet, she needed a hard run in her pelt.

"Look, Reya, I'm sorry. It's just that I care about you. I don't want to see you get hurt by some hotshot just passing through, is all," Marc said quietly, stepping back from her, his step non-threatening and his voice semi-contrite.

The bunching muscles of her shoulders and neck relaxed and thick fur that had been ready to erupt from her pores receded. She wanted to yell that both Dr. Matons and Bethsaida had met and liked Aaron, which was good enough for her. Instead, with a deep breath, Reya forced a tight-lipped smile.

Hoping the incisors receding into her gums weren't visible, she clapped him on the shoulder with a positive-sounding grunt, motioned her head toward a path off to the left, and the two companions took off into the night to finish their patrol together.

Neither said another word the rest of the night.

∞

Funny, he was a successful architect, but his family still considered him the "baby." Yeah, he was a baby all right—a horny one that took every opportunity to touch Reya whenever she was near. He just couldn't keep his hands off her.

When she came to check his stitches, bring him a meal or help him to the bathroom—she waited outside of course, after all he did have some pride—his fingers itched to skim over her luscious form. And after that first kiss, he always looked for a way to get her to bend down or simply reached out to grab her by the hand and pull her to him so he could taste her mouth. She threw herself completely into each kiss they shared and always tasted of apples and cinnamon. Delicious.

To taste but not take her was killing him. Damned weakness royally irked him, but come hell or high water, he'd be up and about as soon as humanly possible just to get the woman underneath him again.

Raising his arms to hold on to the headboard of the bed, he raised straight legs a scant two inches from the mattress and held the position until his stomach muscles burned. Exercising in bed was all he'd been allowed to do while he was on bed rest. He felt stronger than just yesterday, and if Dr. Matons didn't let him up soon he'd call his brothers down here just to strangle the man. *Oh but wait*, he thought sarcastically, *Reya already called them.*

Aaron grimaced at the tongue-lashing he'd received from his oldest brother Austin. His ears still burned from the blistering rant as his brother expressed his outrage and worry that Aaron hadn't called them earlier. "The second the plane dropped off the radar, we were alerted that you were in trouble, but a woman we don't even know was the one to call and let us know you were okay? And a week later, when you were perfectly capable of talking, Aaron," his brother had yelled. Then Anthony joined in on the line and told him off some more before reminding him how much they worried, loved and cared about him. He felt like a child all over again. It was his own damned fault. Being so determined to handle it his way had caused his brothers, his only family, undue stress. Now he felt like a heel for getting on Reya's case for doing what she felt was right. Mr. Blunder? Yep, that was him.

If only he could stick to architecture. Building plans didn't get disappointed. Building plans' eyes didn't fill with sadness when he stuck his finger out at them and told them off. And building plans didn't avoid him when he pissed them off. Aaron couldn't remember ever feeling this lonely. It was a sobering thought.

Reya filled his mind and a wistful smile touched his lips. The woman was smart as a whip. Conversation wasn't something he'd often engaged in with a female, but he could sit and talk to Reya for hours. In fact, that's exactly what they'd done when he'd been able to stay awake long enough. Now that the bruised ribs and kidney were healing nicely, they usually talked about any and everything from the time she came in from scuba expeditions in the early afternoon until she left for patrol at midnight.

A laundry list of everything he needed to do scrolled behind his eyes. The project on Ambergris Caye for his customer in Belize wouldn't wait forever. Thankfully, the blueprints and plans were saved from the wreck and could be delivered. The budget had to be reworked and the deeds on the land secured in his client's name. He didn't even want to think about how much the project plan would need to be reworked, pushing back the grand opening of the posh luxury fitness resort. He absolutely did not want his brothers to handle it. They'd taken care of him all his life. Now he made his own way, was his own man. He had work to do and another million to make for their company. Then again, he'd rather stay here and . . .

When was the last time he'd had a hard time making a decision between getting work done and hanging out with a woman? Hell, he couldn't think of a single instance. Until now. The woman had him so wide open, Aaron couldn't decide if he wanted to go or stay. Nevertheless, he was still pissed off that Dr. Matons wouldn't clear him to get out of bed and travel to Belize City yet.

Unbidden, the conversation from when they'd awakened in her bed early this morning jumped back into his head.

"I assured them you were fine. They'll be here as soon as they can arrange for emergency visas. Next week, perhaps."

"Damn it, Reya!" he'd fumed, "don't get me wrong, I appreciate your not wanting my brothers to be concerned, but the last fucking thing I need is the James clan prowling around Belize, dogging my heels."

Well, at least he hadn't shouted at her, but he'd been so angry and annoyed his face and ears felt hotter than hell. When Reya's eyes narrowed and she barged from the bed, he'd known his "charging bull" face was in full force.

And he didn't even want to think about her patrolling the jungle alone at night. He knew he'd been a royal pain in the ass about it, but it simply didn't matter that she'd done it for years, long before he crash-landed in her bed. In her bed . . . damn, that had a nice ring to it.

Now he wished he'd kept his big mouth shut. The woman had avoided him all day. His chest tightened and it had nothing to do with sore ribs. It wasn't an easy thing to admit, but he was man enough to do so.

Plain and simple, he missed Reya and doing right by her was important.

Brooding would get him nowhere. He had a ton of things to do and what better way to get your mind off a woman than do something else? Besides, he'd decided that this was one woman he wanted to keep, whether she was mad at him or not.

Five

Finally! It was all he could do to keep himself from yelling his thanks to the rafters! Dr. Matons had given him a clean bill of health. While the older man cautioned him to take it easy, he could run, jump, do anything he pleased. Including woo Reya.

As soon as the doctor left Reya's apartments with his big medical bag of tape, butterfly stitches, antibacterial ointments and pharmaceutical goodies in tow, Aaron moved all of his things out of Reya's bedroom into her office. He'd had enough of trying to keep himself from wanting her. But he would do this right. First, since he could get up now, he had no right to keep her from her bed. Second, he had no right to join her there without a true commitment. He was beyond ready, and he would seduce her until she felt the same. If he had his way, soon she'd be banging on the office room door to jump his bones.

Reya's office was perfect for what he needed to do. The woman had everything—state-of-the-art laptop and full-sized desktop computers with all the bells and whistles, including both satellite high-speed internet, phones and, thankfully, a very comfortable futon. It was a bit short for his six-foot-four frame, but he'd make do.

While he worked on getting her agreement to either join him in Colorado or be his woman here in Belize, he could catch up on work. And earn his keep.

Quickly showered and dressed, Aaron put on his own clothes for the first time in almost two weeks. After spending so much time in nothing but a pair of shorts and Reya's sheets, he was thankful she'd had the foresight to have someone wash every article of clothing packed in the black duffel she'd rescued from the plane.

In a form-fitting black tee shirt, comfortable black jeans and a pair of comfortable all-terrain half boots, he made his way down the stairs and into the dining hall.

He almost burst out laughing as Reya looked up from her table where she sat with Dr. Matons and Bethsaida. The woman's mouth had fallen open, and even with Bethsaida poking her in the ribs, it took her a while to finally manage to close it. He walked past her, winked and headed straight into the kitchen.

When he emerged with a crisp white apron tied around his waist and a tray of beverages, one of the young men was showing him which patrons waited for their breakfast drinks. Aaron felt Reya's eyes on him as he delivered a large tray of goodies to a tableful of guests across the room.

He was tiring quickly, but damn it, he had a woman to chase and he didn't have time to waste on getting back up to his full strength. That would come with hard work and nothing less. So he may as well get to it, and now was as good a time as any.

⟡

Lazing in the limbs of a broad tree near the perimeter of the woman's home, he watched through the window. A low growl escaped his throat as his future mate ogled the weak human who'd crashed in their jungle not long ago. He should have finished the man then, but couldn't without harming Reya. And he wanted her to come to him wild and unbroken of spirit . . . so he could enjoy breaking her.

Baring his teeth, he watched the human male move through the food area. Reya's eyes were plastered on the human male as he moved around the room serving other humans. He would have to do something about the man's attempt to insinuate himself into Reya's daily life. It would ruin his plans to ensure she wanted no one but him. And even if she did, she would *have* no one but him. The woman was a jaguar shifter, and she would mate a jaguar shifter. Period.

Reya belonged to him whether she realized it or not. And if she didn't fall in line soon, he would simply take her by force and make her feel the wrath of his bite.

∞

Aaron leaned against the wall in what he hoped was a casual stance. Sweat poured down his back as he tried to make himself useful, running all over the dining room, helping the staff and serving Reya's guests and fellow rangers. How the hell did Reya and Bethsaida run this place by themselves? There was never an idle moment and always something to do. After sitting in bed for a week, he suddenly wished he was back there, at least long enough to get a second wind. A coal black brow rose in question when a short, bulky young man dressed like a ranger strode through the dining area and headed straight for Reya.

As Aaron's eyes followed the bulky man, another one, young, thin but athletic, walked up to him, placed an ice cold pineapple juice in his hands and joined him against the wall, eyes on Reya and Mr. Bulky. Both of them pushed away from the wall and stood at the ready when Reya's back went ramrod straight and her lips tightened.

"So you're the man who crashed in our jungle, eh?" his companion said easily.

Aaron turned and looked the man in the eye. Something about the guy struck him as odd, but he detected no malice. In fact, he looked like an overgrown kid.

"Yep, that's me," Aaron said, holding his hand out in a friendly gesture. "I'm Aaron James. Nice to meet you."

"I'm Marc, one of the rangers. I do patrol with Reya sometimes."

The two moved to a nearby table, sipping cold juice, watching Reya deal with her obviously unwanted company.

"Who's the guy talking to Reya?" Aaron questioned, forcing his voice to sound calm and unconcerned. If he'd been a dog, his ears would be pointing straight up and his hackles showing.

"Name's Trefor, the new director of the sanctuary. She doesn't like him very much," Marc said quietly.

"You don't say," Aaron said distractedly, his irritation rising by the second when the Trefor person sat down next to Reya and wrapped his fingers around her arms, causing her to yank away. Noting the contrast between the other man's golden skin and Reya's darker tones, one side of Aaron's lip curled up, not wanting any other skin against hers but his, damn it. Aaron didn't care if he was the director. Hell, he could be king for all he cared.

If Trefor touched his woman one more time, he was going to get pounded into the floor, right here and now.

"So how long you gonna be here?" Marc queried, pulling Aaron's mind from his murderous thoughts. Setting his cup down, he turned and cocked a brow at the smiling young man. He looked just out of college. Probably had a crush on Reya. What young man in his right mind wouldn't want such a beautiful, self-sufficient woman on his arm? Too bad, this one was taken. Time to make it clear.

"How long? As long as the lady will have me. Clear enough?"

The smile remained on Marc's face, but a chill seeped into it as he nodded and said, "Just make sure you're worthy of her."

With that and a final sip of juice, Marc strode away and made a beeline to Reya's table. One of his hands landed lightly on her shoulder and Aaron's frown was instant as she looked up at Marc and appeared to immediately relax. With a smart-looking smile on his face, Marc said something to Trefor. Two seconds later Mr. Bulky stomped out of the room. As Aaron watched him barrel toward the front door, he couldn't help but notice everyone was talking to someone, whether guest or ranger. He was the only one sitting alone. He felt very much the outsider, and the conspiratorial smile shared between Reya and Marc made him grind his back teeth.

Reya should be looking at him like that, not Marc or any other man. He was, after all, her new best friend, whether she realized it or not.

Six

R eya slipped out of the kitchen's back door and strode purposefully into the jungle. Moving at a good clip, and thankful for well-worn trails and her unusual strength and speed, she figured to make her half-mile trek to the Sittee River in less than ten minutes.

Her stomach danced and the hair on the back of her neck stood on end from the moment she stepped into the dense fauna of deep jungle. A couple of times she'd actually stopped to look around, allowing her eyes to shift to enhance her vision. Everything appeared normal but didn't *feel* normal.

"Goddamn it, Trefor," she yelled when the idiot jumped out at her from somewhere to the right of the path she'd been traveling. He knew she had a diving appointment today and must have come out to head her off after she'd told him to kiss her ass earlier at the breakfast table.

"This seems to be the only way I can get you alone, Reya," he said cockily with a too-confident smile.

"Look, how many times do I have to tell you? I don't want to be alone with you. Not now. Not ever. Not for any reason. Now go away!"

Turning her back on him, she took two steps before his meaty hand landed on her shoulder and spun her around. That hand moved down to her biceps and squeezed brutally. Her shifter senses might be muted in her human form, but they weren't non-existent. If he didn't watch it, she'd have to give him a jaguar ass whipping and see how he liked that. Idiot.

"You're interested in that black-haired giant staying at your place, aren't you?" he snarled into her face. "Everyone is talking about the two of you!"

Snatching her arm away, she snarled right back. "It's none of your goddamned business, Trefor!"

Grabbing her arm again, he pulled her roughly against his chest. She almost giggled at how much shorter he was. Even if she'd wanted to kiss him—and the thought was too disgusting to imagine—she'd have to bend her head to do it. Not like kissing Aaron. Her mind drifted to how it felt to raise her head for his kisses, and how he liked to grab her by her hair and pull her head back so he could nibble on the sweet spot just under her jawline, and . . .

"Damn it, Reya, I'll wipe him from your mind if it's the last thing I do!" Trefor yelled as he grabbed at the front of her camo shirt, ripping the first two buttons off. Now *that* pissed her off.

The change pressed and pushed at Reya, urging her to allow the cat to come out and play. And Trefor would be the toy to her cat as she swatted him between her massive paws. But he didn't deserve to see the majesty of her shifted form. The numbskull wasn't good enough to lay eyes on such beauty. So she shoved him away from her with enough force to make him leave his feet and land hard against the trunk of the nearest tree.

Up quickly, he ran at her and right into a hard balled fist. Her right hook landed high on his cheekbone and he went down in a heap. But the idiot just didn't have enough sense to stay down.

Shaking his head against what she was sure was blinding pain, he hefted to his feet again. Eyes tight with anger and his lips pulled back in a nasty snarl, he yelled like a male banshee.

"You bitch! You hit me. Me! Trefor Dionisio!"

Reya rolled her eyes and looked up at the glorious sky. God, why did she have to deal with all the goofballs? A raging scream erupted from Trefor's throat as he ran at her. Oh this was definitely not good. He outweighed her by a good fifty pounds and if he pummeled into her, she'd end up on her back and might have to shift after all just to get him off.

The world came to a slow roll as one of Trefor's thick arms cocked back and let fly. Reya knew she was more than strong enough to deflect the blow and raised her arm to do just that. She could clearly make out the size and shape of the knuckles headed for her face. The blow never landed.

When time sped up again, she spied a larger hand attached to an even larger body, holding Trefor's fist in a palm just inches from her right eye.

Aaron!

Reya gasped in surprise as he insinuated himself between her and Trefor and smacked the shorter guy in the exact spot Reya had tagged him. Boy, his cheek would be good and sore tomorrow. And probably a few choice colors. God, she sure hoped so. Trefor yelped, lifting a hand to his face while backing away quickly. She giggled when he slammed into the same tree she'd introduced him to earlier before stumbling down the trail back toward the ranger station.

Maybe she and Aaron made a great team after all, both in and out of bed. And the man was sexy as hell even while he was beating the shit out of someone.

"You all right?" he asked gently, taking her face in his powerful, slightly calloused hands.

"Oh yeah. My hero," she sighed as his mouth came down on hers, sweet, searching. Delicious. He tasted like pineapple and hunger. She broke the kiss and looked up into his sinfully handsome face. The gentleness was a thing of the past. Oh he was hungry all right. For hot, wet woman. Judging by the way her womb reacted to that bare and open expression, she'd be both hot and wet shortly.

Instead, she pushed away. She couldn't do this now. She had a boat to catch and had to hurry or it would leave without her. Besides, he still hadn't apologized for his little temper tantrum over her calling his brothers.

"Aaron, I have to . . . ." was as far as she got. He reached down, picked up the duffel filled with her scuba gear and tossed it over one shoulder before reaching beneath her knees and tossing her over the other shoulder.

"Aaron, do you know where you're going?" she asked, noting the path he took through the thick trees. A smack on her backside was his answer, followed by the magical traipse of his fingers over her ass. It sent tingles down the back of her legs. She squirmed against the sensation, earning another smack. Oh God, that felt so good she wished he'd put her down so she could strip out of her pants, lean over and bare her ass to his strong but gently questing fingers.

But it wasn't to be. Sigh. Back to business.

"Aaron, I'm going to miss the boat. You're going the wrong way." When he didn't reply, she started to struggle. "Will you put me down? I've got to go."

Smack! Followed by a soothing rub of his hands all over her butt cheeks.

She stiffened against his shoulder as a pleasure-pain *zing* dove straight for her pussy. Oh yum! When he dipped down into the cleft of her cheeks and played with the little spot between her slit and her little anal hole, a deep shivering started at the base of her spine and spread outward. Oh Lord, he was making her dizzy, and not from carrying her pitched over his shoulder like a sack of potatoes.

He didn't say a word, just kept trudging with her out into the wilds. Reya's keen senses picked up other jaguars in the area. A female resting in the shade not fifty paces from where they strode through the jungle. Another female sounded less than a mile east of them. And they were excited, agitated, yet not in a fearful way. If she weren't mistaken, they wished her well with her love play.

Now this was ridiculous. The man had already won over Dr. Matons and Bethsaida. Now the jaguars liked him too?

Finally, he slowed his stride as they came out of the canopy and into a clearing. Raising a low-hanging thorny branch, Aaron ducked underneath and chuckled at her yelp when it made contact with her backside as they passed. A few branches and thick vines later, he put her feet on the ground in the middle of a beautiful, though small, secluded meadow.

They were well off the trail and surrounded by thick trees and fragrant flowers all laid around a thick carpet of bright green grass. She tore her attention away from the beauty of the place and back to her captor, and the heat behind his sensual gray eyes pulled a gasp from her lungs. Oh was he ever up to something. But he wasn't moving a muscle. Just stood there, looking at her like she was his favorite steak or something.

"Aaron? What's going on?" she asked, a bit wary now. His body language was tense, dangerous. She wasn't afraid he would hurt her, but she definitely wondered what the hell he had in mind way out here. When he started stalking toward her, his body all sinewy grace and deadly intent, her feet backed up all on their own. Eyes wide, she felt her back make contact with a very solid tree. Okay, time to go. Or at least that's what she thought, but even her shifter reflexes weren't fast enough. As soon as her muscles bunched to spring away, he was on her. All over her.

Aaron's hard, lean body rubbed against hers as he pressed her against the towering tree trunk, holding her hands over her head. The thick, long ridge of his cock pressed into her stomach, hot enough to scald through her clothes.

"Aaron," she said breathlessly, the scorching between her legs skyrocketing by the second, "I-I really need to go. Maybe we can get together later?"

As he shifted his hips, something hard dug into her side. Not his arousal. Something small, square and surprisingly familiar—her satellite phone was clipped to his belt loop. The little silver box gleamed dully in the muted light of the canopy of green over her head. With both her hands secured in one of his, he used his free hand to unclip it and flip it open. Too curious to be upset, she looked up at him and quirked a brow. What the hell was he doing?

"Close your eyes and I'll let you call the boat." The words brushed against her ear, low, seductive, determined.

She did as he said, knowing she had only a few more minutes to get to the river.

"Good girl. Now just stand here a second."

Stand here? She didn't have time to stand . . . oooh! Okay, not fair! Warm, sensuous lips nipped at her bottom lip before sliding down to her neck. Her mind screamed for him to stop. Her body, however, wasn't so inclined.

The kiss was gentle, seductive as his lips moved down to the juncture of her neck and shoulder. Then he laid into her, sucking fiercely, marking her until she squirmed against him, her breath coming in shallow gasps. Now the tip of his tongue outlined her ear and she heard a hiss of air float up into the morning sky. When her lungs burned, she realized that air had escaped from her chest as her breath seized in her throat. The man literally took her breath away.

His body kept her pinned against the tree. She wanted to move against him, grind her hips into the delicious hardness at his center. But she couldn't move, except to breathe in the masculine scent of him and let it out on a sigh, a moan or a gasp.

A beep caught her attention but not enough to hold it.

"Reya?"

"Oh yes," she breathed, eyes closed against the assault on her senses. His scent. The feel of his tongue and lips on her skin. The sound of the wind that floated through the trees and mixed with her own breathing. The wild call of colorful birds and the scurrying of insects up the smooth trunks of the trees. The easy burn that flowed out from her core and wrapped around her clit. She felt, heard and *smelled* it all. Now a taste was in order. With a tilt of her head, she caught his mouth with

her own and flicked out her tongue to play with his. He opened
to her and she was lost.

Whimpering with need, she chased his mouth as he tried to
break the kiss.

"Reya, call the boat."

"Huh, why?" she pleaded, again trying to get to his magical
mouth. A mouth that made her want, made her need.

"Tell them you're not going to make it."

She jerked her neck back and asked, "What? I've never missed
a booking."

"Yeah. Until today." As he bent to nip the globes of her sensitive breasts through her camouflage shirt, she fought to free her
hands so she could press him closer.

"Mmmm, that feels so good." When he bit down on the
hard berry of her nipple, she cried out and threw her head
back, unfazed when it made contact with the tree. Boat? What
boat?

"Aaron," she gasped. "Oh Lord!"

"Call them . . ." he crooned, his words full of a promise he'd
damned well better keep.

∞

Aaron flipped open the phone and held it out to her, then changed
his mind, realizing he would have to release her hands.

"Tell me the number," he ground out. The erection pressed
tight against his zipper bordered on pain.

"What? You want me to think now?" she protested.

A self-satisfied smile spread over his face. So she couldn't think,
eh? Good. He'd make sure she was flat-out mindless as soon as the

phone call was made. She would think of no one but him. Not Trefor, not Marc. Nobody. Just him.

Deliberately teasing her, grinding his cock against her fluttering belly, he said again, "The number, Reya. Tell it to me."

She spit out the numbers between gasps. He keyed it in and held the phone against her ear while his mouth played with her skin.

"H-Hello? Hi, this is . . . oh God!" she screeched, when he'd given her a full, openmouthed lick from her collarbone up to her ear. "T-This is Reya Daines. Sorry, I, I'll need you to . . . Jesus!" He'd just bitten the sensitive spot on her shoulder. "I c-can't make it to my dive appointment. Please have Shelly in Hopkins take the crew out for me. She's on standby, thankfully."

Aaron disconnected the call, tossed the phone into the grass next to her duffel and pulled her hard against his body. She felt so good and he'd missed her so much, he just couldn't hold himself back or away from her any longer.

"Baby, I've missed you the past couple of days. Take your shirt off. If I do it, I'll rip it to shreds."

"Then rip it," she whispered. Her gray eyes, so much like his, gleamed with passion.

He grabbed the top of her shirt and buttons flew in all directions as her shirt fell open and hung loosely on her body. He fell on her like a parched man who'd just discovered a fresh, cool drink of water and kissed her everywhere his lips could reach. Her lush, swollen breasts boasted nipples like chocolate candies, her skin like silken cocoa. And it was all his.

So attuned to her arousal, he felt every shudder, every quiver as he all but devoured her until she was a moaning, whimpering mass of want. He kneaded her breasts in his large hands and his mouth moved from one to the other, tasting, sucking, until her knees knocked together.

"Aaron," she gasped. "Oh God, baby, I need more. Please . . ."

Down on his knees now, he unbuttoned her camo pants and slid them down to her ankles. Her strong fingers tangled in his hair as her body undulated like waves breaking over a sandy beach, rushing and eager for fulfillment. He'd always been into the Barbie-doll type, but the flare of Reya's ample hips intrigued him. They reached east and west below a trim waist and made him want to slide into her until she was full of his seed.

"I love your body, Reya, your wide hips, your tight, firm ass. And your stomach, all lean and toned. A man would kill for your washboard abs. But . . ." he paused, kissing a path down the cropped mound of her woman's place, "most of all, I love your pussy. It's like a Dove ice-cream bar. Dark chocolate on the outside, creamy and sweet on the inside."

His mouth slid between her dewy lips, latched onto her clit and sucked for all he was worth. She screamed.

When her knees buckled he caught her, lifted her high and ground his jean-covered erection against her wet mound, and slammed his mouth down over hers so she could taste herself on his tongue. It was the most erotic dance he'd ever experienced. But his woman was insatiable. She wanted more and wasn't afraid to ask for it.

"Aaron, oh baby. Please. Now." Her words pulled at his gut. She was ravenous, starving. Her fingers reached down to massage the bulge in his pants and then a harsh groan emanated from deep in his chest as she unerringly yanked open his belt and unbuttoned his jeans in short order.

"I want you. Deep. Right now," she breathed, each word sending a jolt of sensation directly to his balls.

"You want it? Then take it." His head swam with her scent, her taste so heady and overwhelming, Aaron had no idea how he'd even formed the words.

The warm, humid air of the jungle wrapped around his steel erection scant seconds before the tip was surrounded by the warm, wet caress of Reya's pussy. The rest of his cock was jealous of the head and demanded he sink deep so her wet channel could envelop it, surround it completely.

His hips had a life of their own as they thrusted, his cock stroking the inside of her vagina until they were both grunting, straining for a completion they could only find in each other.

Aaron felt his balls pull close to his body and pressed his sweaty forehead against Reya's as she rode him like a professional bronco, taking everything he had. The tight walls of her cunt milked him until he could hold back no longer. Her toes pointed as her thighs tightened around his back as she came long and hard. A plume of thick cum shot up through his rod like the cork of a shaken champagne bottle, eager to splash against her womb and fill her with his cream.

Sapped of strength, his knees were history. He fell back into the grass, taking her with him where she lay on top of him, cushioned against his body. Chest to chest, her strong legs straddled around his hips. Still buried deep inside her soaked pussy, his fingers played in her hair as hers plucked at the hard nipples of his pecs, causing them to instinctively flex and bunch. The woman giggled as she wreaked havoc on his nervous system. Chest muscles danced, stomach muscles rippled as she tortured him with soft touches and gentle scrapes of her fingernails over his sensitized skin.

"Witch." He let out a chuckle as she tickled his top rib.

"That's Miz Witch to you," she purred.

"You seem to have caught your breath," he queried playfully.

"Mmm hmm."

Her pussy fluttered and his cock stirred wickedly in response, stretching and filling her as it flared back to life. Pushing up on her elbows, Reya looked down at him with amazement.

"Already?" she asked, one of her perfect brows raised a good inch.

"Baby, I've got lost time to make up for." The plan? Fuck her until she couldn't walk or see straight.

Seven

S on of a bitch! How dare he make love to her then decide
to leave! Oh sure, claim it was to finish his original business in Belize City. Claim he was going to take care of a
client so he could return to her with no distractions and concentrate on her. Yeah, whatever.

To further kick her in the face, the man had moved all his
things into her office. Granted, he only had the black duffel she'd
salvaged, but that wasn't the point. He wouldn't sleep in her bed
with her, claiming it was bad enough he'd made love to her without a commitment, and tried to stress the significance of the fact
that it had never been important to him until he'd met her. Sure,
she believed *that* one, all right.

Reya had been so angry, she'd yelled that she couldn't wait for
him to leave for Belize City so she could have her life back. Rage
flared in his steely gray eyes and he'd practically ripped every last
shred of clothing from her shivering body. In spite of his anger,
his touch had been so gentle and his words so sexy, by the time
the last bit of fabric hit the floor she'd practically sobbed with
anticipation.

The loving had been hot, desperate. Both of them took with mutual hunger and gave with unrestrained passion. Caught up in the rapture, she'd screamed words at him that would have normally made her blush, had told him with unrestrained fervor what she wanted him to do to her. In turn, he'd promised and delivered everything she'd begged for.

He'd left her sometime in the night for the futon in the office, leaving her to wake alone. Still, she hadn't wanted to risk facing him and slipped out of her apartment and down to the dining area much earlier than usual.

But she still hadn't managed to avoid him. The second he stepped foot into the dining hall, her body recognized his presence, tingling from her scalp down to the base of her spine. They worked practically side by side in the B&B but hadn't exchanged a single word. The stiff set of his shoulders told Reya she'd hurt him with her accusation that he'd simply wanted a piece of her ass and had no intention of coming back. She hadn't exactly said that, but it was close enough.

Later that morning, she'd made her way down to the boat, tired of the stress and strain of having such an imposing man so near. Aaron's anger and pain were practically palpable, setting her nerves on edge. It didn't help to see his finely honed body, all golden skin and stacks of cut muscle wrapped around long limbs, flex and stretch as he worked with the kitchen staff. Pissed off as she was, the man still made her knees wobble.

On her way to and from her diving spot, there'd been plenty of time to think. The conclusion—her mouth and temper had gotten the best of her, and as much as she hated to admit it, the stinging words had tumbled out before she could stop them. She hadn't meant to be so harsh and only intended to learn his reasons for leaving for Belize City now. But it had come out as an accusation, and a mean-spirited one at that.

With no patrol tonight, perhaps they could talk, clear the air before he left in a couple of days, but when she returned from the river, he'd used the excuse of working late. She guessed it was his turn to avoid her. The rejection wrapped around her heart and squeezed brutally until she fled her apartment with the excuse of needing to see Bethsaida.

And now here she sat on her good friend's balcony, sprawled in a rattan chair, bawling her eyes out. Mega bastard.

"He seems to be a good man, and you're a good woman. Surely two good people can work things out. You'll see," Bethsaida said softly, soothing Reya's hair back from her forehead before handing her another tissue.

"I-I just feel so mixed up and out of sorts. I like Aaron, I really do. But he makes me feel so out of control, it's scary," Reya sniffed. An ache crept up the back of her neck. Crying certainly wasn't helping. And what was she crying for anyway? Hell, she wasn't sure.

"From what you've said, he told you he's never felt this way about a woman before either. So you're at least on an equal playing field. But you'll have to bend, sweetie. Flexible branches don't break, eh?"

"Yeah, I guess. I don't even know if he wants . . ."

"Stop trying to figure out what he's thinking and just ask him, Reya."

Her elbows rested on her knees and her head was in her hands. She didn't say anything, simply thought about Bethsaida's words while wallowing in her self-imposed misery.

"Reya, why don't you go to bed? Things are always clearer in the morning."

"Thanks, Beth. Maybe I'll do that."

Kissing the older woman on the cheek, Reya saw herself out and headed toward her own apartments. Almost to her front door on the third floor, she changed her mind, headed back down to the first floor and made her way out the kitchen doors instead.

She knew exactly what she needed to get her head together. A bit of time communing with the land, air, wind and a few of her wild cousins.

Easing into the surrounding foliage, a quick stop behind a huge tree found her stripped naked in a flash. Dropping to all fours, she felt the power of her gift ripple through the muscles of her legs and up through her back. Each limb trembled, stretched and shrunk. The breath of the spirit of nature traipsed along her skin then sank down through her pores until it filled her soul and pumped through her blood.

Bones crunched as they moved and made way for their new configuration. Her height, or rather length, remained the same, but her strong thighs became lean, bulky haunches, her chest thick and heavily muscled, and her jaw widened. Covered with silky black fur, she laid on the jungle floor. A long pink tongue flicked out over thin lips before snaking out to clean her whiskers.

Padding silently into deeper bush when she was a good distance away, she opened her mouth and let out the frustrated yell she'd been holding in all day. It came out a loud, frightening roar, carried on the wind. The sounds of the insects, loud birds and even louder monkeys quieted as huge paws dug into the soft earth. There was a predator among them.

Muscles bunched beneath her, and she shot out into the night. Two miles from the B&B, her cry lit the night again. This time, two gold and black females flew out of the trees and joined her in the run, romping and playing as they loped under the canopy of huge trees, into the night.

∽

What had he been thinking when he'd volunteered to keep his hands off Reya? For the life of him, the reasons for tormenting himself just weren't surfacing. He must have been crazy to invite this kind of suffering. Maybe a late fever from his injuries had set in, or temporary insanity? His expression was pensive as he wondered if she was suffering as well. But it wasn't about him, not this time. It was about doing right by her, and until she was really, truly his, he had no right to touch her again. Trying to "work" her out of his mind obviously hadn't worked considering he'd fallen asleep with his laptop perched on his thighs and a pile of unfinished business on the coffee table. And now that he was awake, he wanted her more than he had before he'd decided to bury himself in trying to catch up on work.

Rising from the couch, he stretched, trying to work the kinks out of his back. Reya's bed was much more comfortable than her couch by a long stretch. Reya. He wondered what she was dreaming about. Or was she awake like him, trying to push him out of her thoughts like he was?

He looked down at his feet and wondered when he'd walked across the room to her door. Bone tired and weary of heart, he threw in the towel and knocked softly on her door.

"Reya?" he called quietly, tilting his head and listening intently.

Nothing. "Reya," he called again, this time silently turning the door handle and poking his head inside. The room was shrouded in darkness. As usual, the shade was up and the window wide open. He could see the veranda from this window, but unless someone could jump twenty feet horizontally then tear off the screen, the window couldn't be reached from the balcony. After his eyes adjusted to the gloomy gray of the room, an alarm went off in his head.

In two bounds Aaron stood next to a comfortably inviting bed. But Reya wasn't in it. In fact, it looked like the covers had never been disturbed.

He glanced quickly at the digital readout of the little clock near her bed, his hands planted themselves on his hip—one-thirty a.m. Where the hell was his woman? Wait, he couldn't call her that, at least not yet. Fine! Where the hell was his woman-to-be?

Fingers tore through his jet-black hair as he paced until some semblance of reason set in. Perhaps she was out on patrol? He was sure she wasn't scheduled tonight, but she was definitely gone. Maybe she was helping out by taking someone else's shift?

One thing was sure, if she was with that Trefor creep, he'd kill them both. Trefor would go first, with great pain and equal relish. Reya, he'd just have to kill her with cock, uh, kindness.

There was only one problem. He didn't want her later. He wanted to hold her, to kiss her soft lips, to simply be with her, right here, right now. But this pacing was getting him nowhere. His muscles screamed for action, any action. Maybe the time he'd spent recuperating was taking its toll? Perhaps if he just got out for a little while he'd feel better, work off some of his pent-up energy. That way if he came upon Reya, he wouldn't just jump on her and hump her brains out.

The decision made, he stalked into the smaller room Reya used as an office, now his bedroom—idiot!—and pulled his black jacket out of the closet. Reya mentioned her patrols were safe and generally boring, hardly ever coming across a poacher this late at night. Mainly because they couldn't see as well in the dark as the cats they hunted. She might have said that just to make him feel better when he'd expressed concern over her having the night shift in a jaguar sanctuary, but he didn't think so. Besides, jaguars didn't typically eat humans. Other than the recent attacks on female jags, there was nothing to worry about other than an occasional monkey shit bomb out of a high tree or a bird taking to flight.

But his papa hadn't raised a fool. Before he set out, he ducked back into Reya's room, grabbed the extra tranquilizer gun off the shelf in her closet and made sure it was loaded. Finding a pair of sleek night-vision goggles tucked on the top shelf, he grabbed those too, impressed at the quality of the gadgets of this obviously well-funded operation.

Not wanting to wake any of the other guests, he slipped quietly through the living room, out onto the balcony and down the private back stairs. The balmy night air was comfortably warm, nothing like the sweltering nights of a Colorado summer. The tall, wide trees cast shadows across the earth, and his feet made no sound as he walked. Flipping the night-vision goggles down, the world became a brightly lit, though green-tinted, paradise. Suddenly he felt like a mighty hunter out stalking prey, exhilarated, as he moved silently through a jungle he knew teemed with four-legged hunters that lived at the top of the food chain.

After about an hour, he saw something most humans were never blessed to see—a majestic gold and black jaguar. It appeared in the path not more than ten feet from him and stood watching him with a curious tilt of its head.

Aaron stood perfectly still and marveled at the beauty and power of the creature. Given its size and powerful build, he guessed it was a male. The broad, well-muscled chest, strong legs and wide, heavy body moved with grace, its large padded paws completely silent in the dead of the night.

The hackles on the back of his neck rose to full alert. A moment ago, he'd commented to himself about the peace surrounding him at the sound of various chirping insects and rustling leaves as small creatures scurried about. Now there was nothing. Not a single sound met his ears except the deep growl of the large cat as it bared lethal canines.

Aaron's first instinct was to run, but common sense overrode the sudden burst of adrenaline making him tremble. Instead, he raised the tranquilizer gun and aimed. Before he could fire a blur shot out from behind him and tackled the large male.

He watched spellbound as a beautiful black jaguar locked jaws and paws with the threatening male. The gold jag looked like it was going to come out on top after rolling several times with the black cat. But he was up on his feet quickly. No, wait. The black *he* was actually a *she!* And she was vicious, fast as lightning, and gave no quarter to her foe as their snarls filled the jungle. The male delivered a particularly nasty swipe to the side of the female's head and she stumbled.

But all was not lost. Two more jaguars charged out of the foliage and came to the black jaguar's aid. But the male was strong and the three females were having a tough time subduing him.

Maybe someone would hear all the noise and come help? No, he couldn't wait for that. He had to do something. Right now.

Raising the sights on the tranq gun again, Aaron fired at the male. Shit, he missed! The dart lodged deep in the black female's shoulders and she tottered momentarily before flopping to the ground. But the male lay on the ground as well, taken down by the females. Seeing the threat eliminated, the other females took off the moment he hit the dirt. But this male was smart. Too smart. When the females disappeared into the night, he was back on his feet, dancing around wildly.

Aaron's eyes narrowed as he regarded the deadly creature. Something intelligent went on behind the big cat's eyes. It was as if he recognized not only the danger of the downed black but him as a man. The feeling shivered down Aaron's back and settled behind his knees. It was the most uncanny thing he'd ever experienced. And he didn't like it one bit.

Aaron raised the gun and aimed it right between the gold male's eyes. He'd be damned if he missed this time. Taking a bold step forward, he growled at the crazed jag, prepared to pull the trigger. At the hard glint in Aaron's eyes, the male came to a decision and took off into the deep jungle.

Behind him came a soft growl followed by . . . a moan? Jaguars didn't moan, did they? Turning back to the female that had more than likely saved his life tonight, he stared down at the ground in awe and went completely still. The moan was louder now, but the cat's body was shivering and shifting, the bones repositioning themselves under the skin. Shiny fur receded into the pelt, replaced by sleek, smooth skin. The bones of the shoulders and head made a squishing sound as they shrank and rearranged.

The sucking and popping noises made his stomach dance as he watched the cat transform.

Kneeling down next to the animal, Aaron removed the tranq dart from her shoulder and ran his hand through a tangle of soft, thick hair. Shock was quickly replaced by concern as his eyes roamed over the tall, muscular, very naked frame. Reya.

Removing his jacket, he quickly covered her sleeping, bleeding form, threw her over his shoulder in a fireman's hold and took off as if her life depended on it. And judging by the amount of blood oozing through his jacket from the wounds she'd sustained, her life just might.

Glancing up at the sky, Aaron hissed a prayer under the weight of Reya's body. He hadn't prayed since he was a teenager when his father lay at death's door. *Please let Reya be knocked out from the tranquilizer and not so still because she's dying*, he pleaded out loud as her warm blood ran thick from the wounds on her back and the backs of her legs, and over his hands where he held her close to his body.

While they trekked at a speed Aaron hadn't known he could move, he listened closely for the sounds of any large, dangerous animals with canines crashing through the trees behind them. Adrenaline-fueled legs pumped tirelessly as he weaved through the tangle of trees back to her B&B near the front entrance of the sanctuary. All was quiet except for the occasional distant roar that sent chills up his spine and anger coursing through his heart. Anger that some wild cat had injured his sweet, loving Reya. His own adorable, precious . . . whoa! Precious? Adorable? How about dangerous with claws, literally! His woman was a shifter, and it seemed a very capable one.

It sure explained a lot. Now it made sense why she usually patrolled alone in the middle of the night with no night-vision goggles and no weapons. Even when learning biology and evolution as a child in school, he'd never bought in to the idea that plain old humans were alone on this great big planet. Did he believe in fairies, ghosts or elves? No. But people with a different genetic makeup that allowed their bodies to change? Well, sure, why the hell not? And the fact he'd never expected to meet such a being didn't change reality—a sleek, lovely and changeable body was draped over his shoulder, thoroughly unconscious.

He should be more upset at the discovery, at least amazed by it. He didn't have time to worry about the fact that his woman was a different species. She was hurt and it was all his fault. Now she needed him in the worst way.

Damn, she's heavy, Aaron thought as he hitched Reya's unconscious form higher up on his shoulder and shot up the steps, thankful he'd left the door to her private veranda unlocked. He ducked inside, careful of Reya's dangling arms and legs, and headed for the bedroom.

Easing her down off his shoulder and onto her stomach, Aaron was out of her apartment in a blink to bang on the door across the hall.

"Dr. Matons!" he yelled at the top of his lungs. Who cared it was the middle of the night, or rather the early dark hours of morning? His woman needed help, and right-damned *now*. Aaron's huge fist made contact with the door again.

"Dr. Matons! Open up, it's Aaron!"

Seconds later, a frazzled doctor yanked open the door, dark hair tousled, eyes wide with concern and lips pressed into a thin line.

"She was attacked in the jungle. Jaguars. Unconscious," was all he could get out as he yanked the doctor behind him and down the hall into Reya's apartments.

Together they slowly and carefully removed his blood-soaked jacket from her naked form. Some of the blood had dried and caused the jacket to stick to the wounds. Thankfully she was unconscious as they removed it.

"What happened?" Matons asked, clenching his teeth against what Aaron assumed was a mix of concern and anger. After all, it was apparent both the good doctor, Bethsaida and the staff all loved Reya.

"I was aiming at a jaguar. He was about to attack me, so I tried to shoot him with the tranq gun. I shot Reya by mistake."

"How the hell could you mistake her for a jaguar, Aaron?" he asked calmly, easing the last of the jacket plastered to Reya's ripped and torn flesh.

He didn't miss the stiffening of the doctor's spine as tension set in, nor the tight set of his mouth as the blood drained from his face. The flicker of concern as it passed over the older man's forehead made it clear he saw Aaron as a possible threat.

"Because, Doctor," Aaron growled, lowering his head to look at the man eye-to-eye, "she was a damned jaguar when I shot her! She saved my ass. Now do something to help her instead of just standing there questioning me." Backing off just enough to give the doc a little bit of breathing room, Aaron let his fingers stray to Reya's thick black mass of hair and idly stroked through the softness. He closed his eyes and took a deep breath, trying desperately to get ahold of the possessiveness, the helplessness suddenly assailing him. What if she never woke up? What would he do if he lost her? A lump formed in the back of his throat. He couldn't get a single word out for the next few moments.

Never taking his eyes off her, he finally said, "Please, Doc. I owe her my life several times over. She means everything to me." Forcing a bit more grit into his voice, he followed up with, "Now move your ass. Help her."

After what seemed like endless moments of sizing each other up, Aaron's relief was almost palpable when the doctor turned away from him with a half-cocked smile and began digging in his bag for supplies.

"Get a soft cloth and water," the doc said as he pulled a sterile syringe out of his goody bag. "Clean the wounds as well as you can, first with warm water, then cool."

"But she's not moving," Aaron said, unable to keep the desperation out of his voice. Hell, he was so scared for Reya, her chest barely moving and her pulse much too sluggish. It was all he could do not to yell, scream and rant at the doctor who moved just a little too slowly.

"She's not moving because the tranquilizer is meant for large game animals. It's obvious you know that Reya fits into that category, but only when she's in her shifted form. Once human, her metabolism changes to fit her body and the drug has a much more potent affect. She'll be fine in a few hours. I'm more concerned about infection than I am about her sleeping."

"But . . ." Aaron sputtered, touching firm fingers to her wrist again just to make sure she still had a pulse.

"Stop worrying. Those wounds of hers will be all healed in a few days."

"Are you serious?" Aaron asked incredulously. The wreck on her back would have downed the heartiest man, but he was supposed to believe Reya could just shake it off in a few days? Then again, she wasn't quite human. It would stand to reason that her body might behave differently than his. But hell, he didn't feel like being reasonable. He wanted her awake, telling him he'd been a big jerk, telling him anything for that matter.

"Trust me. She'll be fine. You get a cloth and water, I've have to go pick up a few things." With that, Dr. Matons left the bedroom. A quiet but finite snap of the door told Aaron the doctor had left the apartments.

With a basin full of clean, warm water, Aaron moved to the side of the bed. His stomach muscles clenched wildly as he took in the sight of the damage done to his woman's body. Her back was a mass of criss-crossed, angry, open lashes. The oozing pink and white raw flesh contrasted wildly against her dark skin.

Unable to take the sight of her ravaged body, Aaron dimmed the lights as he began to work, easing a soft cloth over the worst of the wounds. He changed the water in the basin three times before managing to clean all the cuts and dried blood. Where the hell was the damned doctor? It had been more than an hour since he'd left and there was still no sign of the man. When Reya awoke she would need something for the pain.

He wished he could give her something to forget her ordeal. Hell, he wanted something to help *him* forget. To erase the memory of the regal form of the gold and black jaguar squaring up to pounce on him, fangs bared with a menacing growl in its throat.

Then the beautiful black-furred cat appeared. Almost as large as the male, her smooth coat reflected the pale moonlight as she barreled into the one meaning to attack him.

According to what Reya had taught him about the jaguars in the sanctuary, hunting together was almost unheard of with these solitary animals. Yet the black cat and two other majestic gold cats coordinated their efforts in order to protect him, fight for him.

Even when she'd thought he was leaving her for good, thought he didn't want her, she'd come to protect him. Had sacrificed herself for him. God knows he didn't deserve such a woman.

Closing his eyes, he could still see the aggressive jag's claws ripping into Reya's flanks. His ears couldn't seem to push away the anguished roar that escaped her throat as the flesh of her back was torn open. He'd come so close to losing her. Trying to shake the memory, Aaron inadvertently dug his fingers into Reya's tender flesh through the soft cloth.

A quiet moan rumbled through Reya's too still body. Aaron looked down and immediately pulled his hand away. Flipping the cloth over in his hand, he grimaced. Fresh blood. Her blood. Rinsing it again, he ran it over her now fevered skin and braced himself when the sound came again. Something about the low sensual quality of Reya's moans wrapped firmly around his balls and gently squeezed. Damn and double damn. The woman was hurt, and here he was getting horny over the way she moaned as he cleaned her up. Boy did he need help.

His eyes roamed over her nakedness in appreciation. She was a beautiful woman. And not just her facial features, but everything about her was exquisite. A brilliant mind, full of knowledge of everything from medicine, to big cats, to the latest and most popular anime movies. Physically, she was perfect—firm, toned, with everything in abundance. Her arms were cut and well defined, her stomach rippled and ridged. Breasts and hips were full and ample. Lush. All covered in rich cocoa skin.

Aaron had never really been into muscular women, but then again, he'd never had the pleasure of undressing one. Making love to one. Gently, slowly caressing every inch of delectable skin over solid muscle. And there was no doubt Reya was what he preferred.

As his fingers ran over her skin, the contrast of his fairer golden skin was sensually beautiful to him against her darker tones. His mind flitted to the memory of the sight and feel of his long, tanned fingers sliding into her silky, tight depths, so dark on the outside but pink as cotton candy on the inside. His unruly cock stirred. Damned good thing she was injured and unconscious, otherwise, he wouldn't have been able to resist dragging her underneath him and burying himself to the hilt in her hot pussy.

Eight

Ooooh, that felt so good. Something cool and soft traipsed over her back with easy strokes. She wasn't sure what it was, but it was so nice she didn't really care. Before the coolness touched her skin, her back burned with such ferocity the pain reached beyond the tranquilizer to penetrate the peaceful darkness of unconsciousness. Half awake now, the intense fire from the deep claw marks was a dull ache rather than raw, pulsing pain.

Boy that tranq had really knocked her on her . . . oh God! The tranquilizer dart! It had pierced the deep muscle of her shoulder. A tranq dart shot by Aaron! She remembered hitting the dewy grass in her jaguar form. Considering she now lay in her human body, there was no doubt that her secret was out. Aaron knew she was a shifter.

This was definitely not good. He'd already left her bedroom with his lame excuse of wanting to "do right by her" but she knew the real reason. It was because he was trying to find a way to bow out gracefully. Well, if he needed a reason, her being a shifter was definitely it. Now that he knew who, or rather what, she was, he'd run hell for leather back to the States.

Embarrassed and more than a little frightened that Aaron knew her deepest, most closely guarded secret, Reya's words came out on a rush as her groggy mind suddenly cleared and snapped fully awake. Trying to rise, she found herself eased back down to her stomach.

With more than a hint of panic she blurted, "What are you doing to me?"

"Easy, baby. Dr. Matons is on his way."

The soft sheets under her bare flesh were damp from the cool liquid being dribbled over her raw wounds.

"Does this feel all right?" Aaron's voice was soft and full of concern. That couldn't be right. He should be running and screaming, or something. Anything other than being so sweet to her. "Did you hear me, Reya? Is this pressure all right? I don't want to hurt you."

"Uh-well . . ." she stammered. Maybe her wits were still out in the jungle. They certainly weren't anywhere near her head right now.

"Relax, baby. I'm sorry if this hurts, sweetheart, but these scratches are deep. Dr. Matons told me to wash your wounds as well as I could while he went to get a few things."

No censure or hostility in his voice? Was he just being nice until he could make sure she wouldn't change and bite him in the ass?

"Reya, I doubt you feel like talking about this now, but you were incredible," he said softly but with something that sounded a lot like pride. Man, that rogue must have slapped her in the head harder than she thought—surely she was imagining all of this.

"I mean, hell, I don't know what to say," Aaron continued. "That big male would have had me if not for you and your friends.

Baby, it was the most amazing thing I've ever seen! It was just, like . . . wow, Reya!"

Wow? Amazing? Was he crazy? Her aunt had always taught her that she must keep her abilities under wraps. Aunt Sulu had always said that it was hard enough being a black female, let alone one who could turn into a jaguar and rip you to shreds. But here was the most handsome man in the universe complimenting her on her abilities.

"Does anyone else know?" he asked softly.

It took her a moment to get her head around his question, too caught up in her disbelief that he wasn't running out the door.

"Reya, does anyone else know, baby?"

"No, well, yes. Dr. Matons and Bethsaida. No one else outside of my family, which consists of only my aunt Sulu." She listened to the water trickle into the basin as Aaron dipped the cloth into the water, wrung it out and bathed the ridges on her back again with cool water. She hissed long and loud at the pain, wishing she'd remained knocked out a little while longer. Each cut felt like a hive of bees had landed on the open wounds and started stinging her repeatedly. It took all her concentration not to flinch with each stroke of Aaron's hands.

"So you're a black panther, eh?"

She sniffed, throwing her nose up in the air as much as she was able considering her position on her stomach. "There's no such thing as a black panther."

"Well, you sure looked like . . ."

"I didn't say there weren't black cats, just not black panthers. I'm a jaguar, a melanistic one."

"Mellon-what?" he asked, pausing midstroke with the cloth.

"Melanistic, Aaron," she chuckled, then winced before explaining that melanism was a hereditary trait, an abnormality of one of her cat genes associated with coat coloration and markings. He lifted her hair out of the way to run the cloth over the back of her neck and paused. The second her neck was exposed, every muscle in her body went taut.

"Reya, what the hell happened to you?" he asked angrily, pressing a little too hard with the cloth. She yelped.

"I'm sorry, baby. But these scars, what happened?"

She knew exactly what he was looking at—the scars hidden in her hair just above her nape. Something she'd never shown or shared with anyone. Ever.

"Look, Reya, understand me when I say I'm not willing to go another day pretending I can leave you alone. Hell, I can't even stay mad at you. You are, as of this moment, stuck with me. So your choice, tell me now or tell me later. But you will tell me so I can kill the son of a bitch who did this to you."

Well, damn, wasn't he pushy? Her heart melted. Even as he growled the words, his touch was gentle and caring. After a few moments of silence and weighing her options, she decided that some of the mysteries she kept were no longer wanted and spilled the whole sordid tale.

"Both my parents were shifters. But unlike lions, jaguars aren't social creatures. We're pretty solitary and don't mate for life."

"Wanna bet?" Aaron snarled, pausing the cloth midstroke at the base of her spine.

"Do you want to hear the story or not?" she said firmly, tucking her head into the fold of her arms to hide a grin. His response was a single grunt, which she took as a yes.

"Anyway, after my mother conceived, my father disappeared. It's what was expected so none of my family was shocked, surprised or even concerned." Another humph from Aaron, but she continued.

"One day, when Reyna . . ."

"Reyna? Who's Reyna?"

"My twin sister, my littermate," she whispered, fighting back the tears that threatened every time she thought about her sister. A sister she would never see again until the hereafter.

"We were really young and hadn't mastered our shifting abilities yet. We'd just slipped into our jaguar forms unexpectedly when my father showed up. My mom tried to run him off, but he was feral, infanticidal actually."

"The man was a baby killer?" Aaron asked incredulously.

"In large cats, it's not uncommon for adults to kill cubs. My, uh . . ." she paused and took in a shallow breath. "Reyna didn't survive. My mom survived long enough to get me to my aunt's home. My aunt Sulu raised me. From that day until I was grown enough to take care of myself, she never let me out of her sight. That woman was a stern old biddy, but she loved me and always looked after me, even after I was a grown woman. She raised me to understand the importance of secrets and survival. The keys to any shifter's survival."

"Secrecy? Don't you think the world would be amazed at what you can do?"

"Yeah but after they finished being amazed, they'd try to cut me up as this week's biology project."

She sighed when his hands settled on her backside for a moment, gently stroking and kneading the flesh. She loved when he touched her ass. The man was almost reverential about it. Then he moved lower, bathing the cuts across her hamstrings.

Just then, Dr. Matons came in. Reya was somewhat surprised. The doc knew all she needed was a good wash and a painkiller. Give or take a day or two of rest and she'd be good as new. When he walked in and winked at her, she knew exactly what he was up to. Meddlesome old matchmaker.

"How are you feeling, my dear?"

It was a stupid question. She hurt from the back of her neck to the heels of her feet. The pain accompanied the myriad slashes covering her body. How did he think she felt?

"A strong narcotic would be nice," she growled, then grinned when he winked at her.

Aaron left the room and returned with a glass of water and a straw. When she raised her head and quirked a brow at him, he said, "Well, it's not like you can sit up right now with all those cuts everywhere."

"Dr. Matons," she pleaded, "will you please tell him?"

"I already did, my dear. He's aware that you'll be fine in a day or two. Already your cuts are beginning to heal, but you're going to be quite sore until then."

Dr. Matons stuffed a couple of little, white pills into her mouth, and Aaron was right there ready with the water, fitting a straw between her lips.

"What is it?" she asked, hoping he remembered that certain drugs made her queasy.

"Tylenol with codeine. Two now. Two in four hours."

Aaron stroked a large hand through Reya's hair. "I'll see to it, Doctor."

"Good," he said, his eyes locked with Reya's drooping ones. "I'll let Bethsaida know you won't be down in the morning."

"I'll be down to help," Aaron said resolutely.

Now what kind of sense did that make, Reya wondered as the painkiller started to take effect. He would be in Belize City tomorrow morning.

As if he'd read her mind, he looked down at her and said, "I'll be here, Reya. I'm not going anywhere until I'm sure you're all right."

"But your brothers are meeting you . . ."

"They can reroute and meet me here instead. Besides, they'd love to meet their soon-to-be sister-in-law," Aaron said lazily as he took a tube of antibiotic ointment from Dr. Matons's fingers and began to ease it lovingly into the slashed skin on her calves.

"Sister-in-what?!" she gasped.

"You heard me. Marry me?"

Her mouth dropped open and stayed there. He wanted to marry her? Even after learning she was a shifter? Her eyes went as wide as they were able, given the swift arrival of her latest groggy state. Lord knew she wanted him, but they hadn't known each other that long. And what about his brothers? What if they didn't like her? And what if Aunt Sulu didn't like any of them?

"Aaron . . . I-I, well . . ." Her mind was a jumble of questions and muted excitement, but in seconds the codeine won the fight with her head as Aaron's fingers smoothed the antibiotic up the backs of her thighs, lulling her into a deep, healing sleep.

The last thing she remembered was wishing she could stay awake long enough to tell him to linger on her ass. And to say she'd be honored to marry him.

Nine

He couldn't decide whether he should be seething mad or deliriously happy. His brothers absolutely adored Reya, doted on her. They'd come down on Cockscomb Jaguar Sanctuary like a pack of flirtatious mother hens. Hell, he couldn't even wrap his mind around how they managed to baby him, flirt with every woman in sight, including his own, and have everyone still love them like sons. Austin and Anthony James had even managed to thoroughly charm Bethsaida and Dr. Matons was a close second.

Now they were working on Reya. The bastards had stormed right into her bedroom while she was still in bed. *Reya, you're just so beautiful. Oh Reya, we're so glad you've caught yourself a James boy. Reya, we look forward to going scuba diving with you. Reya, it's so nice and green here, unlike dry-assed Colorado. Reya, your bed-and-breakfast is exquisite.* Shit, it was Reya this and Reya that. On and on it went. It didn't matter that their compliments on Reya's B&B were warranted. He had to admit, it was a well-designed structure with the best amenities, and if the James boys knew anything, they knew architecture. But they were damned annoying, flirting with his woman like shameless hussies, er, hussie-men!

And Reya loved every minute of it. Had even had the nerve to tell him how good-looking all the James boys were, him included of course. He'd wanted to smack her as she went on about how tall Austin was, how he looked so much like Aaron. Oh and then there was the Ode to Anthony's Dimples. Damned woman. And she still hadn't agreed to marry him. Admittedly, he asked her when she was half delirious with pain and enjoying a nice dose of pain meds. But still!

She'd sat in the damned bed, skinning and grinning up at Austin and Anthony as they brought her anything and everything her little heart desired. Hell, there wasn't anything left for him to do because his thickheaded brothers had taken care of all of Reya's needs.

All they cared about was the fact that she was the woman he wanted to marry, and they were busy sinking their claws—that word held new meaning for him—into Reya to secure her as part of the family. And all because he wanted her. As if he couldn't do it himself. Damned meddlers.

Aaron's spine stiffened as his head filled with a possible explanation for his ire—he was jealous! Nah, that couldn't be right, could it? No. Hell no. Absolutely not! He'd never been jealous over a woman in his whole life. But then again, since he'd met Reya, he'd had all kinds of new emotions dancing around his brain.

Right now both Austin and Anthony were downstairs filling in for him and Reya in the dining area, no doubt trying to run the kitchen by now. And here he sat on the side of Reya's bed, grumbling about all their playboy-laden clucking. A resigned sigh huffed from his chest. May as well get over it. After all, they meant well.

Aaron tensed at the feel of fingertips traipsing down the middle of his back. His breath hitched as warmth spread from his spine, wrapped around his kidneys and dove straight for his heart. Only one touch could do that. Reya's.

"I thought you were sleeping," he said quietly without turning around. The lid of Reya's laptop snapped closed as Aaron braced himself. Any second now his brothers would somehow sense his woman was awake and come barging into her apartments to kiss her feet.

"I was asleep, but I like being awake much more when I can wake up to you here with me," she drawled. Her voice was low, sweet, and held him completely in thrall. God, he loved this woman. He set her laptop on the nightstand and turned to face her. She took his breath away, all tousle-headed, and her lips tipped up in a sensual half smile. Her gray eyes twinkled in the dim early morning light that filtered in through the closed blinds. Oh she looked so ready to be loved.

"How are you feeling, baby?" he asked quietly, a lump in his throat he hadn't noticed before.

She stretched sensuously, lacing her fingers together. He could see her toes point and flex under the light covers as she tried to cover a very unladylike yawn. He liked that about her. No cutesy eyelash batting or pretense. Just Reya. And what you saw was what you got. Well sort of, he thought as the image of a sleek black jaguar filled his mind. He grinned.

"What are you smiling about, Aaron?"

"Nothing," he mumbled, closing his eyes a second, trying to clear the image of Reya in her shifted body, purring at him as she licked her paws. "Nothing, Sweet. Let's take a look at those wounds."

"I told you I'd be fine in a couple of days. See for yourself."
The timbre of her voice was a playful purr as she raised her arms
over her head, taking her nightshirt off in one move. The shirt
was tossed carelessly toward the foot of the bed as she rolled over
to her stomach and watched him over a well-formed shoulder.
Fingers wrapped around the post of the headboard and her body
writhed slowly, sensuously against the soft sheets. Aaron's Adam's
apple bobbed up and down roughly in his throat at the sight of
all that smooth skin rubbing against the bedding. Her full breasts
pressed into the mattress, and he could see the swells spilling out
from underneath her body, peeking at him. His mouth watered,
jealous that the bed enjoyed her sweet Hershey's Kisses nipples
instead of him.

Reya raised her head scant inches from the bed, her gray eyes
finding him from underneath her lashes. Was that a smile or a
smirk gracing her luscious mouth? Then the little hellion wiggled
her ass at him. His cock responded, the base warmed and thickened until the ridge pulsed as it pressed against the zipper of his
pants.

"See any wounds, lover?" she crooned, just before her tongue
left a wet path over her top lip. What had she asked him again?
Something about wounds? In truth, he wasn't looking for any.
He was looking at the teasing cleft between her ass cheeks, overwhelmed with the sudden urge to taste it.

"Aaron?" she questioned, a hint of "bad witch" in her words,
"you all right?"

Oh, he was plenty all right. It only took a second to determine
there wasn't even a scar on her lovely back. But he had to check
to make sure, didn't he? Hell, yes!

Rising from his side of the bed, he gathered up the laptop, his scheduler and her satellite phone and stalked from the room. A brief stop in the living room and the items were dumped unceremoniously on the couch, the front door dead bolt slid home and the back door secured. He left his clothes next to the laptop in a heap.

Reya's eyes went wide as they zeroed in on the lengthening, flushed cock jutting out from between his legs. Rain sounded on the roof overhead and Aaron had the sudden urge to let nature in. He raised the blinds and opened the window, letting in the sound of the summer storm and the smell of the surrounding fauna. With eyes closed, he inhaled as it swirled into the room, mixed with Reya's unique musky scent and filled his lungs.

Easing onto the bed next to her, he felt her muscles bunch and tighten as he fought to control the lust quickly consuming him, but every second spent watching the daylight play over her skin drove his need a notch higher until he practically shook with it.

"Well, I'm all healed up, handsome. Care to take a closer look?" Her thighs spread just enough for him to glimpse the treasure glistening between them.

His fingers itched to sink into that treasure. Instead he decided, forced himself, to savor the beauty of the arousing woman spread out before him. Besides, he knew how much she liked him to play with her ass. So he set his hands on the path from the base of her spine down and across the supple cheeks, causing them to quiver at his touch. Putting his nails into play, he gave her a teasing, barely there caress that set her teeth on edge—he could tell from the audible snap of her teeth coming together on a groan.

Deep breaths became gasps. Gasps became moans as her body

writhed under his hands, making him want to make her crazy. Something inside of him wanted her to be so crazy for him she would beg, scream.

Kneeling behind her up on the bed, Aaron gently pulled her up by her hips until her luscious ass was in the air, legs spread wide. Shoulders and chest writhed and rubbed against the soft sheets. When her fingers began to yank and pull at the bedding, the uninhibited response only spurred him on more.

Gently parting her plump folds, he gently licked the crevice at the top of her ass, playing with the sensitive skin just above her tight, puckered hole until she shivered with anticipation. Eyes closed, he imagined what it would feel like sinking his steel-hard cock into that tight hole. One day. One day soon. But tonight was for her pleasure. A single finger sank into her pussy's wet dewy heat as he tongued her ass, rimming the quivering hole until she cried out.

"Oh! Aaah!" she panted anxiously, almost whimpering with pleasure. But he had a goal to reach—a blistering orgasm, complete with screams from his woman for his cock. Just the thought of her milking him dry made him pick up the pace just a bit. His wet tongue left her ass and traveled down to her soaked pussy, teasing the little space between her asshole and her creaming cunt while his finger worked in and out. The little ripples along her sleek, muscled walls drove further into sensual mayhem, if that were possible.

Aaron pulled back and forced himself to wait for her words. Didn't take long.

"AJ, please!"

AJ? No woman had ever called him by his nickname. No

woman had ever gotten close enough to even figure out what it was. It sounded perfect on her lips and made him want to please her even more, made him want to make her scream it, yell it, shout it from the highest mountain.

Raising his head just enough to ask, "Please what, baby?"

"Please lick me. Please . . ."

The first swipe of the whole length of his tongue against her slippery folds earned a keening growl from deep in her chest. Oh yes, that's what he was after. Replacing a finger with two, Aaron practically buried his face into her dripping pussy. She was sweet and spicy, like the apples and cinnamon she always munched on. His tongue tasted and teased then sucked furiously on her flesh until her body went taut and rigid. Orgasm number one in the bag.

Loving had never been more fulfilling. And he wasn't even inside her yet.

∞

Reya marveled at the fullness of her closely shaved lips, inflamed and swollen as Aaron worked her pussy into a mound of frenzied need. Engorged and achy, she craved the fingers and tormenting tongue playing over her body.

This man never left her unsatisfied, his loving slow and giving, then escalating to wild, frenzied fucking. Long, hard and deep.

The latter is what she needed just now.

"Fuck me, Aaron!" she yelled into his ear. "Oh God, please!"

"Call me AJ again," he hissed between his teeth, the sound urgent, like the sizzle of water splashed into a roaring flame.

With a speed and strength that amazed her, Aaron flipped her onto her back. With a mind of their own, her long, strong thighs automatically fell open as his wide chest settled between them.

Each finger reveled in the slide of luxurious silk locks as she buried her hands in his hair, holding him firm against her burning cunt. Oh such a talented tongue. It lapped, pulled, pressed and sucked until she was mindless with lust.

But he didn't have enough hands! Reya's body wanted his touch everywhere at once. Lifting a hand to the tightly drawn buds of her nipples, she matched the rhythm of his mouth, tugging when his lips tugged, pulling when his teeth pulled on her clit, caressing when his tongue caressed her pink slit. Just as one breast began to feel neglected, one of Aaron's larger hands joined in the play. He squeezed and palmed her full globes, sending sweet sensation through every pore in her body.

When he hummed against her writhing core, orgasm sped through her blood with such force, it skyrocketed into the sun where she melted with the speed and heat of a solar flare. The glowing power of the feline rose up, the change rippling just underneath her skin, fighting for dominance. She'd never experienced this kind of primitive need, the urge to be taken in the change. And by a human? It was beyond her imagination. For the first time in all her young years, Reya found herself battling the animal instinct to mate.

Her mate was over her now, chasing her lips as she battled the change and the need to catch her breath. But Aaron gave no quarter.

"Open for me, baby. I want it all, heart and soul." His mouth locked to her and the flavor of her nectar on his tongue was exotic and heady, like the jungle that surrounded them. The wonder of the intensity of their lovemaking was enough to give her the control she needed to subdue the regal beast within.

"Hold on to me, Reya. I can't wait another second to sink into that sweet pussy."

"Aah, God, AJ! Give it to me!" she belted to the ceiling.

"Is it all mine?" he asked, gritting his teeth as he plunged.

"Yes!" There was no doubt what was coming. Wrapping her arms around his broad back, she held on for dear life as the heart-shaped head of his cock slipped into her welcoming heat just before the long, veined ridge of pleasure slid home. Arms wrapped around each other, anchoring their bodies together, he rode her into oblivion. Hard. Fast. Slick. Wet. A wild mating frenzy. But the untamed cat stayed just there, right on the edge of her consciousness, watching, waiting to be freed. Aaron's loud yell exploded from his chest. The knowledge of the meaning of that feral sound triggered her own roar as her clenching channel gloried in the splash of his scalding seed against her cervix, sating her urgent need.

∞

As he stroked her spine, they lay quietly and listened to the deep boom of the thunderheads passing over. He hoped it wouldn't delay his flight. The plan was to fly to Belize City, meet with his client briefly then he and his brothers would head out to Ambergris Caye to survey the land they'd purchased for the project. They had to wrap up these final details so they could break ground on time. Luckily his unexpected, unfortunate, very hard landing hadn't affected the project plan as much as he'd thought. Even if it had, meeting Reya made it all worth it.

Last night Marc had come by to see how Reya was doing and to deliver some information about the jaguar that had attacked her. The whole place was in an uproar over it. The rangers were even thinking about shutting down the sanctuary to visitors until the cat was put down. Marc, after meeting Aaron's brothers, all huddled around Reya as they were, told them the jag had been spotted by two other rangers, always at night and always in the same spot Aaron and Reya had run into him.

The man promised to look after her for the couple of days Aaron and his brothers were in Ambergris Caye, but the thought of leaving her alone, even with a so-called "good friend" like Marc, made him uneasy. Choice? He had none.

"Promise me you won't go on patrol alone," he asked quietly, kissing the top of her head.

"Aaron, I've been doing this a long time . . ."

"Yeah, and how many times have you been injured by a male jaguar who happened to be after a human?" His arched brow and tight set of his chin dared her to gainsay him, but he knew she'd try to think of something.

"How many times? Well, uh, never."

He was actually surprised she hadn't added a few more uh's or er's to that statement. Raising his head, he looked down at her like she was someone else, earning a giggle and a slap on the chest. Damn, she was strong. But she wasn't arguing with him, so he counted his blessings and left it alone. Sort of.

"Promise."

"Fine. I promise," she whined.

"Now was that so hard, baby? And," he said nuzzling her ear, "you have yet to agree to marry me."

"There just hasn't been time to talk about it, now has there? Not with all the hot lovin' you've been laying down on me." She turned her head and nipped his ribs.

"Laying down on you . . . I like the sound of that," he drawled, turning quickly and sweeping her underneath him.

"Aaron, it's already seven a.m., you're going to make yourself late." Her voice was a blend of highly charged thunder and gentle rain. Just like the storm overhead. What a potent mix she was.

"That's fine as long as I make you come while I'm making myself late." Oh, did he ever enjoy the tremble working its way down her lush body when he swiped his hot tongue down her neck. Yes, trembling was good, but panting was better.

The unsteady quaver of her husky voice sent what could only be described as pure male pride spreading through his chest. The woman sounded like a horny toad on overload, and it was all his fault. The press of her strong thighs as they wrapped around his hips had him bracing himself against the surge of pleasure as he slipped into heaven.

"But what will your brothers think?" she squeaked out on a pant.

"They'll think I'm a damned lucky bastard, is what." Then he moved and the ridge of his cock caused just the perfect amount of friction deep inside her heat.

"Ooooh, I think I can live with that."

Ten

Aaron loved flying. Even when he'd piloted their company jet alone, it had given him a thoroughly enjoyable feeling of freedom and peace while gliding through the air among the clouds. It was the closest to heaven he'd ever been . . . until Reya. This time flying wasn't so impressive, or even welcome. As they sat on the jetway in Dangriga awaiting clearance for takeoff to San Pedro on Ambergris Caye, his finger circled around the rim of his coffee cup as he stared absently into the steaming dark brew. He wished he was sharing it with Reya.

"Missing Reya already, lil' bro?"

Aaron's head popped up at the sound of his tormentor's voice. When his eyes met Anthony's, he couldn't help but grin along with his brother. He still couldn't get over the fact his brothers had insisted on peeking into her room so they could kiss her goodbye on the cheek as she slept.

"Bethsaida should be looking in on her now . . . if she's awake yet," Aaron said, unable to keep the smug, self-satisfied look off his face as he looked down at his watch. Reya was usually up with the chickens. But it was now eleven o'clock in the morning, and he'd be amazed if she was able to move from the bed. He'd left his woman well loved and plenty satisfied.

"She's a keeper, Aaron. Such a nice mix of feisty and sweet," Anthony said appreciatively as Austin chimed in. "Not to mention beautiful."

"Yep, you picked a good one," Anthony continued, "real good. That woman of yours is as smart as a whip and has a head for money. She even asked about investing in your project in Ambergris Caye, you know, being a private shareholder. She thinks it's going to take off as soon as the word gets out about what kind of facility it is."

Aaron hadn't known that. Reya wanted in on his deal? And she hadn't even seen the blueprints or financial projections? She trusted his judgment that much? He felt like the Grinch when his heart swelled ten times larger than it already was.

"And," Anthony said around a bite of fluffy, butter-smothered biscuit, "she's got you plenty pussy whipped."

"What?" Aaron gaped, ready to protest. When both his brothers pinned him with an amused but unflappable stare, he snapped his mouth shut. Him? Pussy whipped? Hell, when had that happened?

"So, what about her family?"

"Family?" Aaron lifted a brow in query at Austin. "Well, she's got an aunt in the States, somewhere in the bayou of Louisiana."

"Not what I meant," Austin said quietly, signaling to the crew member for another cup of coffee. "Are they going to have a problem with the fact that you're a white boy from Colorado?"

Aaron stared dumbly at the both of them, his face the picture of a total lack of comprehension. Hell, he hadn't given it a second thought. Did Reya care that he was white? Not likely. If she had, she would have said something or blown him off before he'd gotten much past "hello." He put it out of his head and answered with clear conviction.

"No, Reya doesn't care, and if she doesn't care, her aunt won't either."

"They sound like good people. But you are whipped though." Aaron rolled his eyes. Anthony had always been the philosophical one. A regular male talk show host. "But whipped is not necessarily a bad thing, especially when your woman cares for you."

"Oh, shut up already, Anthony!" Aaron snapped, but there was no heat behind his words. The smile spread across his mouth was too big.

"Congratulations, Aaron," Austin quipped with a grin, raising his mug of coffee in a salute.

After landing safely, the three brothers boarded a boat and headed out to the caye. In the middle of surveying the view of the barrier reef near the new resort site just off Ambergris Caye, Austin turned and asked, "So, I take it you'll be staying in Belize for a while?"

Aaron thoughtfully regarded the most perceptive of the bunch. How did Austin always seem to know what he hadn't figured out yet? They hadn't discussed where they would go from here. Forget the fact Reya hadn't said yes to his proposal yet.

"I'm sure we'll spend some time in the States," Aaron said, noting their coordinates and the angle of the boat. "But Reya has a passion for that jaguar sanctuary. It's the only one in the world, so she has to be there to do her work. Give me a drafting table, a satellite phone and a computer and I can work anywhere."

"She's back to her patrolling this afternoon, eh?"

"Yeah. Actually tonight she'll be . . ." Just then, the hairs on the back of Aaron's neck stood at full attention and sent a tingle of dread straight to the pit of his stomach. The second he thought about Reya out in that damned jungle patrolling for poachers, the bottom dropped out of his gut. He shook the feeling off and concentrated on getting the rest of his notes together for their meeting with their customer in less than an hour.

"She'll be what?" Austin asked.

Serious eyes on both Anthony and Austin, Aaron said, "I told you about the jaguar that tried to attack me, right?" When they both nodded he continued. "Reya saved my ass. She promised she wouldn't go out into the jungle until the rogue was put down, but . . ." Shit! There it was again, a damned alarm pounding inside his head that screamed something was wrong. And this time, as much as he tried, he couldn't push it away.

"Damn it, tell the captain to turn the boat around," Aaron said through clenched teeth as he strode toward the back of the boat for the portable phone in his duffel.

"Aaron," Anthony called, "what the hell is wrong?"

"I don't know, but I just have this strong feeling that Reya's in danger. I can't explain it, but if I don't get back to that damned wildlife sanctuary and fast, my woman is history."

It was obvious they hadn't felt the cold chill of warning he had, but his brothers would back his play. They just had to, and Aaron wasn't disappointed.

"It makes sense, Aaron. If you had it out for her, when would you strike next?" Anthony asked on a growl, eyes flashing with anger as he headed toward the captain, yelling over the din of the yacht's engines. "Hey, turn this thing around! Get us back to San Pedro. Right now!"

Understanding dawned in Austin's eyes. His jaw ticked as he answered Anthony's question. "I'd strike the second she was alone, as soon as her man was out of sight." Seconds later he was on his satellite phone calling the airstrip in San Pedro, giving them an hour to get the jet cleared and ready for takeoff to Dangriga. A car would be waiting to cover the twenty miles from the airstrip to the wildlife sanctuary.

Aaron was on the satellite phone he'd borrowed from Reya. Urging the speed dial to dial faster, he felt his chest tighten as he waited to connect to the spare she promised to carry with her while he was gone. No answer.

∽∾

"I can't wait until the rainy season is over. I like that it's so green everywhere, but all this water is getting on my nerves," Reya gritted through clenched teeth as her boot landed with a splash in a deep puddle. "Marc, you all right? You've been awful quiet."

Reya couldn't recall a single time during the year they'd been friends when Marc wasn't open and upbeat, but for the last couple of hours he'd been quiet and reserved. She almost wished they'd run across a poacher just to break the weird silence between them.

"I'm fine. Just have a few things on my mind," he said quietly, looking around as if he expected King Kong to come bursting through the trees. Not afraid but . . . overly cautious.

She scented jaguars on him again. The aroma was weak, but she was curious why he, a human, smelled like female jaguar all the time, even in the middle of a downpour. Damn it, her senses just weren't as sharp when she was in her skin. The urge to drop to her knees and transition was so strong she clamped her jaw tight and came to a dead stop. Something was dead wrong.

"You all right, Reya? What is it?" Marc asked with sudden concern.

Now this seemed more like Marc. "No I'm fine. My, uh, my knee is a bit sore. Trudging through all this mud is kind of pulling on it," she lied. Hell, it hadn't sounded convincing to her own ears, but Marc didn't seem to notice.

"Oh no," he gasped.

"What?" she asked, grinding her back teeth, willing her body not to grow a pelt.

"I left the radio in the jeep. Maybe we should head back?"

"Head back?" she asked in disbelief, her discomfort momentarily forgotten. They were on a circular route and would exit the trail in the same area they'd entered. The man's suggestion didn't make the least bit of sense. "Marc, we drove an hour into the park and hiked another hour. We've only got two hours left before we have to head back and our path is going to take us to the exact spot where we started. Let's just keep going rather than backtrack."

Just then a series of roars filled the area off to their left. Female jaguars. Extremely agitated female jaguars. The next roar came from behind her. Reya wasn't afraid, but when she turned to Marc to ask if he had his tranquilizer gun on him the words froze in her throat. His typically smiling eyes were narrowed in menace, golden blond brows snapped together until they met in the middle of his forehead. He was obviously as agitated as the females whose growls and snarls began to encircle them.

"What do you think is wrong with them?" she asked breathlessly as her own hackles rose at the strangeness of the situation. What the hell made a pack of female jaguars coordinate on a hunt? It just wasn't the norm.

"They should be pretty used to us. I think they've scented a poacher," Marc said quickly, backing up toward a copse of trees. His explanation made sense, and if it was a poacher, they had to get to him before he either took a jag down or the jags took him down.

Her hand was on the strap securing her tranq gun over her shoulder. Before she could pop the snap that allowed the piece to fall into her hands, Marc withdrew a pistol from the belt holster obscured by his jacket. Not a tranquilizer gun, but a fucking 9mm handgun! What the hell was going on here?

"Reya, you go take the left trail, I'll head off to the right."

"But, Marc . . ." Reya tried to protest, but he just shoved her toward the direction he wanted her to go. "Don't worry, we'll be all right." After a quick, supposedly reassuring hug, he gave her a strained-looking wink and headed off into the trees.

The second she was alone, all the growling, snarling and roaring ceased. Just stopped, as if it had never happened. Danger lurked, she could feel it creep up her spine and tighten around the nerve endings of each vertebra. Forget stripping out of her clothes, something told her she needed to shift and right-damn-now.

Instinctively dropping to her knees, her thick pelt exploded out of her pores so quickly, a burning sensation covered every inch of her skin. Canines exploded into powerful jaws and muscular arms became stocky forelimbs. Senses sharpened as special sensory whiskers sprouted around her snout. The smells of the surrounding fauna exploded as her keen nose picked up even small changes in the air pressure.

Gray eyes glowed in the coming twilight as she stood completely still, surveying her surroundings. All was quiet, but the hairs on the back of her powerful neck danced all the same.

Suddenly a blur shot past her right side. The rogue!

In a flash, she was right behind him as they became two streaks running with the wind. Wait, where did he go? One second he was right in front of her, the next, he'd turned a corner and disappeared. She slammed to a halt, large paws sliding as she dug into the wet earth.

Zip!

Owww! What the hell? She looked back at the dart sticking into her flank. *Aw, hell, not again*, she thought as her muscles refused to cooperate with her brain. She heard a faint snuffling sound and realized it was her as she slumped down onto the cool, muddy floor of the jungle.

The jet landed without a hitch and the brothers sped toward the reserve. It was only eight o'clock, and Reya wasn't due to go out until almost eleven tonight. Thank God they'd arrived in time. All three James brothers barreled into a completely empty common dining area at twilight.

"Bethsaida!" Aaron bellowed, heading for the kitchen. "Bethsaida!"

Running through the swinging double doors, a wash rag in one hand and a pineapple in the other, Bethsaida came to a screeching halt.

"Aaron! Oh, thank God!" she yelled, dropping the cloth and the fruit to the floor.

"What's wrong? What's happened?" Anthony took the upset older woman into his arms.

"Reya is missing!"

"Missing? How? She's not even due out on patrol for several more hours!" Aaron bellowed. His heart sank into his toes as his heart rate pounded with adrenaline and fear-filled palpitations. It didn't even faze him when Bethsaida yelled right back, just as angry and unsettled as he was.

"Damn it, she's gone!" Bethsaida screeched. Tears gathered and fell unchecked down her brown cheeks. "She went out with Marc on his shift . . ."

"Marc? Why?"

"Aaron, let her finish. Can't you see she's upset?" Austin admonished.

Hell, all he cared about right now was answers. He opened his mouth to give his brother a heartfelt "fuck you" when Bethsaida spoke up.

"Because his usual partner came down ill. The last time I talked to her was more than three hours ago. They were out in the rain and she said something about poachers, but the connection was poor."

"Then why didn't she answer when I called? It was around the same time."

"Her last words were something about the battery. I guess it was low because right after, the line went dead. But I'm afraid, Aaron. I swear I heard roaring in the background."

Shit! What if she was hurt? And worse, what if she'd been attacked again?

Five minutes later they all stormed into the ranger's office.

Trefor stood behind the main desk. An instinctive step back accompanied his first glance at a raging Aaron headed right for him. If he hadn't been so anxious to find Reya, Aaron would have begged the man to say one wrong word so he could beat the shit out of him. But right now, Trefor was their best hope of finding Reya. Alive.

"Trefor, what time were Reya and Marc supposed to be back?" When Trefor looked at his watch a little too slowly, Aaron growled a warning.

"Two hours ago," the stocky man stammered. "They're probably at Reya's place with Bethsaida getting a snack."

What a dimwit, Aaron thought. Trefor believed the very woman standing in front of him was in the dining room feeding Reya? How had the man ever become the director of a wildlife sanctuary? Maybe he'd have an accident, or perhaps one of the big cats would mistake his beefy head for a dumb deer in the headlights. After all, the gene pool was overdue for a good cleansing.

At Trefor's dumb-as-a-bucket-of-soaked-raisins look, Bethsaida lost it. She stepped nose to nose with him and screamed like a drill sergeant. It was rather impressive.

"Listen, you idiot! My Reya is missing and you're going to arrange a party to go look for her. And I mean right this minute, or I'm going to find a very sharp kitchen instrument and gut your sorry ass!"

But Aaron wouldn't dare trust Reya's safety to such incompetence.

"Better yet, my brothers and I will take care of it." Aaron leaned forward and hauled Trefor halfway over the counter he quaked behind. "Listen, idiot, I want the keys to a jeep, a map of the route they were supposed to take, and I want it thirty seconds ago. You!" he snarled, motioning to another ranger standing off to the side, taking in the scene. "Yes, you! Give us each a pistol, fully loaded, and a tranquilizer gun. You guys form your own teams, take a radio and check in every twenty minutes. As for the James boys, we're out of here now. The rest of you can catch up."

Eleven

The groggy aftereffects of the tranquilizer faded quickly and her heart rate automatically kicked up at the feel of cool air against her very naked body. No, she must control her physical reactions or she'd give herself away. She lay perfectly still. There was no sound, but it was no assurance that she was alone. Back in her skin, her senses somewhat muted, all she caught was the damp, musty smell always present in deep, canopied jungle. Forcing her breathing to remain at a slow and even pace, Reya cracked her eyes open just enough to peek at her surroundings. It looked like some kind of stone cave, probably one of the many ruins they were forever uncovering out in the bush. Just enough light filtered in from somewhere to tell her it was close to twilight.

That meant she was late returning from patrol. Hopefully someone would notice her missing and think to look for her. And what happened to Marc? Oh God, had the rogue jag gotten him? Oh, please let him be okay, she prayed silently.

"I know you're awake, Reya."

Wait a minute. She knew that voice. "Marc? What the hell is

going on?" she asked incredulously, sitting up and drawing her knees in close to her body to hide her nakedness. "And why don't you have any clothes on?" she asked, bewildered.

Blowing off her question, he took a step forward with a cold response. "Shift, Reya."

"Shift? What are you, crazy? And who the hell are you anyway? You look like Marc, but I don't recall my friend being such an asshole," she snapped from her perch on the hard dirt-packed floor.

Her neck snapped sideways as his hand shot out and slapped her so hard bright points of light danced behind her eyelids.

Oh hell no! Nobody slapped her like a bitch and got away with it. Nudity forgotten, she stood up to face her agitator, hands perched on her bare hips. With a glare, she hissed through gritted teeth.

"You touch me again and I will kick your feral ass, Marc!"

"Shift, Reya, and we'll see."

What was his obsession with her shifting? And how the hell did he know she had the ability?

"I said shift. Now," he snarled, stepping much too close for comfort. Reya stood her ground as a furious blush of anger crept across her bare chest and up her neck. The change was just under the surface, on the verge of breaking free. She'd always kept keen control of it, but this asshole was pushing it! But her aunt Sulu hadn't raised her to be a fool. Whatever this rabid and certifiable nut had planned for her, she must have to shift first. This seemed like a good time to stall and maybe just get some answers.

"Marc, what's the deal with this shift stuff?" she asked dumbly, urging him to spill whatever he knew or *thought* he knew.

"What, you thought I was a blithering, muscle-bound clod like Trefor? I know exactly who, or rather what, you are, Reya."

She'd perfected the deer-in-the-headlights look as a child and slipped it onto her face with ease. "What are you talking about, Marc? Why are you being such an ass? And with me of all people?"

"I've known for a while that you're a shifter. A beautiful, black jaguar shifter and you are going to be my mate."

"I can't mate with you! Eww, that's just too nasty." Shit! The words slipped out before she could clamp her lips shut. His fist flew, and she barely got an arm up to block the punch that landed on her forearm with a sick slapping sound. That would have really hurt if it had reached her face.

"Look, Marc, I'm marrying Aaron, okay? Don't do this. You've always been a good friend to me." *Until now*, she thought. "Besides, why would you want to mate a shifter anyway?"

Her question was answered by the sinewy popping and crunching of rearranging bones as they moved and settled in their new positions. Eyes wide, she stood still as stone while goose bumps erupted from neck to knees at the familiar, quiet hiss of lengthening and stretching muscles. A gasp escaped her throat at the bombshell dropped on her.

Before her stood the regal gold and black rogue that had challenged her for Aaron after his plane crashed and had later attacked him. Hell, attacked and injured her. Reya had never seen anyone shift so fast. Then again, she'd never met another shifter outside her family. Her head tilted in question as another thought came to her. The dead jaguars.

"Yes, Reya, I was the one that attacked the females in the sanctuary. It

wasn't a poacher who didn't have time to recover the furs without detection." He spoke directly into her head in a perfect imitation of their dimwitted director Trefor.

"But why?"

"They refused to mate with me. And their choice was the same as yours—accept me."

"Or?" she asked, tilting her head at the crazy jaguar before her.

"There is no 'or,' Reya."

In his skin, he was already stronger than her. In his pelt, he was several times faster and stronger. Reya backed away slowly, more than wary of his intentions. If he attacked her in her skin, she'd be laid up for weeks recovering. But if she shifted, healing would occur faster, but she'd be giving in to whatever he had planned for her.

"I'm disappointed you've chosen the human male. I would make a much better mate, Reya. I would even break with typical jag behavior and stay with you long after our cubs are born. Maybe even mate for life."

Her mind flashed to a terror-filled night so long ago when her sister and mother fell under the claws of an infanticidal jaguar shifter. Her father. She had no intention of mating with a shifter, jaguar or otherwise. She'd fight him tooth and claw first!

Just before she allowed herself to succumb to the change, the lightbulb in her mind clicked on. He wanted her to shift so he could fuck her in the change! Not only was he a bastard, he was a sneaky bastard.

Stalking slowly toward her, canines bared, Marc padded silently across the stone floor of wherever they were. He pounced. Reya screamed with anger and jumped back, just out of reach of a powerful swipe aimed at her calves. His roar chilled her blood, but she forced her legs to move again, unable to suppress another scream as claws tore across her back. At least it was just a few shallow cuts across the newly healed muscles rather than the deep gouges he'd obviously intended.

"I will have you underneath me, Reya, in your skin or in your pelt. Your choice." The words were snarled with such vehemence she actually flinched.

Damn it, she was a goner, definitely no match for a fully grown male jaguar determined to sink his barbed cock into her body and hump her brains out. If she shifted, there'd at least be a fighting chance.

The decision made, she dropped to her knees and let the change ripple through her and prayed she'd be fast enough.

∞

Aaron adjusted the night-vision goggles a second time. Something loomed just ahead of them, but with no definable shape. They'd passed the jeep assigned to Reya and Marc a couple of hours past. Where the hell were they?

Glad his brothers were there, he signaled to Austin.

"This is search party two. We're less than fifty yards from a big mound-looking thing almost two hours from Reya's jeep's position. Can't make it out. Anybody have a clue what it is?" Austin whispered into a wired headset. One of the rangers searching another part of the reserve called back.

"There are some new dig sites, recently discovered archaeological finds in your sector, search party two It's probably the Mayflower archaeological mound. Right behind it are some stone structures that were just excavated."

A vicious roar sounded just ahead. Sounded like it came from the dig site.

"Search party two, this is search party one, do you need assistance? We hear cats in your area."

One of those cats could be Reya. Aaron knew he had to protect her and her secret at all costs.

"No, we're fine. Stay clear and just continue searching your areas. We'll radio back if there's anything to report," Aaron answered quickly, clicked off the radio and signaled silence at his brothers' raised brows.

Removing his headset, he whispered a simple "trust me" and pulled his weapons from their borrowed holsters—a lethal pistol in one hand and a tranquilizer pistol in the other.

His whole body stiffened, not from the new roar reverberating in the air but the sound of Reya's screams echoing through the bush. The first scream had been rage and frustration. The second was pure terror and pain.

Like a burst of compressed air, all three of them took off into the darkness of the jungle, legs pumping furiously, tearing through the thorny branches toward the dig site. Ignoring the scratches and tears on their faces, arms and clothing, they flew through the thankfully cleared trails and into a dense mass of vines and ferns.

There was no trail here, just a huge mound rising up out of the ground, covered with brush and vegetation. Making their way around, Aaron signaled Anthony and Austin to go to the left while he flew off to the right. If their luck held, they'd meet up together at the rear of the structure.

Adrenaline sent his heart up into his throat as it pounded from a combination of fear and hope. If anything happened to Reya he couldn't even wrap his head around what he'd do. The only thing he could see in his mind's eye was a curtain of pulsing red rage and black fear. Please, God, let him get to her in time.

The next scream froze the blood from his brain all the way down to the middle of his chest as it faded into nothing.

Just as he hoped, his brothers pushed aside the overgrown vines and thorns at the same time he did right in front of a low stone ledge that led into a newly uncovered structure of some sort. Thankfully, there was a string of dim electric torches lining the walls, obviously part of the excavation effort. Raising their night-vision goggles, Aaron again motioned for silence as they moved cautiously into the building and down a narrow earth and stone hallway to the sounds of scrapes, growls and snarls.

Toward the rear of the building, the hallway curved then opened up into a wide room. Three pairs of eyes widened at the sight of two muscular jaguars fighting to the death. Aaron recognized both cats.

"No!" he bellowed, jumping in front of his brothers as they raised their guns to fire. "Don't shoot!"

"What the hell?" Anthony yelled. "Move out of the way, Aaron!"

"No, don't shoot the black one! Oh shit!" he yelled as Reya was bowled over by the male rogue. Damn it, she'd been distracted by their arrival. The sneaky male took complete advantage of the situation, ran head-on at her and plowed her into a stone wall. Stunned and disoriented, his woman lay on her side, trying desperately to make it to her feet.

Aaron ran toward her, shaking off the groping hands of his

family who were trying to protect him. He understood his brothers' fear and need to keep him safe. But right now, he needed to save Reya and nothing else mattered.

"Aaron, what the hell are you doing?" Austin bellowed, trying again to grab hold of him as he ran toward the big cats.

"No! Get away!" Aaron screamed wildly, waving both guns like the crazed male he was. But the damned cat was too close to Reya. He couldn't shoot for risk of hitting her by mistake. And they'd already been down that road.

Trying desperately to hold on to consciousness, Reya turned her head enough to bare a set of wicked, long fangs, but to no avail. The rogue pounced on her, covering her semiconscious form with a fully erect jaguar cock prepared to take her.

He could not let this happen. Damn it, he had to distract it long enough . . .

Mere feet away from Reya, the male jag turned on him and attacked. With two hundred and fifty pounds of muscle and bone behind the blow, the impact sent Aaron's tranquilizer gun flying across the room and scuttling across the floor. But his pistol was pinned under his body as the jag's teeth sank into the vulnerable space between his neck and shoulder.

"Get clear, Aaron, damn it!" Anthony called frantically. Aaron knew there was no chance in hell of getting a clear shot with the jaguar right on top of him. His only chance was to get his weapon from where it was pressed into his stomach.

The crunch of teeth against bone echoed in Aaron's ears, but all he registered was the sight of Reya, lying much too still against the wall.

The male had hurt her. A rage beyond comprehension or control filled him with new strength, new heart, new determination to avenge his woman.

Anthony and Austin were on either side of him now, deftly avoiding the sharp claws of the big cat on his back. Suddenly he was free, turning to see the huge male bearing down on him again, the razor-sharp maw headed straight for his skull.

No match for the strong jaws, primal instinct kicked in, erasing any hint of fear. He raised his gun. The jag batted it away and it joined the tranq gun across the room. Raising a fist, he shoved it down the jag's throat, effectively choking him. Now the tables were turned as the rogue struggled to get free.

Scooting back, Aaron rolled clear just as the loud pop of two handguns echoed in the ancient chamber they were in. He looked back to see the jag lying still, his head and chest oozing blood.

A low, tired groan caught his attention. Reya.

On unsteady feet, Aaron eased around the dead jag's body to Reya's side just as she stood up. Even in the dim light of the torch-lit shelter, she was beautiful. Scratches, wobbly furred legs and all.

"Uh, Aaron," Austin queried, gun still raised. "That's a fucking jaguar. Step away, little brother."

"Real slow . . ." Anthony finished the sentence.

"It's okay. She's a friendly jaguar. Saved my ass more than once from this cat you just shot." Aaron sank to his knees and buried his face into the neck of the most beautiful creature any of them had ever seen this close up. In pain, but apparently all right, she licked his hand as he ruffled the thick hair behind her ears.

"Oh God, Reya. I was so afraid I'd lost you this time. I love you so much, I don't know what I would have done. This is the last time you're out of my sight, I swear," he whispered fervently into her ear.

So unique, even if she weren't a shifter. Beautiful, strong, capable and fearless. What more could a man want? Well, actually he did want something more. And now was as good a time as any to try to get it.

For her ears only, Aaron said, "You never gave me an answer to my question. Will you marry me, sweetheart?"

Ducking her head under his hand, astonished gasps sounded from the amazed men standing near the entrance as she purred loudly. He would take that as a yes.

Looking up, laughter bubbled up out of his chest at Anthony's and Austin's astonished expressions. What a Kodak moment! Pretty sure he'd never seen that look on either of their faces in his entire life, Aaron chuckled then winced as the punctures in his neck pulsed. He'd forgotten all about the bite from the dead cat. But he'd worry about that later. Right now was for family.

"Can your new brothers pet you, sweetheart?"

The large black jaguar flopped to the ground, laid her head in Aaron's lap and licked her paws. Nobody moved. After a moment, her large gray eyes turned on the two James brothers, standing with their mouths hanging clear down to their knees. With a muted roar and a little encouragement from Aaron, they too kneeled on the dirt-packed floor to touch the silky fur of a regal black jaguar.

∞

While his brothers dragged the lifeless body of the rogue male out to the main trail, Aaron sent Reya home under the noses of

Anthony, Austin and the search parties. An hour later, a radio transmission flashed through from the ranger station. Reya had been found. She'd been attacked by a rogue jaguar but managed to make it back to the station.

Way to go, sweetheart, he thought, impressed with her ability to sneak past a whole pack of humans walking around in the pitch-black of the jungle with night-vision goggles. And she must have hauled ass to make it back so fast. Hell, he wouldn't mind being a shifter!

Aaron radioed back that the rogue had been killed. But where was Marc?

Later, as Dr. Matons saw to her injuries, Aaron swore she was never getting out of his sight again. Reya explained Marc's whereabouts and his temper hit a new high as he tried to control the murderous urge to go back to where they'd left the body and kill him all over again.

Marc was a shifter—a two-faced, lying, killing, woman-stealing shifter. And now a dead shifter. When the bastard died, he'd remained in his animal form. Without the life-energy to fuel the change, his carcass would give away no secrets. Aaron's beautiful Reya, and those like her, would keep their secrets and remain safe and undiscovered for yet a while longer.

Epilogue

Enjoying the cool ocean breeze at the rear of the brand-spanking-new high-class fitness center, Aaron stood on the private pier built just for Reya and marveled at the radiance beaming across the face of his new wife. The breeze whipped her black curls around her head and the sun kissed her cocoa skin. His eyes drifted lower, admiring the sparkling white bikini hugging her curves. The woman made his mouth water.

"Hey, you two!" came a high-pitched, but sweet, call from the wide balcony above. "Don't stay under too long, children. Our plane is leaving in less than two hours."

"Yes, ma'am," Aaron called up to an older woman, the spitting image of Reya in thirty years. Aunt Sulu. After Reya refused to get married without her only family present, Anthony and Austin had taken it upon themselves to surprise their new sister-in-law. In truth, she had them all wrapped around her finger. It didn't matter which finger, the pinky or the thumb, they were all well and truly caught up over her.

They'd sent a jet for Aunt Sulu and flew her all the way to Belize to attend their wedding then talked her into staying for a month to get to know Reya's husband and his doting brothers who were, as Aunt Sulu put it, "good-looking with muscles as big as melons and sweet as old-fashioned pecan pie."

Waving to the short, little dark-skinned woman with graying locks down to her waist, Aaron took Reya's hand as they walked to the end of the pier.

"I still can't get over your love of water," he grinned, pulling her into his arms. "I thought kitty cats didn't like water?"

"Actually, most big cats are very good swimmers."

"Your skin looks so yummy when it's wet. Can I have a taste?" he teased.

She wrapped her arms around his neck, lifted her lush lips for his kiss and purred. God, he loved when she purred deep in her throat like that. It made him think of *being* deep in her throat.

After a quick peck on the neck, she pulled her scuba mask down and fell backward with a splash into the azure blue ocean.

Aaron was right on her tail. Literally.

One Night with You

SHILOH WALKER

One

How could a simple look make her feel like that?

Shifting around in the chair, Bo hoped he couldn't tell how nervous she was. False hope—Logan always seemed to know how she felt. He always had. But she could pretend, right? Pretend that she felt totally comfortable in the dark, quiet Lexington restaurant with its flickering candlelight and soft music. Pretend that she didn't feel self-conscious in the red silk that draped her body. Pretend that she knew how to handle the looks he kept giving her.

If she faked it long enough, maybe she could actually convince herself it was all true. That she knew how to wear silk and sip wine and smile a sexy little smile at the gorgeous man staring at her. But she didn't think it was going to happen.

Bo was more comfortable wearing jeans and a tank top while she worked a photo shoot. She'd rather the silk be on some bone-skinny model she saw through her camera lens instead of on her. She'd rather be riding through rain and snow on her dad's ranch and taking pictures of a newborn foal—even helping to deliver it. She'd take the blood and gore and afterbirth or dealing with demanding models and demanding agents. She'd take those experiences any day of the week over this one.

At least she knew how to handle those.

"You don't have to look so nervous."

Bo didn't see the point in lying. She looked at Logan and smiled a little. "I'm not used to this kind of place, that's all." Okay, so maybe that wasn't the complete truth but that wasn't exactly lying, was it? Because there was no way she was going to tell Logan that he was the real reason she was so nervous. He had a bad habit of making her feel like she was still the skinny teenager she'd been when they had first met instead of twenty-one years old.

Logan glanced around and smiled a little. "I thought about going to the Roadhouse but they don't have crème brulee."

Even though her belly was pleasantly full from dinner, the thought of crème brulee had her mouth watering. "You got me," Bo said with a grin.

"You and your sweet tooth." The waiter showed up and Bo sipped her wine in silence while he ordered. Just one dessert.

As the waiter walked away, she looked at Logan and cocked a brow. "I hope you don't think I'm sharing."

His pale brown eyes dropped to her mouth and that nervousness returned. "I'm not hungry for dessert." Bo thought the look on his face said the opposite. He looked like he was starving but she had a weird feeling he wasn't interested in food.

∞

He was hungry all right, but food was the last thing on his mind. Well, maybe not the complete last thing. He could picture up some very worthwhile fantasies involving the crème brulee and Bo's mouth.

Watching her eat the rich dessert had him as hard as if she had reached over and wrapped her hand around his cock. Of course, just watching Bo do anything did that. She could be sitting at a table doing yearly taxes and he'd be hard. But the look in her eyes when she had taken that first bite . . . her lashes had fluttered closed and she had moaned like a woman on the brink of climax.

That thought only made his problem worse. He was dying to get her out of here, get her someplace where he could see how she really sounded when she came. Get her someplace quiet so he could strip that red silk away and touch her . . . And if he kept thinking like that, he was going to be stuck in this chair for a while.

He had plans for the rest of the night and they didn't include sitting here waiting for a hard-on to subside.

Another soft *hmmmmm* of pleasure escaped Bo's lips and Logan's control snapped. He reached for his wallet and dug out a couple of bills. The waiter saw him and started in his direction but Logan had no desire to wait for him. Bo looked up at him as he stood over her chair. The fork was still between her lips. If he didn't know better, he'd swear she was doing it on purpose when she slowly slid it out, taking time to lick it clean. She glanced down at the dessert in front of her and said, "I'm not done."

"Too bad. The way you are with sweets, you'd lick the bowl clean if I let you," Logan growled. He pulled the chair back and held out a hand. When she stood, he pulled her up against him and slid an arm around her waist. Their gazes met and held as he lowered his mouth.

She tasted of the rich, decadent dessert, wine and heat. Sheer, unadulterated heat. Desire and hesitation, curiosity and want—there were a million contradictions in her kiss and it was enough to drive him mad. Control snapped. He could feel it, all but hear it in the little cracking noises as she leaned into him. One fisted hand lay against his chest, clutching the lapel of his suit. Through the layers of clothing, he felt the warm weight of her breasts, the soft little curve of her belly—

"Ahem."

Logan tore his mouth away from hers and looked at the waiter. "Shit," he muttered.

Bo's spiky black lashes lifted, revealing smoky gray eyes fogged with desire. She moaned a little and leaned toward him again for just a second. Then it was like she realized where they were. She blushed, the soft pink flush starting at the low neckline of her dress and spreading upward to her face.

Without saying a word, Logan took her hand and led her out of the restaurant. Home hadn't ever seemed so far away.

The drive to the old farmhouse where Logan lived normally took thirty minutes. This time, it took him less than twenty, speeding most of the way, the gas pedal nearly pressed flat against the floor. "Are you in a hurry?" Bo asked as she looked out the window.

He just glanced at her.

In the faint light coming off the dash, he saw her eyes widen, watched as her lips parted and she licked them nervously. *Moving too fast*, he told himself and he wasn't thinking about the speed limit either. *Slow down. Slow down.*

When he got to their street, instead of taking the long winding drive to her house, he took the shorter paved one to his. Bo glanced over her shoulder toward her home but didn't say anything. He wasn't going to do anything stupid. At least he hoped not. Logan had a little more control than that. He thought.

He hoped.

But when Bo accepted his hand a few minutes later, Logan knew he was kidding himself. He helped her from the car but once she stood in front of him, he didn't let go. Instead, he rubbed his thumb back and forth over her soft palm and stared at her.

Her heart-shaped face tipped up so she could look at him. Thick black lashes framed a pair of wide, misty gray eyes. She'd cut her hair. Once, her thick black hair had fallen nearly to her waist and Logan had had a hundred dreams where that hair had fallen around them while she straddled him and rode him through orgasm after orgasm. A thousand dreams where he fisted his hands in the thick silk.

It was short now. Spiky short, a little longer on top, with a tousled look. It suited her. Even he had to admit that, though he still daydreamed about how she would look, kneeling in front of him, that silky hair falling around her shoulders while she took his cock into her mouth.

Logan stared at her as he trailed the fingers of his other hand up her other arm, over her shoulder. He pressed the flat of his palm against the soft skin of her collarbone, his thumb resting in the delicate notch at her throat, his fingers curving over the slope of her neck.

Her lashes drooped low, shielding her eyes from him. He wanted to see them. Had to see them. Had to know if he had even half the effect on her that she had on him.

"Look at me, Bo." Her lashes lifted and he found himself lost in the smoky, innocent seduction he saw in her eyes. His hands tensed. He moved into her, his weight pressing her up against the side of his car. Her mouth opened as his came crashing down on hers.

He swallowed the ragged groan and thrust his tongue into her mouth. Under his hand, he could feel the pulse in her neck. It beat against his palm—wild and erratic. He kept that hand pressed against her neck and skimmed the other up her side. When he cupped her breast, Bo's pulse kicked up a little and she gave one soft, erotic little groan before arching into his hand.

Bo had once shot some pictures of a tornado as it cut through the Kentucky countryside. The wild power of it had been exhilarating and terrifying at the same time. The destruction it left behind had been heartbreaking. If you threw some fire into the mixture, that just might sum up how it felt having Logan touch her. Exhilarating, terrifying, seductive and destructive. He had one hand at her neck, the other cupping her breast and the heavy, solid weight of his body pressing into hers.

Bo wasn't a virgin. She'd had one semi-serious boyfriend since she'd left home for college and she had thought she knew how arousal felt. She was so fricking wrong. This kind of arousal was devastating in its intensity. Mind-blowing. Logan pushed his knee between her thighs and Bo automatically tightened hers. He pushed up and her dress rode up her thighs, exposing them to the chilly night air. She barely noticed the cold. She was too focused on the heat of his body and trying to breathe. He slid a hand down her side, cupping the curve of her hip. Mindless, Bo rocked against his thigh. Her panties—already wet—slid slickly against her flesh.

"Bo—"

She moaned and turned her head, trying to catch his mouth with hers. He kissed her back, a deep, hot kiss that stole her breath. The hand at her neck slid around and fisted in the short choppy strands of her hair. He pulled, arching her head back. Logan's mouth left her but he didn't pull away, not completely. His lips pressed against her neck, followed by his teeth as he bit her. The feel of his mouth against the sensitive flesh there was like throwing a match on something combustible. Bo could feel herself exploding.

His hand tightened on her hip as if he knew what was happening and his mouth came back up, smothering her scream with his lips. He shifted against her, cupping her ass in both hands and wedging his hips between her thighs. He pressed against her. Her panties were so wet, she might as well not even be wearing them for all the protection they provided. He rocked against her and Bo shattered.

The world spun around her, her feet leaving the ground. Reflexively, she clutched at Logan and realized he'd picked her up. They were heading toward his house. Blood rushed to her face and she blushed hotly as she realized what they had just done— right in front of his house. In full view of the road and anybody who might have been inside the old farmhouse.

Fortunately, Bo's house was hidden by the curve of the road and set far enough back that it was unlikely her dad might have seen. But what if Logan's brother was home?

Oh, shit.

Still struggling to get her breath back, she pressed against Logan's chest. He lowered his head and kissed her hard and quick. He did put her down but only long enough to fish his keys out and unlock the door. Her legs wobbly, she leaned against the wall and licked her lips. *This is moving way too fast*, she thought. But she couldn't quite find the words to tell Logan that.

Slow down just didn't want to come out. She opened her mouth to say something but he turned his head and looked at her. The hungry, hot light in his gaze made the words die before she could even say them. He reached over and caught her hand and when he pulled her against him, Bo couldn't resist. She leaned into his body and tipped her head back so she could stare at his mouth.

In a thousand years, she wouldn't have ever admitted to him how often she had thought about kissing him. She'd thought about it since she was old enough to think about kissing boys and all the years she'd known him hadn't changed that. Now she thought about kissing him and all sorts of other things—things that would have made her dad blush and maybe lock her away for fifty years.

But they were fantasies. Fantasies weren't meant to come true and when they did, they were rarely as good as you'd hoped. At least, that had been Bo's view on it. Until about fifteen minutes ago. Because Logan's kisses were a thousand times more potent than anything she could have imagined.

His touch even more so. The way her body lit up when he touched her could get addictive. She could start craving it. *Dangerous ground there, Bo.* She didn't want to crave anything. Didn't want to need anybody. Needing usually led to loving people and that never ended well.

Logan slid his arms around her waist and she gasped when he lifted her off the ground again. This time, her body was pressed full against his, from the chest down. His thighs rubbed against hers as he carried her into the house. Her breasts pressed flat against his chest, her belly against the hard wall of his abdomen and lower where she could feel the hard ridge of his cock.

The door banged shut behind him as he kicked it. The wall felt cool against her back as he turned and pressed her into it. His hands stripped her jacket away and then his own. The time to try to slow this train down was rapidly getting away from her but she couldn't find it in her to care. At least not yet.

His hands came up and cupped her breasts. Through the silk and the thin layer of her bra, she could feel him—hard, hot and strong. His thumbs circled her nipples. Then his hands pressed flat against her chest, slowly rising higher. Bo leaned her head so she could watch his face. His eyes glittered and he had the look on his face of a man starving.

She felt the tug at her neck and then cool air. Her dress fell to her waist and then her bra fell to the floor. He sank to his knees in front of her and took one nipple in his mouth. Bo cried out. She cupped the back of his head in her hands, fisting her fingers in the dark waves. *Time's up* . . . Like some little countdown clock in her head, the voice sounded and Bo realized she'd hit the point of no return with him. Pulling away now wasn't going to happen.

She had gone and thrown herself into the tornado and now she was lost in it. His hands slid under her dress, stripping her panties away. He pulled her to the floor and shoved the skirt of her dress up to her waist and lay between her thighs. The feel of his mouth against her sex had her screaming out his name. He growled against her and the vibration of that made her shudder. One big hand cupped her ass, squeezing gently. The other slid up the soft skin of her inner thigh, his fingers tracing random little patterns that took him closer and closer to the heart of her.

He circled his tongue around her clit, sucked on it, pulled away so he could mutter something against her flesh that made no sense, then he kissed her again, his mouth full against her, his tongue stroking around and around, in and out. Light, teasing little touches that had her rocking and circling her hips up to meet him. Ready to scream, ready to explode, Bo hooked her legs over his shoulders and squeezed. He laughed hoarsely and pressed her thighs open. He pulled away, propping his weight on his elbows so he could look up at her.

His mouth was wet. Wet and gleaming. From her, Bo realized with a jolt. She flushed a painful shade of red but in the next moment all thought of embarrassment was gone as he lifted one hand and pressed it against her mound. The world shrank down until there was nothing and no one, except for them. He slid one finger inside, easing past the squeezing muscles of her sex, pushing deeper and deeper until he could go no farther.

He lowered his mouth and licked her again—a soft, thorough caress around her clit. Then he pushed a second finger inside her and repeated the caress with his tongue. She bucked and screamed out his name, coming hard and fast.

She never had a chance to come down from the second climax. Before she could even catch her breath, Logan was on her. She felt him press against her, the smooth thin shield of a latex condom and then he was inside her. His mouth covered hers and one hand fisted in her hair, holding her still for his kiss.

He took her in one slow, thorough stroke, pushing inside her relentlessly until he could go no deeper. When he was seated inside her, he lifted his head and stared down at her. His eyes glittered as he studied her face. Something unreadable crossed his features but Bo couldn't quite decipher it. "Put your arms around me Bo," he muttered, breaking the tense silence. "Hold on to me."

She did.

His arms slid under hers, curving her shoulders and bracing her body. "Don't look away from me," he rasped. His voice was a harsh, guttural sound, unbelievably erotic.

Their gazes held as he pulled away and then surged back inside. Slowly at first, watching her face with an unsettling intensity. He shifted a little on her body and when he pushed back inside her, it brought him into close, complete contact with her clit. Her breath hitched in her chest and she bucked against him. A slow smile turned up the corners of his mouth and he slid his hand down her side, over her hip, until he could catch her leg just behind the knee. He repeated the caress on her other hip and then he rocked back, bracing his weight onto his knees as he pushed her legs into the air.

He fell forward, his shoulders wedging her thighs apart. Then he started to pump against her again with slow, almost lazy strokes. Bo felt the nameless, indescribable ache settle inside her, deep and hot, centered around her clit and her sex. He pushed into her, stroked her flesh where she stretched around him, muttered her name, kissed her quickly and roughly. She moaned out his name and he kissed her again and again. His rhythm changed abruptly from lazy and teasing to hard and driving.

It exploded inside her. She would have screamed out his name, except his mouth came crushing down on hers. Within the sensitive grasp of her pussy, she felt his cock swell and then jerk. His hips hammered against her, his hands squeezing so tightly that it bordered just this side of pain.

Bo gave herself up to it, lost herself in it, as he pounded away at her. Her vision dwindled down to darkness. His lips gentled against hers, pulled away to trail a line of kisses to her neck and then he collapsed against her.

"You're not going anywhere."

Bo glanced toward the sound of Logan's voice and blushed. She hoped he couldn't see her very well. The only light in the room came from the clock on the bedside table and the watery moonlight filtering through the shades.

Bo couldn't see well enough to find her clothes, so she hoped that meant he couldn't see her.

Couldn't see how embarrassed she was. Couldn't see how nervous she was. How scared she was. That would be bad, bad, bad. Cuddling against him, letting him hold her half the night had felt way too good. Too natural. She'd been right in thinking that Logan was somebody she could see herself needing. Loving. Part of her already loved him. The little girl in love hadn't ever completely faded. It wouldn't take much to push those feelings of first love into the real thing.

She knew it wouldn't and that terrified her. Love. She couldn't do love. Didn't want it. Wouldn't risk it.

She cleared her throat and hoped she could manage some kind of normal tone as she said, "It's past midnight Logan."

"I don't care." His hand found her wrist in the darkness, manacling her to the bed. She felt the mattress shift as he moved toward her and then his other hand came up, cupping her chin. "Open your mouth," he muttered but he didn't even wait to see if she did. He kissed her, using his tongue to part her lips.

The man kissed like he was some warrior intent on conquering and Bo loved it. She heard foil rip and then he tumbled her back onto the bed. "Logan . . ."

"Bo . . ." he teased, his voice low and rough. He spread her legs and pressed against her.

Her breath caught in her chest and Bo closed her eyes, reaching up to grip his shoulders. Irresistible. Logan was so irresistible. He always had been. As hard as she tried not to let herself think about things like love, Logan had always managed to sneak past her guard. She'd managed to deal with it just by telling herself daydreams and fantasies were harmless.

They didn't come true.

But tonight, one of her deepest fantasies *had* come true and Bo didn't want to think about how much this night would change things for her.

His mouth covered hers and his hips circled against hers. She felt the hot, heavy length of his cock pass over her sex, once, twice. On the third pass, she tilted her hips up and tried to take him inside.

"Such a hurry," Logan muttered. He didn't want to rush this

time. It had taken an hour to get her into his bed. After that first, fast fuck just inside the front door, they'd dozed on the hardwood floor for a few minutes. They might have stayed there half the night if Bo hadn't suddenly thought about Dustin. Logan was pretty sure that Dustin had gone out with some friends, but since he didn't really want another man seeing Bo naked, he'd figured they should move.

Then he'd picked her up, planning on carrying her to his bed. But she had rested her head against his shoulder and looked up at him under the fan of her lashes. Just that simple look, her eyes sleepy and satisfied, her hair tousled from his hands, had undone him. He had lowered his head to kiss her and had ended up taking her on the small landing of the stairwell, her back pressed to the wall, her legs wrapped around his waist.

They'd made it into his bedroom for the third round, even if they'd only made it halfway onto the bed. He had bent her over the mattress and pushed into her from behind. The round, firm curve of her ass had driven him to distraction and he had thought of a few dozen dirty little things he wanted to do to her.

But now he wanted to make love to her, soft and slow, so that she came with a sweet sigh. He bussed her mouth with his and traced the outline of her lips. "You taste so good," he whispered.

She whimpered into his mouth and her fingers dug into his shoulders. Her hips rocked against his in a desperate, demanding manner. Logan cupped a hand over the subtle swell of one hip, slowing those hungry, demanding motions. Then he pressed his hips against hers, letting the weight of his body crush her into the mattress, effectively caging her in.

His cock rested against her belly and he rocked against her. Her skin was soft as silk. He'd remember how she felt for the rest of his life. A perfect night, but it wasn't going to be enough. He thought after fifty or sixty years with her, he might be able to take the edge off. Maybe. Possibly. He spread her thighs and pushed inside her.

"Look at me," he demanded. He pushed her hair back from her face with one hand and cupped her cheek. "I want to watch you."

Her lashes lifted and a blush stained her cheeks as she stared into his eyes. She flexed around him. Logan groaned. Those little rippling caresses as she neared climax were designed to drive a man insane. She got so damn tight and so hot and those little muscles gripped his dick like a hungry, greedy fist, milking him to distraction.

"This isn't over," he whispered into her mouth. He canted her hips up and drove into her hard, fast, taking her deeply. Those rippling caresses got stronger, her pussy got tighter and her breathing got rougher. She started to scream and he swallowed it down.

Her legs came up around his hips, squeezing like a vise. Her back arched and her hips pumped against his in a frenzied rhythm. "Not over," he growled.

Logan tore his mouth away from hers, shoving up onto his hands. He pulled out and slammed back into her once more. They climaxed together. She shuddered and bucked and cried out under his body. Logan felt like he was frozen, his orgasm dragging on and on. When it ended, he felt drained. Emotionally, physically, mentally.

And more complete than he'd ever felt in his life.

"Not over," he murmured against her breast.

⟨∞⟩

"She . . . *what?*"

Logan stared at William Martin, certain that he'd heard wrong.

Will lifted a shoulder. "Asked her when she'd be back and she didn't know. That girl, she can't stay in one place for longer than it takes to catch her breath." The expression on his face was puzzled, disturbed and resigned. Logan had seen that same expression on Will's face a thousand times before and he usually sympathized. Right now, though, he wanted to grab the older man and shake him.

"What kind of fucked-up joke is this?"

Now Will shoved off the doorjamb and gave Logan a look that made him feel about thirteen years old. Graying black brows dropped low over eyes that were the same misty gray as Bo's. "You have a problem, son?"

Logan closed his eyes and made himself take a deep breath. "Did she say where she was going?"

The hard glint was still in Will's eyes but he relaxed back against the door. "Milan, I think. Someplace in Italy," Will said. He shrugged. "Tore her room apart looking for her passport."

"Milan."

Milan? "You let her go to Milan?"

Will narrowed his eyes. "Logan, I don't much care for your attitude right now. Bo's a big girl. Legally, I have no say over whether or not she decides to take off to Milan. She can go to Tokyo. She can go to Australia."

"She's practically a kid." *Hypocrite—you weren't screwing a kid last night.*

With a shake of his head, Will said, "Bo hasn't been a kid for a long, long time, Logan. You and I both know that." He sighed and rubbed a hand over his head. Then he studied Logan thoughtfully. "Between you and me . . . no, I don't like my baby trotting over to parts unknown. But it's her choice. She had a call a few days ago. The job in Milan opened up unexpectedly and somebody gave her name. It's a big opportunity for her. She only had a few days to decide and when she decided to go, I wasn't going to tell her to pass it up. It wouldn't be fair to her."

Big opportunity, my ass. She'd run from him. That's all there was to it. Slowly, carefully, Logan took another deep breath. "I need to talk to her."

Will just grunted. "She's supposed to call tomorrow. I'll let her know."

But Bo didn't call. Even later, he barely got a chance to speak to her. Oh, he tried. She didn't return his calls. He called her and she either didn't answer or rushed off the phone before he managed more than, "Hi." Okay, maybe he didn't actually say, *Hi.* The first time he'd demanded she get her ass back home.

The second time he'd tried to make some sort of apology but he was pretty sure he'd ended up yelling then too. He had figured he'd wait until Christmas. She'd come home for Christmas. She wouldn't leave her dad alone for Christmas.

And she hadn't. But it turned out that she talked Will into flying to her for Christmas. Logan had tried calling again. She'd hung up on him again. He had written her. Sometimes the letters had come back. Sometimes they hadn't. But she'd never answered.

The days stretched out into weeks and months and by the time Bo finally stopped running, nearly four years had passed.

Two

Four years later

L ogan Wallace was a patient man.

Always had been.

Hell, patient didn't even begin to describe him. He figured as far as patience was concerned, he ought to rank right up there with the saints. He was content to sit back and wait—watching and debating every little step he took in life. Damn near everything in life could be gotten if one was patient enough. That was what Logan had always believed.

Unfortunately, though, his patience was about ready to bite him on the ass.

Bo's sudden return home six months ago had come at a seriously bad time for him. She could have come home at any time during the past four years but she had picked a time when he was in the middle of a very ugly undercover case. It had him working nineteen hours a day so he'd decided to wait until he could actually focus completely on her instead of the meth-dealing bastards he was investigating. Working the case from the inside, he was able to make it home maybe once a week or so. Hell, Bo had been home two weeks before he'd even known.

It had taken two precious months to close that case. After everything had been tied up he was finally free to pursue Bo. He'd made a few overtures, called her, gone by to see her but she had retreated each and every time. Even though he'd been pissed off and frustrated, part of him understood. He'd moved too fast last time. Regaining the ground he'd lost was going to take time.

So he had waited, willing to give her all the time she needed after how badly he'd messed up before. But that bad call was going to cost him everything, because during that time Bo had started dating his damn cousin.

And now they were getting married? Who in hell got married after a three-month engagement? And they'd only dated for two months before that.

Married! Bo was getting *married!*

Son of a bitch. Married to Logan's cousin. David McNear had always had a thing for Bo. Logan had known that. Hell, half the men in the county had a thing for her. But Logan had also known that Bo was *his*. He'd waited for her. He'd bided his time. Six years older than she, he had sat back and watched as she'd gone from coltish teen to rebellious coed to sleek, sexy, svelte woman. And he had waited.

She was his, after all.

He'd known it the minute she had climbed out of her father's truck when she had moved into the old ramshackle farmhouse across the road from his parents' home. Logan had taken one look into those big, misty gray eyes and he'd known. He'd felt like a damn pervert for it too—in his sophomore year in college and drooling over a high school girl.

He had brooded every time she had batted her lashes at some high school punk and he had silently gritted his teeth through the three years she had been away at college in Chicago. Bo had graduated from high school a half year early. She'd also been taking college courses in high school so she had graduated from college a full year early.

That damn investigation. If it hadn't been for that, he could have gone after Bo the minute she returned to Kentucky. Instead he had been forced to wait two long, awful months and that had given David the chance to work his way into Bo's life.

"I'm going to kill the bastard." Shit. What if David had touched her? Logan clenched his hands and fought the urge to plow his fist into a wall. If he killed David, it would make the next family get-together really tense.

Logic dictated that it wasn't completely fair to blame David. David didn't know how Logan felt about Bo. Hell, *Bo* didn't know how Logan felt. She'd been running from him for close to four years now.

Since that night, their second date. The night he'd fucked her blind, marking her, binding her to him. Or so he had thought. But when he had gone to her the next day, she'd already left. Spent almost four years running around the globe. Milan, Tokyo, London. When Bo did something, she did it to the extreme. He knew that about her but he hadn't expected her to run from him.

He still didn't understand why she'd run, or really why she had been avoiding him. Each of her visits home had been quick and spur-of-the-moment. Will never knew when to expect her. The few times he had seen her on those random visits, she was careful never to be alone with him. As often as possible, she'd avoided seeing him altogether.

She wouldn't talk about that night. She acted like she'd rather that night had never happened and part of him wished it hadn't, because now he had even less of her than before. Before, they'd been friends. Now?

Now, it felt like—nothing.

Logan had been terrified of rushing her again after how badly he had screwed up before. He'd wanted to give her time. He'd screwed up, after all, by moving too fast and scaring her away. If waiting was going to be the penance he had to pay in order to win her back, so be it.

All that time, Logan had waited so patiently—all those years while she was busy growing up, while she was in college—he'd waited all that time. But then when it was the most critical that he take care, he'd moved too fast and scared her away.

He didn't think he had any other choice but to give her a little more time. He loved her more than he loved to breathe and he knew they belonged together. He could wait until she saw it. Even if it killed him. He'd been telling himself that ever since she had run away. It was the only way he stayed sane.

When she hooked up with David, just the thought of those two together had been enough to have him seeing red but he had kept it together because he *knew* Bo belonged with him and sooner or later, Bo would come to her senses. A few months, that was all it would take for Bo to see that David wasn't right for her. A few months and she'd be bored out of her mind.

But he'd waited too long.

Instead of dropping David after a few months, she was marrying him.

"Bastard," he muttered. David had been one of Logan's best friends growing up. They were close and not just because they were related. But Logan wanted to pound his cousin into the ground.

Marrying Bo. No. No fucking way.

Maybe Logan should have tried to talk some sense into her sooner. Like the second he'd seen that rock on her hand. But give a guy a break—he'd been in shock. What in hell was she thinking? Marrying David. *Shit.*

Apparently a prolonged engagement was a load of bull too because in exactly two weeks, they were walking down the aisle at St. Paul's and Logan was expected to be one of the groomsmen. "My ass."

"You're a moron." The words echoed in the room and Logan wondered if he had gone and lost his mind over this. "You're talking to yourself again."

Logan glanced back and realized that Dustin was standing at the doorway to his office. It looked like his brother had been standing there awhile. "Go away."

"You going to keep standing there or go out and talk to her?"

Logan closed his eyes. He hadn't told Dustin a damn thing about his feelings for Bo but then again, Dusty was his brother. They shared the same dark brown hair, though Dusty wore his long enough to pull it back in a stubby ponytail. They had the same long, rangy frame. Dusty's eyes were a dreamy blue, surrounded with spiky lashes that had put him on the wrong end of serious teasing as he grew up. Half the time, Dusty seemed unaware of anything outside his horses and his land. But Dusty was a hell of a lot more aware than most people gave him credit for.

Dusty was sharp and too damn observant. The two of them knew each other as only brothers could. Logan didn't have to say a thing to Dustin, because Dustin knew. Dustin probably always knew. Which meant Dustin was probably aware that Logan was losing it.

He turned around and leaned back against the wall. He sighed tiredly and rubbed his hands over his face. "It's too late, Dusty."

"Ain't too late until she says '*I do*'," Dustin said. Then he lifted a shoulder in a shrug and said, "But you'd better say something before then. Can't believe you've let it go this far."

Logan mumbled under his breath. He looked out the window. Out in the distance, he could see Bo. She was riding Mist—or she had been riding. Right now, though, she was still as a statue.

He couldn't see her clearly, but he didn't have to see her face to know it was her.

Marrying David. The words kept circling through his head like a litany. "Shit. I'm going insane."

Dustin laughed. "Ya think? Go talk to her, Logan." But Dusty's words barely registered and Logan was only distantly aware that Dusty had left.

Going insane. It wasn't a far stretch, as far as he was concerned. Insanity would explain how he'd gone this long without saying anything.

He'd gotten measured for a fucking tux. But damn if he'd wear it. David probably wouldn't forgive him but Logan wasn't standing up at the church and watching as the woman he loved married somebody else.

He stared at her, watching as she sat on Mist and stared out into the distance. He didn't know what she was looking at. Probably the impossibly blue sky. The sun was shining so brightly, it hurt the eyes. He could tell she had a camera but even if he hadn't seen it, he'd know she would have one on her somewhere.

Bo's cameras were as important to her as a cop's gun. Not just a tool of the trade but something she considered vital. She was probably out there taking pictures of the terrain or the clouds drifting through the sky or something like that.

Logan clenched his jaw. He wanted to hit something. Wanted to beat something bloody—preferably his cousin's affable face. He just bet that Bo was about as happy as could be, as content as the proverbial cat and cream. Daydreaming about her upcoming wedding and how perfect her life with David was going to be.

At that, Logan laughed. There wasn't much humor in the sound, though. He felt so bitter, it almost made him sick. He *knew* Bo. Her marriage to David would be sheer hell for her. She'd have David wrapped around her finger and ground into the dirt in no time flat.

David had the problem of wanting to take care of a woman. Coddle her. Protect her. And in Bo's case, that would be smothering her. She might like the pampering for a while but it wouldn't take long for the novelty of that to wear off and then she'd be miserable.

Bo didn't realize it yet but she *would* be miserable.

David would be miserable too. "Stopping that wedding would be doing them a favor," Logan muttered. He scrubbed a hand over his face and turned away from the window. He caught sight of a picture on his desk. It was the only picture on the desk, one of the very few he had in the house.

It was Bo. He'd taken it himself one weekend when she'd come home from college for a few days. They'd gone out riding one fall day and she'd spent most of the time taking pictures with the Canon EOS Rebel her dad had given her just before she left for school.

She had looked so beautiful that day. So happy. So perfect. It had been before she chopped her hair off and Logan could still remember how she'd looked, that long thick hair escaping from the braid to frame her face, her eyes bright with laughter.

He'd wanted to grab her, haul her against him and kiss her until she couldn't see straight. Then he wanted to strip her naked, spread her thighs and taste her. Fuck her hard and deep and then do it all over again but slower.

"You going to tell me about school or just snap pictures all day?" he'd asked her when they stopped for lunch. When she'd lowered the camera, he had grabbed it away from her. He'd planned on just putting the camera back in the case but he'd looked at her. Grinning, with her hair blowing across her face. He'd snapped a quick picture of her before tucking the camera away.

She had looked happy.

Logan's lids drooped and he thought of the way she'd looked Christmas Eve. She had been smiling, yeah. She had looked happy enough. But David didn't make her face glow. She didn't look as happy with David as she had looked with Logan.

"Why in the hell is this happening?" he muttered.

But he knew the answer to that. It was happening because he had let it happen. Logan closed his eyes and rested his forehead against the windowpane. How many mistakes was he going to make with her? Rushing her like he had. Then, when maybe he should have moved a little faster, he hadn't.

He should have gone after her. It didn't matter if she was seeing David or not.

That was what he should have done.

Ain't too late until she says I do.

But now it was too late. Logan had to do something before she married David but he didn't know what. It wasn't purely selfish. Logan wanted her, had always wanted her, but it wasn't just that. It wasn't even the bone-deep knowledge that she belonged with him. *To* him. Sounded archaic but hey, there it was. She belonged to him and even though she didn't know, he belonged to her.

Both of them would be miserable marrying anybody else. He wanted her happy. If he thought there was a snowball's chance in hell that she would be happy with David, he'd walk her down the aisle himself. He might drink himself into oblivion and stay drunk for weeks after but he would do it. If it would make her happy.

Slowly, he turned and looked back out the window. She was still out there, high on the ridge. He could do that—give her away to another man. He could do whatever it took to make her happy, no matter how much it hurt him. He loved her—what else could he do but want her happy?

"You're marrying the wrong guy, Bo."

Ain't too late until she says I do.

⤜∞⤏

Bridal jitters.

Hell, these weren't jitters. Jitters sounded like such a small thing. Like aftershocks or something. She wasn't having jitters—she was having quakes that would register 6.0, complete with emergency alerts and fire truck sirens.

The warning system was all in her head of course but every time she thought about the wedding, it was with a pealing of alarm bells that made her gut tie itself into knots.

Up until a few days ago, she'd had herself convinced she wasn't making a mistake. She just needed time to get used to the idea of getting married. She was twenty-five years old. She could take care of herself and had been doing just that since she'd landed her first job, a pure stroke of luck while she was still in college.

Bo had money in the bank, she had a great career and she had a man who adored her. What more could she want? Logically, there shouldn't be anything.

So why was she so miserable?

From the corner of her eye, she saw a horse and rider approach. She didn't even have to see him to know who it was. Logan. Nor did she have to see him to react. Her skin felt hot and tight. Her heart banged away within her chest with a force that made her breathless. Her muscles felt like putty. Only one person on Earth had that effect on her and she'd been running from him for four years.

Like she sensed her rider's mood swing, Mist shifted and Bo reached out a hand, soothing the mare.

The bastard always did this to her. She'd had a serious crush on him the entire time she was growing up. Getting away from him at college had seemed to make it a little easier and it had been so damn necessary. Bo liked keeping a certain distance between herself and everybody else. Except her dad, and even with him, there were some boundaries she didn't want to cross.

Her mother's death had hit both of them hard and William Martin had always been there for Bo but he never really recovered from Isabo's death. Bo didn't ever want to go through the pain her dad had gone through. Sometimes it made her feel like a coward.

Bo looked like her mom, though she did have her dad's eyes. She'd been named Isabo Dawn, after her mother. She'd been Bo pretty much since birth. Her memories of her mother were vague but they centered around a woman so pretty that she'd looked like an angel in Bo's eyes. She'd loved to laugh. She'd loved to dance.

Isabo had loved life, plain and simple.

Bo preferred to hide from it. And she'd been doing pretty well, until Logan. He'd shattered her defenses four years ago and if she let him close enough, he'd do it again.

All the more reason to marry David, she told herself. She liked David. She even loved him. He was funny. He was sweet. He made her laugh. She'd marry him and in a year or two, they would talk about having kids.

Maybe. The kid thing was still a maybe for her. She might be able to maintain distance with those around her but having kids would shoot that straight to hell. So the jury was still out on that one. David had already told her that it was her decision.

Bo grimaced. Too often, David's answers were along those lines. *Whatever makes you happy, Bo.*

Lately, Bo had been thinking, *How about an argument? If an argument will make me happy, will you give me one?*

David didn't argue. He persuaded and cajoled or he went along with her. Bo hated to admit it but that was fast becoming boring.

Logan's never boring. The minute that little voice whispered those words inside her head, Bo wanted to scream. No. Logan wasn't boring. Her palms went damp just thinking about him. If she took off now, she just might be able to avoid him. She'd been doing that for too long.

Ever since . . . Bo winced and shied away from that thought. She didn't want to think about that night. She couldn't think about that night.

"You going to take off running again, Bo?"

Shit. She took a deep breath and hoped her nerves weren't showing on her face. She'd gotten very, very good at hiding her emotions but Logan tended to shatter her control.

"Don't know what you're talking about," Bo lied as she looked at him. Mist shifted a little as Logan and Dervish drew closer. Absently, Bo stroked a hand down the mare's neck. She made herself look at him as she responded and wished she hadn't.

"Don't you?" There was a smile on his face. A cool, knowing smile that was completely maddening. And sexy as hell. Everything about Logan was sexy as hell. He was just an inch or two taller than her. She was five-nine and she liked being able to meet his eyes head-on, without looking up.

She loved his shoulders. Always had. She loved watching him while he worked with his brother in the stable, worn cotton clinging to the sleek muscles underneath. She liked how he looked in a suit. An agent with the local DEA department, Logan was just as comfortable in a suit and tie as he was in denim and cotton. He spent a lot of his time undercover, which meant he spent more time in the casual clothes but he could wear a suit better than most of the male models Bo had met.

He was better looking than most of them too. Hard, male

looks instead of glossed up pretty-boy looks. Thick chestnut brown hair that curled just a little when he forgot to cut it, eyes the palest brown. When she'd first met him, he'd had dimples when he smiled but over the years those dimples had deepened to slashes that bracketed a mouth that wasn't as hard as it looked.

She ought to know. That one night had forever imprinted the memory of how that mouth felt. She realized she was staring at his mouth and she jerked her eyes away but not soon enough.

He smiled a slow, lazy smile that seemed to say he knew exactly what she was thinking about. Blood rushed to her cheeks. Damn it.

Bo had been dealing with her feelings for Logan for a long time and she knew damn well that if she let him in on how nervous she was, it would be that much worse. She took a deep, slow breath. Even if she was still blushing, she made herself look back at him and answer. "No, Logan. I don't know what you're talking about."

And it wasn't a lie, not right now. The look in his eyes could make her forget her name, so recalling something he'd said thirty seconds ago was difficult.

He didn't push. He glanced around and nodded to her camera. "You've been sitting out here for a while. Something wrong?"

Only an entire world of things, Bo thought but she didn't say that. "Just thinking." As she spoke, she lifted the camera and snapped a picture of him. He didn't blink. Logan had been around her long enough to know that a camera in her hands rarely remained unused. She had hundreds of pictures of him. More than anybody else in her life, though she'd never let him know that.

He was still smiling but the smile changed, grew sharper, almost icy. She suppressed a shiver and snapped another picture. "Thinking about your wedding?" he asked. His tone was silky smooth. If it wasn't for that smile, she'd almost believe that he was just expressing casual interest.

Yeah. Casual, my ass, she thought sourly. "Just thinking."

He urged Dervish a little closer, until they were practically knee to knee. He leaned in and said, "About what? You look so serious for a girl who ought to be riding high on the world right now."

Irritated, Bo tugged on Mist's reins, guiding her mare a short distance away. "I'm just *thinking*," she repeated. "I've got an assignment coming up in Alaska, one in Japan, a wedding in two weeks and I'm still trying to keep an eye on my father. He still isn't acting like himself and I'm worried. I've got a million things on my mind, okay?"

If she thought Logan would let it go at that, she obviously didn't know him very well, he figured. A million things on her mind wouldn't make her look like that, not if she was happy. She had already looked miserable but when he'd mentioned the wedding, her eyes had gotten darker and her mouth flattened out into an unsmiling line. She had a pinched, pale look that made him think that maybe Bo had as many doubts about her upcoming wedding as he did.

"So are you nervous?"

Those pretty gray eyes narrowed and Bo drawled sarcastically, "Gee, I'm about to become a bride. What do *you* think, Sherlock?"

Logan shrugged. "I don't know. I think you're looking kind of miserable. Like you really aren't looking forward to wearing that white dress."

Her brows dropped low over her eyes and she jerked on Mist's reins, putting a little more distance between them. "What in the world do you know?"

He stared at her for a long, silent moment before he finally answered. "You. I know you. And you don't look happy. You so sure you want to get married, Bo?" He closed the distance between them and before she could move away again, he reached out and grabbed the reins.

She gave him a cool, dismissive glare. "I *am* getting married. Since when have I ever done anything I didn't really want to do?"

Well, she had a point there. Logan acknowledged it with a grin. "Just tell me one thing. Are you happy?"

Bo blinked. Her tongue slid out and wet her lips. Her voice cracked a little as she repeated, "Happy?"

"Yeah. You know the meaning of the word, right? Are you happy?"

Her lips curved up in a smile, cool and confident. Her voice was rock steady and she never even blinked as she replied, "Yes. I'm happy." If he hadn't been looking into her eyes, he just might have believed it.

But those eyes? They were lying.

∽∾

Late that night, Logan sat in his office, his hand wrapped around a half empty glass of whiskey. The fire across the room had burned down until the only light it gave off was a red glow.

The bottle on the desk had started out half full. Now, even the most optimistic couldn't call it much of anything except for empty. He was bordering on being really drunk and totally wasted. The whiskey was gone but he still hurt inside. He could empty another bottle and it wouldn't do anything for that pain.

Bo was getting married. In two weeks. To somebody Logan considered to be one of his best friends. It was going to kill him, he knew it. And her.

His parents had been trapped in a loveless marriage. Bo's mother had died when she was young and her father hadn't ever loved another woman enough to remarry. She didn't understand the hell of being married to somebody you didn't belong with. But what in the hell could he do about it?

Stop the wedding. Well, yeah. "Could do that," he said to himself. His voice was so damn slurred, nobody would have understood him. But since he was talking to himself, it wasn't an issue.

"Stop the wedding," he mumbled. Then he snorted. "How'm I gonna do that?"

An insane idea, no doubt brought on by his drunken state, danced through his mind. If he kidnapped her, she couldn't get married.

Could she? Can't get married if you don't show up for the wedding. He squinted a little and tried to think past the fog of alcohol. It did make sense.

She might hate him. "She doesn't belong with him," he said with the complete, utter confidence of somebody who was either shit-faced in love or falling-down drunk. Logan was both and he knew it. But the idea still made perfect sense.

Well, maybe not perfect sense. "It's illegal." So the plan had one little flaw. Still made really good sense. So maybe it was a little bit illegal but he could always arrest himself after, right?

Logan shoved up from his chair. The room swirled around him and he slapped his hands against the desk to keep from falling over. The room stabilized a little and he tried taking one step away from the desk. So far so good.

If he had a handrail all the way over to Bo's house, this just might work. But the desk was only so long and if he wanted to keep moving forward he was going to have to let go of it. First step—good. Second step—good.

Third.

Hell. He hit the floor and was still drunk enough to find it funny as he lay there, drunk out of his mind and snickering. He had to get up. Find Bo. Yeah. 'Cause it still all made perfect sense. Kidnap Bo and she couldn't marry David.

Perfect sense. The ceiling spun around overhead and he closed his eyes. All those circles were making him dizzy. He wanted to sleep. But Bo . . .

Then he sighed and stopped fighting it. Bo would be there in the morning and the plan would still make sense in the morning. He'd fix it then, because she couldn't marry David. Logan couldn't bear to see that sad look in her eyes get any worse.

Three

Morning came and with it, the hangover from hell.

Clarity also came but it wasn't the kind of clarity he might have expected. Because the idea still made sense. Bo wasn't in love with David. If she was, she wouldn't have looked so miserable.

But she was stubborn and if she'd made up her mind to marry Logan's cousin, it would take a cataclysmic event to change her mind. Or maybe an illegal event with somewhat questionable motives. Logan had no problem admitting that, for purely selfish reasons, he didn't want her marrying David. But he also knew that if he'd looked at Bo and seen happiness in her eyes, had known that she loved David and wanted to marry him, he would have let go.

At least, he was pretty sure of that. Logan would have been miserable and he would have thought about beating David into a pulp. On a regular basis. He might have even moved away, just so he wouldn't have to see his cousin, his *friend*, with the woman Logan loved. But she wasn't happy and she didn't love David.

Logan knew he was leaving a vital part out of his reasoning. David. He didn't want to think about David too much and he wouldn't let himself look too closely at his reasons for avoiding it either. But one thing he was certain of, David wasn't going to be happy married to Bo, either. Even if David was in love with her, he wouldn't be happy because Bo wouldn't happy.

When he added it all up—Bo's stubbornness, her unhappiness, the unhappiness that would result between Bo and David if they went through with the wedding and the fact that Logan had been in love with her his entire life—he figured he could do one of two things. He could do the wrong thing and let Bo marry somebody who'd make her miserable. Or he could do another wrong thing by kidnapping her. Give himself a few days to convince Bo that he was the only one who could make her happy.

In the long run, it wasn't a hard choice. Granted, his libido was all for the one that involved getting up close and personal with Bo. He was all for that. He wouldn't deny feeling a little bit of guilt over what he was doing to his cousin. David might never forgive him. But Logan knew he couldn't forgive himself if he let Bo make a mistake that made her miserable.

So his guilt over David might make him lose some sleep but it wasn't going to stop him.

It would take planning. A couple of little white lies. He didn't want anybody worrying about Bo. Not her dad, not her friends—not even her fiancé. That word left a bitter taste in his mouth. He couldn't even think it without sneering.

Still, as much as he wanted to pound on David's face a little, he didn't want his cousin thinking that something bad had happened to Bo. It was his weekend on call but he had a few favors to call in. Arranging everything was child's play and oddly, sort of exhilarating.

He cruised through Friday and considered it a good sign when Bo's father came by the house where Logan lived with his brother. "You and Dusty going to be around this weekend?"

"I won't be," Logan answered. "Dustin isn't going anywhere though." Dustin never went anywhere. His brother lived and breathed the small horse farm. "You need something?"

Will shrugged. "Just a hand. I . . . ." his voice trailed off and unless Logan was mistaken, the old guy was blushing a little. "Thinking about going up to that new casino in French Lick. A . . . friend invited me."

With a wide grin, Logan tucked his hands in his pockets and rocked back on his heels. Well, this was going to be even easier than he'd thought. "A friend. Do I know this friend?"

Will gave him that glowering, irritated glare.

Logan stopped smiling. He thought he managed to keep the pleased smirk on his face. Or mostly. Twenty minutes later, he watched as Will mounted the old gelding and headed back to his home.

"You're up to something."

Logan looked up to find Dustin watching him with knowing eyes. "Up to what?"

Dustin shrugged. "Beats the hell out of me but you're up to something. How come I'm going to be helping Bo out by my lonesome?"

"He's got stable hands. They'll be helping." He didn't say anything about Bo not being around. Dusty was a smart guy. He'd put two and two together soon enough.

A small, satisfied smile curled Dusty's lips. Dusty's summery blue eyes darkened when he was mad or thinking. He wasn't pissed off right now so that dark blue could signify a problem. "Saw you talking to Bo yesterday. Finally. What did you two talk about?"

In a level voice, he replied, "Nothing you need to worry about."

The smirk on his younger brother's face just got wider. "Really. So, is she ready for her wedding?"

"You'd have to ask her," Logan replied easily.

"Hmmm. Maybe I'll do that when I see her tomorrow."

Logan smiled. "Yeah. You do that."

∞

Sleep didn't come easy for Bo. Her dad had left in the middle of the day, leaving a note on the counter while she was in town stocking up on film, books and chocolate. Extra on the chocolate. She needed the fortification right now. Chocolate didn't solve the problems but it kept her from biting her nails down to the quick while she worried.

Of course, if she wasn't careful, she wouldn't fit into her wedding dress. Lying in her bed, she stared up into the darkness and grinned. *I'm sorry, David. I can't marry you. I ate myself out of a dress. No hard feelings?*

But as quick as the lighthearted thought came, it passed. Was she really having that many doubts? The razor-winged butterflies jumping in her belly certainly seemed to think so. With all these doubts, was she really doing the right thing or just the convenient thing, going through with this wedding?

She tried to picture herself with David in another year. Ten. But none of the images ever came into focus. Even the thought of their upcoming honeymoon in Spain just wouldn't come. If she couldn't even imagine her wedding night, all of two weeks from now, there was no way she could picture a year or five years from now.

Bo closed her eyes and imagined herself in her dress. It was a fairy tale princess of a dress—silk and tulle and lace. She could see herself wearing it. But what she couldn't see was herself walking down the aisle to stand in front of two hundred people while she said her vows to David.

When she tried to make herself see the groom, his face just wouldn't come to her. She knew what he looked like—dark hair, dark eyes, one of those sweet, boy-next-door smiles that drove women nuts. Bo adored his smile.

But his face just wasn't clear. The only face she could see clearly was Logan's. Bo groaned and buried her face in her hands. "What am I doing?"

But Bo had absolutely no clue. David's marriage proposal had been spur-of-the-moment, said almost jokingly. Bo's response had been given in the same tone. *Sure, I'll marry you. You're easy to be around.*

He was. She didn't feel as on guard with him, though she suspected part of that was because he just couldn't get in close enough to hurt. She hadn't really been that serious but then he showed up the next day with a ring. His dark brown eyes had been gentle and full of understanding as he said, "I know we were mostly joking . . . but . . . ." his voice trailed off and he pulled the ring out of his pocket. "I want to marry you, Bo."

Bo had said *yes*. At the time, she'd meant it.

Now? Now she just didn't know. She didn't know what she

was doing. She didn't know what she wanted. She didn't know who she wanted.

Liar.

Who she wanted? His face was as clear to her as her own. More. Those pale brown eyes, that hard mouth that felt so good against her own.

Logan.

Bo wanted Logan. She'd always wanted him. Had daydreamed about him for as long as she'd known him. He'd been her first crush. He'd been her first love. He'd also been the first man she'd ever run from. Okay, the only man she'd ever run from but that man could get inside her skin, inside her head. Logan would get close to her. He was already in her heart but if she let him, he'd get under her skin, inside her soul and she'd never get him out.

Somebody getting that close was dangerous. And losing somebody who got to her like that?

"You're not ever going to sleep if you keep this up," she mumbled. Sleep seemed even further away than before. Thinking about Logan definitely didn't instill calm, soothing thoughts. She had a deep, throbbing ache between her thighs—she felt too hot, too itchy and too restless. The smooth, silken sheets felt rough and scratchy against her skin and the loose T-shirt she wore felt too tight.

Frustrated, she kicked her way free of the sheets and covered her eyes with her forearm. The cooler air helped just a little but that aching deep inside just got worse. It was a feeling she was familiar with. She'd been dealing with frustrated arousal for the past four years. Experience told her that nothing would help.

Well, one thing might. But that wasn't an option. As tempting as it might be to throw on some clothes and go find Logan, it just wasn't an option.

"Go to sleep," she mumbled to herself. She flopped onto her belly and pressed her face against the pillowcase. It felt cool against her skin. It took a concentrated effort to pull her thoughts away from Logan and think of something else. Not her wedding, though. That was almost as bad.

Instead, she daydreamed. Thought about Mist. Thought about the assignments she had coming up. Slowly, the tension in her muscles dissolved and the exhaustion started to weigh on her. Half asleep, she rolled onto her back. Half-formed dream images danced through her mind and when Logan's face appeared in the darkness, she smiled. "You don't ever leave me alone, do you?"

∽∞∽

At first, he thought she was awake.

It wouldn't change his plans even if she was awake but it would be easier if she slept. But when she looked at him in the shadows, her eyes were cloudy with sleep and unfocused. She sighed a little and he watched the shallow movements of her chest. Her nipples pressed against the T-shirt she wore, hard and erect. His mouth watered a little and he had to stop himself from bending over and taking one nipple and then the other into his mouth.

Not here. Wasn't going to do it here.

He held still until her eyes fluttered closed again and her breathing slowed. Once he knew she was really asleep, he reached into the pocket of his jacket and pulled out a cloth.

She was going to kick his ass for this. Hell, if he knew anything about Bo's temper, he wouldn't be surprised if she called the cops on him and had his ass thrown in jail for a day or two, make him sweat.

Logan was fully aware how risky this was. It was completely wrong and if he got caught, he could lose his job.

But none of that stopped him. Because if he didn't, he was going to lose Bo and that just wasn't acceptable. Logan was desperate, he didn't see too many options open to him so he was going to do this and damn the consequences. As long as Bo realized what an awful mistake it would be to marry David, he didn't care what she did.

Her body tensed a little when he slid an arm under her shoulders. He murmured into her ear and she cuddled into him, pressing her cheek against his shoulder. Guilt tore into him when he covered her mouth and nose and when she bucked and struggled, he almost—*almost*—gave up. Too close now, though. He pressed his lips to her brow and muttered, "I'm sorry," over and over until the chloroform knocked her out.

"It's for the best, Bo, I swear." Quickly, he grabbed a few of her things and tossed them into the bag he'd brought. Then he wrapped the sheet and one of her blankets around her. He lifted her in his arms and five minutes later, he had her tucked inside the front seat of his car. He'd parked just before the bend in her drive, out of view, and he'd been waiting three hours now for her to settle down and go to sleep.

It was late, nearly one a.m. and he had a good three-hour drive ahead of him. The coffee in the thermos tucked under his seat was still piping hot and strong enough to keep him awake for the next twenty-four hours, had he been inclined to sleep.

Sleep wasn't an issue, though, not right now. He'd had the

pleasure of committing a major felony with his eyes wide open and his mind completely clear. He kept waiting for some voice of reason to speak up. Like the voice that piped about the illegality of this whole damn idea. But if that voice had much of anything to say, it was drowned out by the louder, adamant demand that he not let another day go by with her wearing David's ring on her hand.

It was a cool, clear night. Stars shone bright in the moonless sky and the air drifting in through his partially open window smelled of honeysuckle and hayfields.

All in all, Logan figured it was a great night for kidnapping.

By the time he exited the highway, the sky in the east was just a little bit fainter. Four a.m. and hardly a car in sight. He got to the turnoff in record time. Gravel crunched under the tires and next to him, Bo moaned softly. She squirmed around a little. The faint light coming off the dash was just enough for him to see her make a face and then her features smoothed out and she sighed, settling back into sleep.

Don't wake up, he mouthed. He'd driven this road a hundred times but usually not before dawn. The road sloped off to the right and some twenty feet down lay Lake Cumberland, stretching on for miles and miles. The twists and turns in the road required attention and he figured it would be hard to pay attention to the road if she woke up and started pounding on his head with her fists.

So her sleeping for the next twenty minutes would be good.

For once in her life, though, Bo made things easy on him. She not only slept the next twenty minutes, she didn't wake up when he opened the door, came around the car and lifted her out. She cuddled into his chest, turning her face toward him and nuzzling him.

The feel of her in his arms, all sleepy warm and soft, made his gut go tight with need. If he laid her down on his bed and stripped away the T-shirt she was wearing, he could run his hands over that amazing body, fill his hands with her breasts, grip her hips and hold her still while he rocked against her.

If he went down on her, would she come awake with a moan?

She had before. Logan had vivid, almost painful memories of that one night. He'd woken her up just like that, licking and nuzzling her soft, sweet pussy. She had been climaxing when she awoke. The look in her eyes was sleepy satisfaction and a dream-like, dazed pleasure.

Hunger hit him like a punch in the gut. Hard and vicious.

He carried her up to the porch and had to shift her weight around so he could unlock the door. The inside of the cabin smelled like cedar and wood smoke and some of that potpourri crap that one of Dustin's girlfriends had brought.

The cabin wasn't one of those luxury deals, although Dustin and he had fixed it up a lot since it had passed to them. The plank wood floors were new, the couch was overstuffed and comfortable enough to fall asleep on and the fireplace was huge. The deck in the back faced toward the lake and there were a couple of Adirondack chairs alongside the hot tub.

He wanted to see Bo in that hot tub. His dick throbbed and he tried to focus on something that didn't involve Bo naked.

Of course, images of Bo naked had been intruding on his thoughts for more than a decade now. Stopping that process was going to be hard.

∽∞∾

The mattress was lumpy. Bo shifted around and tried to find a more comfortable position, still clinging to sleep. The pillow . . . She smacked at it with her hand and reality intruded just a little more. A funny smell. Lavender and vanilla. She opened one eye. Then the other.

At first she didn't understand what was in front of her. A golden wall—the warm, mellow gold of wood. She could smell cedar somewhere under all that vanilla and lavender. She slanted her gaze upward and saw a window with panes of sparkling glass framed by simple, sturdy, dark blue curtains.

Her head felt kind of funny, her memories of the last night all fuzzy. She was trying to process everything going on but her head just didn't want to work.

A hand on her hip from behind. Bo yelped and drove her elbow back as hard as she could. It connected with a hard stomach and she heard a muffled "Ooph" as she scrambled out of the bed.

She spun around and stared in shock. It was Logan. His hair was rumpled, his lids low, gaze sleepy. He was dressed. Bo looked down at herself and saw that she still wore the long, plain white T-shirt. She blinked. Looked back up at Logan. He was still there.

Bo tried rubbing her eyes and looked back. He was *still* there. "What the hell is going on?"

"Morning, Bo."

She snarled at him and went up to the bed and kicked one of the bedposts. Pain shot up her leg, just a little more proof that she wasn't dreaming. "Don't *Morning, Bo* me, you jackass. Where in hell am I? *What* am I doing here?"

He rolled out of bed and came around the foot of the bed. Yeah, he was still dressed but the shirt was unbuttoned. The plain blue cotton framed a hard, muscled chest and Bo realized her mouth was watering. He reached out toward her and she backed away. "You're at the cabin." He kept coming and when she backed into the wall, he reached up and planted his arms on either side of her, pinning her in place. "Remember the cabin I told you about?" he murmured. He lowered his head and nuzzled her neck. "I told you about it at least once. Right before you hung up on me."

Bo squinted up at him. He'd lowered his head like he was going to kiss her but Bo turned her head aside. "I've hung up on you plenty. No, I don't remember a cabin. Nor do I remember me telling you that I'd like to come to this cabin. Take me home."

He didn't seem to mind that she wouldn't let him kiss her. He nuzzled her neck, licked her there and then bit her softly. Bo had to bite her lip to keep from moaning when he leaned into her and rocked his hips against hers. She felt him through the thin cotton of her shirt and through his jeans—hot and hard. Desperate, she squeezed her eyes closed and pushed against him. "Damn it, Logan, take me home."

"I will. Sooner or later." He did lean back, though, looking down at her hands. He looked back up at her and there was a dark, almost scary look in his eyes. He wrapped his fingers around her left wrist and lifted, bringing it to his mouth. Bo's eyes widened as he slid her ring finger into his mouth. He gently tugged back and she felt her engagement ring slide off. She caught a glimpse of the gold band as he reached up and took the ring out of his mouth.

"I hate that ring," he rasped. His hand closed in a tight fist around it. Bo was temporarily speechless. Apparently, he decided to take advantage of the fact. His mouth came down on hers hard, almost punishing. His tongue pressed against her lips. Reality intruded and she tried to turn her head away. She felt a big hand cup the back of her head, holding her still. At the same time, he used his other hand to cup her cheek. He pressed right *there*, at that sensitive place right along her jaw, forcing her mouth open.

Bo wanted to be outraged. She wanted to be pissed at his rough kiss, at the hard, unyielding strength and the way he used it on her. But she wasn't.

She was so damn turned on, she felt like she just might melt all over him. His tongue came inside her mouth and she groaned hungrily. She arched up against him, opening fully. His hands left her head, traveling down over her shoulders, down her arms. Distantly, she heard something fall, felt it bounce off her foot. "Hate that ring," he muttered again, lifting his head just enough to say that against her mouth and then he was kissing her again.

He was all over her. Bo felt like he had ten hands and wanted nothing more than to drive her insane. He palmed her ass, caressed her breasts, jerked at her T-shirt and tore it away from her. His mouth left hers and moved to her breasts. No soft, gentle kisses there either, he licked and bit her nipples, had her teetering on the point of pain and she cried out and begged for more.

His jeans felt rough against her naked thighs, abrading her flesh as he pushed against her. "You're so hot," he muttered as he sank down in front of her, kissing a straight line down from her breastbone to her navel. His hand cupped her and he dipped one finger inside her sex. Bo clenched around him with a force that damn near hurt. "So wet. Melting for me."

Hell yes, she was melting. Bo felt like she was turning into a boneless little puddle, melting all around him and over him. His mouth replaced his fingers and he plunged his tongue inside her. In quick, rapid succession, over and over, until she climaxed with a scream. She shuddered, slamming her hands against his shoulders to keep from collapsing. Logan slid his tongue around her clit and then he pushed it inside her again. She felt a gentle suction and she wailed. Her nails bit into his shoulders and her knees wobbled. She couldn't stay upright. No way.

He moved, standing up so fast that Bo swayed. Her legs folded under her and she would have sunk to the ground in a boneless puddle, but he lifted her and braced her against the wall. At some point, between going down on her and standing up, he'd shoved his jeans out of the way. She felt the bare length of his cock against her belly as he spread her legs and moved between them.

"Look at me," he growled.

Bo could hardly breathe, could hardly see and didn't even have the strength to wrap her arms around him. But she forced herself to lean her head back and try to focus on his face. "Don't look away." She blinked, barely comprehending his words.

Her feet left the floor. He caught her under the knees and shoved them high, hooking them over his forearms as he pressed against her. "Don't look away," he muttered again.

He pushed inside her, huge and hot as a branding iron. Stretching her. Filling her. She cried out as he filled up the empty ache she'd been living with for four years. His eyes, that pale golden brown, stared into hers with an intensity that seemed to burn. "Tell me you thought of this, the two of us."

His voice was a hypnotic growl and it never even occurred to Bo to *not* obey him. "Every day," she whispered. Every day, every night, until she ached with the sweet pain of the memories. She arched up and tried to pull him closer. He held himself back, though, staring down at her. She reached for him and he somehow managed to capture her wrists, even with her legs hooked over his elbows. He pressed them flat against the wall, effectively pinning her. She couldn't move—Logan held her in a way that kept her open for his use, exposed to his eyes and it was so damn erotic she almost came just from the feel of his hands trapping her.

He pulled out slowly, inch by incremental inch and she'd never been so aware of every little movement. He surged back inside, keeping his pace slow as he pushed deep inside. So deep she could feel the head of his cock butting against the mouth of her womb. He held there for long, excruciating seconds and then he pulled out and started the process all over again, just a little bit faster. Then faster, faster, until he was slamming into her full force. The wooden wall bit into her back, his hands squeezing her wrists hard and tight. His cock jerked inside her and reflex had her squeezing down in return. And still, he kept going, so hard and so fast. Pleasure and pain blurred and she screamed.

His mouth covered hers, an animalistic snarl coming from him as though the sound of her screaming was exactly what he had been waiting for.

The orgasm grew inside instead of fading away and every time he shafted her, it seemed to grow just a little more out of control until it finally shattered her. Blood roared in her ears and for a minute, she couldn't see, feel or anything as she bucked and shuddered and screamed her way through climax.

Shaky, hot, all but dying inside from the pleasure, Bo tried once more to reach for him and this time, he let go of her wrists and let her. She wrapped her arms around his neck and cuddled into his chest. Logan lowered her legs and wrapped his arms around her, stroking a hand up and down her back.

Tears stung her eyes but Bo wouldn't let them fall.

❦

His hand came up to lie on her belly. He'd carried her to bed and Bo was still too shaky to argue. The warm, heavy weight of him wasn't helping either. Her body was hungry for more. She wanted to turn into him and snuggle close.

It was all she could do to lie still. When he touched her, she felt it clear down to her toes. His voice was sleep-rough as he said, "I didn't wear a rubber."

That was a fact that Bo was excruciatingly aware of, thank you. She glanced at him and then went back to contemplating the plank ceiling. "I'm on the pill." She'd started it in preparation for getting married. Up until then, she hadn't needed it. She hadn't been sleeping with David. David hadn't seemed to mind when she had shied back. They hadn't slept together before he'd proposed and after, Bo knew he had just assumed she wanted to wait.

David was sweet like that.

Sweet. Handsome. Sexy, even. But she didn't get all gooey inside thinking about David.

The bed shifted beside her and from the corner of her eye, she could see Logan pushing up onto his elbow. He was staring at her. His hand rubbed in slow circles around her belly. How such a simple touch could feel so erotic, she didn't know. "I didn't mean to let it go that far, so fast. I . . ." his voice stopped abruptly and he took a deep breath. "Look, I meant to wear a rubber."

"Meant to . . . sure." She tried to tug away from him but he wouldn't let go. "Look, I'm protected. I'm clean."

His eyes had a weird, shuttered look to them. When he nodded, it was stiff and jerky. "Yeah. As a whistle." Then his gaze lowered to her lips. Bo squirmed again but he rolled on top of her, effectively trapping her in place. "Bo." He muttered her name against her lips.

Low against her belly, she felt the length of his cock. He was hard and throbbing. She kept waiting for the voice of reason to speak up but when she opened her mouth, it was to kiss him, not tell him to stop. With a groan, she wrapped her arms around his shoulders.

Like he had been waiting for just that, he wedged his hips into the cradle of hers and pushed inside.

Filling her. Completing her. That simple, that easy, all the confusion and doubts and questions fell away and for that time, nothing mattered but his hands, his mouth and his body, touching her, stroking her, kissing her. Taking her higher than she'd ever been.

By the time they came back down, she was exhausted and it seemed perfectly natural to fall asleep in his arms.

Four

inally." Bo saw the sparkle of her engagement ring by the wall, mostly hidden by the curtain. She knelt down to pick it up and started to put it on but something stopped her.

She was still wet from Logan. She could feel the remnants of their lovemaking on her thighs. Her body was so hotly satisfied that she wanted to purr like a cat. Putting that ring on, that glaring reminder of her promise to David, just seemed wrong.

Behind her, Logan said, "You put that on in front of me and I just might go ballistic."

She gave him a cold look. "If you didn't want to see me wearing David's ring, maybe you shouldn't have kidnapped me." Her lips curved in a mocking smile and she held his gaze as she slid the ring on her finger.

Muscles flexed and rippled as he rolled out of the bed and headed her way. He reached for her hand and Bo closed it into a fist. She angled her chin up and said, "Leave it *alone*."

"Why?" He cupped her chin in his hand and stared into her eyes with a dark, turbulent gaze. "Give me one good reason, Bo. You don't love him."

"The hell I don't." She tried to jerk away from him but he wouldn't let go. Once more, he crowded her back against the wall and Bo couldn't help the hot, eager rush that flooded her at the feel of that long, lean body pressed against her own. She *did* love David. She always had.

She just didn't . . . her thoughts whirled to a halt as Logan pressed his mouth to hers. "You might love him—in a way," he whispered against her lips. "But you're not in love with him. You can't honestly look at me and tell me that, now can you?"

Bo should have just lied. She should have looked into his eyes and said just that. *I am in love with him.* She could do that. She *should* do that. But she didn't. He lifted his head just a fraction and his eyes bored into hers. "Say it, Bo and you can leave right now. I won't say a damn thing to David about this and I'll even wear that damn penguin suit and watch you marry. But you have to tell me. Can you do that?"

She closed her eyes. "Why are you doing this? What do you want?"

Logan shrugged. "In the long run, everything. Right now? All I want is an answer and one night with you. Give me those two things and I'll leave you alone."

Bo stayed silent and a small, humorless smile curved his lips. "You want to go home, then you'll answer me," he murmured just before he covered her mouth again. His kiss was hard, rough—a conquering—and he made no attempt to hold back.

His head lifted. Bo was gasping and sweating and she couldn't see anything beyond his mouth. The anger in his voice, though, penetrated the fog of need surrounding her. "You don't love him the way a woman should love a man she's going to spend the rest of her life with. A man she wants to have kids with. You don't love him like that. If you did—you never would have made love with me."

His words were like a cold splash of water. Bo was mortified but it was more than that. She was furious. She was dismayed and confused and so many other things that she couldn't even begin to name. But the fury was the easiest for her to handle. So that was the one she latched on to. Her lip curled in a sneer. *"That was making love? You shove me up against a wall and shove your dick inside me—after kidnapping me—but you can call it making love?"*

She regretted the words almost as soon as they left her lips. But she didn't make any attempt to take them back. Logan didn't do fury the way she did. Instead of burning hot, the madder he got, the colder he became. Cold was good. Cold meant distance and Bo desperately needed the distance now.

He backed away slowly, his hands leaving her body with infinite care, almost like he didn't trust himself. "I didn't hurt you. I'd never hurt you, Bo." His voice was stiff, icy.

The sound of it, the look in his eyes, made a queer ache form in the pit of her belly and Bo wanted to cry. She swallowed. But she didn't say anything. She really didn't know what to say.

His eyes burned into hers. Pissed off. Oh yeah. He was pissed off. But she thought she also saw something else. Hurt. *God . . . I'm sorry. I didn't want to hurt you . . .* "Logan . . ."

"Maybe my hearing is fucked up. Did you tell me to stop? Even once?"

Covering her face with her hands, Bo wished she could just disappear. She'd give anything to be anywhere but right here, right now. She jumped when he spoke right in her ear. "Did you, Bo?" he asked, his voice silky soft.

She looked up. His expression almost had her sidling away from him. The wall wouldn't allow her to back up farther but she could already see a line of retreat if she just inched her way around him. *Coward.* Bo set her jaw and looked up at him. She'd been running from him for the past four years because of that one night. Because of what he'd made her feel, what he'd made her hope for. It was that, really, that had made her run. After the night they'd shared, if she hadn't run . . . she could just see them together. She'd fantasized about just that for so long.

And if she was wrong, if Logan didn't want much more than that one night, Bo wasn't certain she could handle it. Cowardly *and* weak, she thought bitterly. *Damn it, you're pathetic, Bo.* She swallowed. Met his gaze head-on and said in a level voice, "No, I didn't tell you to stop."

His hand cupped her cheek and she turned her face into his touch, needing it. Holy hell, she'd missed him. The past four years had been like she was slowly bleeding inside. Dying, bit by bit. She missed him. She'd adored Logan for more than half her life. Idolized him. He was one of her best friends—he was the one she ran to when she needed somebody, whether it was advice, a shoulder to cry on or somebody to yell at. And he'd always been there.

When she had run from him, she had cut herself off from that. His thumb stroked over her lower lip. Just that simple, chaste touch was enough to have her senses sizzling. She sighed raggedly.

"I'd never hurt you, Bo," he murmured. His voice no longer sounded so stiff and distant. It was soft, low and rough—hypnotic.

He pressed his mouth against her neck, tracing a light pattern on the sensitive skin there. "Never."

Her voice shook as she answered, "I know that, Logan."

"Do you?" he asked quietly. He nuzzled her neck and then lifted his head so he could bite her ear. That soft, careful nip affected her in so many ways. Her knees buckled and she would have collapsed to the floor if he hadn't wrapped an arm around her and braced her body against his own.

He kissed her then, a soft, gentle kiss that was a seduction all on its own. The hand cupping her face moved down to curve around her neck, his thumb resting just above her pulse. She arched up, tried to take the kiss deeper but he eased her back with the hand he kept at her throat. He lifted his head. Their gazes locked. The look in his eyes was enough to melt metal, so hot, the pale golden brown dark with desire.

He wrapped a hand around her wrist and lifted it to his mouth, staring at the discolored marks there. He kissed the faint bruises on her wrists and shame twisted in her belly. She'd always bruised easily—always. The night they'd spent together, she'd had bruises on her wrists, ankles and thighs but not because he had hurt her. He hadn't, not once. But she knew he didn't like seeing those dark marks on her. "I was rough with you," he whispered against her flesh.

She blushed. "I loved every second."

He looked at her from under his lashes. He looked so serious. So solemn. "Maybe you didn't tell me to stop." He rubbed a thumb over the bruises on her wrist and said, "But that wasn't how I wanted this. I waited four years to touch you again and then I fucked you up against a wall."

He might not be pissed anymore but the broody, intense look wasn't much better. The tension in the air was enough to choke her but she managed a smile. "I don't have any complaints."

"Oh, I know." He touched the tip of his tongue to her wrist and then pressed an openmouthed kiss to her palm. "You screamed out my name. I loved hearing it. I'm going to hear it again. But I had a different idea in mind, the first time I touched you again."

Seduction could be torture. The sweetest, hottest, most erotic torture imaginable but still torture. Bo couldn't breathe. Logan had carried her to the bed and she'd gasped when he picked her up. That was probably the last good breath she got and it had been who knows how long ago. Minutes, hours, maybe even days.

Logan lay between her thighs, sucking and licking her with a slow, almost lazy thoroughness that had her teetering on the edge of climax. She'd been teetering on that same edge for ages, it seemed. He pushed his tongue inside her pussy, stroking in, out, in, out . . . oh. *Oh*. She moaned out his name and reached down, fisting her hands in his hair. She rocked her hips against his mouth, tipping closer and closer to the edge.

Then he stopped.

He lifted his head and stared up at her. It took a couple of seconds to catch her breath and then she looked down at him. Once she did, he smiled.

That smile shook her down to her very core. It was full of sensual promise but under that was something deeper. Something she was too scared to think about. It was what lay under the promise that had scared her into running four years ago. And coward that she was, she wasn't ready to face it now either.

As though he could sense her mental retreat, his smile faded just a little. But he said nothing, covering her body with his, taking her face between his hands and pressing a soft, rather chaste kiss to her lips. There was nothing chaste about his taste, though. Bo blushed as she tasted herself there and under that, the hot, heady taste of Logan.

"One of these days, you'll stop pulling away from me," he whispered and there was a determined glint in his eyes.

He pressed against her, the length of his cock hard and hot and pulsating. By contrast, his mouth was soft, almost gentle on hers and he kept the kiss light and easy as he pushed inside her so slowly, stretching her, filling her. Bo felt the burn of tears sting her eyes and she tried to blink them away. One after another broke free, sliding out of the corners of her eyes. Logan lifted his head and saw them—the feel of his lips kissing those tears away only made the ache in her heart worse.

You've ruined me for anybody else, Bo thought bleakly. But she didn't say anything. Instead she pressed her mouth to his. Every last minute of this—she was going to live it to the fullest and carry those memories for the rest of her life.

She wrapped her arms around his neck and gave herself up to him. She brought her legs up, hooking them over his hips and rocking up to meet each slow thrust. He moved with exquisite slowness. She was so acutely aware of even the smallest detail. The way his breathing hissed out of him when she clenched her muscles around his cock. The way the gold of his eyes darkened as she ran her hands over his shoulders. The way his harsh, rough face softened when she kissed him.

He jerked inside her and Bo moaned, tilting her hips more, trying to take him deeper. He slid a calloused palm down her side and cupped it over her hip, guiding her up at a high angle. Now she could feel him sliding back and forth against her clit as he pumped lazily into her.

Time fell away. The world fell away. Her wedding, her concerns about her dad, her stress over upcoming assignments, all of it fell away under the stroke of his hands, the brush of his lips and the movements of his body against hers. He took her to a place where nothing existed but the two of them as he took her from one heart-shattering climax to another.

Sweat gleamed on his body as he lifted his head to look down at her. His breathing had gotten harsh and ragged, coming in hot little gusts. Their gazes locked, held. His hands sought hers and their fingers intertwined. Like that, staring into each other's eyes, hands linked, they gave in to the demands of their bodies. She sobbed out his name and he groaned hers. As she clenched around him, each little caress milked his cock until she'd emptied him completely and utterly.

He lay between her thighs with his head between her breasts. His breath sawed in and out of his lungs but eventually slowed. Bo was drifting off to sleep when he eased off her and lay beside her. He worked his arms around her waist and pulled her close against him. Bo cuddled into him, rubbing her cheek against his chest. His hand cupped the back of her head.

Just before she fell into total oblivion, she heard him murmur, "You can't run away this time."

Five

They napped for a little while and then Logan woke her up, making love to her again. He left her dozing and the next thing she knew, she smelled bacon, eggs and pancakes.

They ate. They made love. He got a bag out of his car and she opened it to find several changes of clothes. She showered—then had to shower again when Logan came up behind her in the bathroom and pressed her up against the wall again.

Her back wasn't ever going to be the same but oddly enough, Bo didn't give a damn. Sore, sensitive muscles winced as she dressed. Logan stood by, his dark, possessive eyes watching every move she made.

They walked through the woods without speaking, just enjoying the peace and quiet and each other. Bo couldn't remember the last time she had felt so . . . right. Being with Logan felt right.

But it was wrong.

She knew it was. And the darkness of that knowledge kept intruding on her thoughts throughout the day, until she could scarcely think past it.

You can't run away this time.

No. She couldn't run. Even if he had put the keys in her hand and put her butt in the car, she couldn't run away. Not this time. Time enough would come when she'd have to walk away but until that second came, she wasn't going to think about it.

∽

Or at least, she was going to try to not think about it. Her head had other thoughts, though. They'd returned to the cabin after their walk and spent some time in the hot tub. By the time they got out, the deck was nearly as wet as they were.

Hunger finally drove them into the kitchen where they ate as Bo sat on Logan's lap. Night fell with the two of them back in bed, where Logan shoved her thighs apart and used his mouth on her until she screamed herself hoarse.

They fell asleep with his arm wrapped around her waist, banding her against him. He didn't let go of her, not once throughout the night.

But Bo barely slept. *You can't run away this time.* His words echoed through her mind, disturbing her off and on throughout the night. Each time when she managed to drift off, those words came back to haunt her.

As a result, morning dawned with her in a worse than normal mood. No amount of coffee was going to help, either. She lay wrapped in his arms and wanted to cry. Sunlight filtered in through the narrow gaps in the curtain and she could see dust motes floating around the bright streams of light.

The cabin was cool. Under the covers with Logan wrapped around her, she felt all toasty warm and comfortable. She didn't ever want to move. But with morning, reality came crashing down.

She had screwed things up royally. She never should have started going out with David. She never should have let it drag on as long as it had and she never should have agreed to marry him. Shame flooded her as she realized she hadn't just been trying to fool herself. She'd been using David as well.

Right now, in the cool, quiet morning, she could even admit to herself why. Bo was in love with Logan and always had been. She didn't like it. Love was messy. Love was painful. Her dad had gone through hell when her mom died.

It was something Bo hadn't ever really wanted to experience, that deep, tearing loss. It was part of the reason she'd always held herself a little apart. With David, it had been easy. *Any* of the other guys she'd dated—holding herself apart had been easy.

It wouldn't be with Logan.

She was in love with Logan. She didn't like it—hell, the thought of it flat-out terrified her. She suddenly had that insane urge to take off running again. Running far, far away and this time, maybe she'd stay away more than four years. A decade might work.

Marrying somebody else wasn't going to fill the void in her heart.

But letting herself believe in a happily ever after with Logan didn't seem like much of an option, either.

She felt it when he woke up. His sigh drifted across her shoulder, warm and soft, and he stretched a little. Bo could feel the length of his cock against her bottom. The rigid length throbbed. Involuntarily, she pushed back against him.

His chest vibrated against her back as he rumbled, "Morning." His hand stroked up her side to cup her breast and Bo closed her eyes against the wave of want that washed through her.

Logan, seemingly oblivious to her inner turmoil, lifted up on his elbow so he could nuzzle her neck. Tears stung her eyes and Bo closed them so he wouldn't see. "Playtime's over, Logan. Let me up."

He stilled. That tense, eerie stillness of his that she always hated. Slowly, he lifted his head so he could look down at her. Bo could feel the weight of his stare and she opened her eyes, only to wish she hadn't. That hard, intent gaze focused on her face and Bo had to fight the urge not to squirm away. He made her feel like he could see right through her. "You haven't given me your answer," he said. His voice was silky soft but no less intimidating for it.

But she wasn't going to let him push her around. Logan was a bully. She loved him but he was a bully and always had been. Carefully, she reached up and closed her hand around his wrist, tugging on it until he stopped caressing her. "I don't owe you any answers, Logan. I never have."

His lids drooped over his eyes, shielding them. A tiny, humorless little smile quirked at his lips and he murmured, "You so sure about that? Not even for what happened four years ago?"

Bo blushed hotly as blood rushed to her face. But she wasn't going to get into this with him. She wasn't going to bare her soul, not with Logan. "What about what happened four years ago, Logan? We had sex. That's all."

His hand came up, curving over her neck. Bo swallowed and she felt the light pressure of his hand against her throat. His eyes blazed and his face no longer looked so expressionless. But the rage she saw there was just as unsettling as the complete lack of emotion. "Just sex," he murmured, stroking his thumb up and down her skin. "That's all."

He nudged her thighs apart with his knee. He pressed up

against her and Bo clenched her jaw to keep from moaning out loud. "And last night? Just sex?" He pressed his lips to her throat, his tongue stroking the skin just above her pulse. "You want me to believe this was just sex too?"

"What else could it be?" she demanded raggedly.

He rocked against her, cuddling close so that the head of his cock caressed her clit. He didn't answer her. Instead, he said, "I want that answer, Bo. You want to leave here, you answer my question. Do you really love him? Can he make you feel like I do?"

Furious and hurting, Bo shoved at his shoulders. She bucked against him, trying like hell to get away from him. "What is this? Some sick game of one-upmanship? I know you're competitive, Logan, but this is ridiculous."

"Competing?" His mouth came crushing down on hers and he pinned her thrashing body to the mattress. His hands came up and caught her wrists, manacling them to the bed. He used his hips to pin her lower body in place as he kissed her. Deep, hard and rough—there was nothing of the tender lover he'd shown her in the middle of the night. Nothing. Once more, that strange, irrational fury seemed to be driving him.

He was furious over something and he damn sure wanted her to know it. "You think this is about some kind of competition?"

He lifted his head and snarled at her. Then he lifted up and shoved away from her. He climbed from the bed and moved to the other side of the room, like he didn't trust himself to be that close to her.

Her voice shook as Bo said, "I don't know what to think, Logan. Four years ago, you took me out to dinner—exactly two dates— and then you fucked me blind. Yesterday, you kidnapped me and spent the night doing the same thing all over again. I don't know why and I don't know what else you want from me."

"I fucked you blind four years ago because I love you, damn it!" He shouted it so loudly that it was a wonder the glass didn't break. He crossed the room and bent over the bed, planting his hands on the mattress by her head and looming over her. "Get it? I love you."

His voice dropped and he said it again, "I love you."

Bo felt like the bottom of the world had just opened up beneath her feet. He hadn't just said that . . . had he? He was looking at her, staring at her with a weird look in his eyes. He had an expression on his face that was . . . gentle. Or at least it seemed gentle. Bo didn't want to trust that look at all. She couldn't. Tears blurred her vision and she shoved against his chest. "Let me up."

"Bo . . ."

Her voice broke as she screamed, "Damn it, let me up!"

Logan's face went blank and he slowly withdrew. Bo scrambled out from under him and climbed from the bed. With stiff, jerky motions, she grabbed a shirt from the foot of the bed and shoved her arms into it. She groaned as his scent surrounded her. Her hands shook as she tried to button it. Shaking too badly to manage it, she ended up just overlapping the edges and crossing her arms over her chest to keep it closed.

"Bo? Look at me." She jumped as Logan moved closer and when her eyes met his, she had that deer-in-the-headlights look.

He reached for her and she backed away so fast, she tripped over her feet. Logan tried to catch her but she smacked at his hands. She stumbled away a little bit and said, "This is insane."

"No." He kept his voice soft as he closed the distance between them. "This is the sanest thing I've done in quite a while. I love you."

She flinched a little and hugged herself even tighter when he reached out for her. But oddly enough, that made him feel a little bit better. He knew Bo—better than she knew herself. He knew that look in her eyes. He'd seen it before.

She was scared. Bo didn't handle scared very well.

Had she looked like that when she'd run away from him four years ago? He captured her face in his hands and used his thumbs to arch her face upward. Still her eyes wouldn't meet his. Nervous too. "Why did you run away, Bo?"

"I didn't run." Finally her eyes met his and her chin went up stubbornly. "I had an assignment."

"Yeah, good excuse. And was part of the assignment refusing to take my calls? Refusing to call me back? Hanging up on me? Was that part of your assignment too?" Logan asked. "What about coming back home and hooking up with my cousin? Was that an assignment?"

He wasn't mad, though. It was the first time he hadn't gotten mad when he thought about her with David. "No answer for me, Bo?" He rubbed a thumb over her lower lip. She jerked back and ended up hitting the wall. Logan followed her, pinning her there.

Her face was hotly flushed and her eyes glittered up at him. "What do you want me to say? Fine. I ran away from you. So what?"

"I already know you ran," he muttered. He dipped his head and licked her lips, tracing the outline of them with his tongue. "I've known that since it happened. Now I want you to tell me why. Although I think I already know."

If she could have melted into the wall, she would have done so, Logan mused. She had already pressed herself hard and flat up against it, holding herself completely rigid. He didn't have to ask anything else—he knew.

Bo didn't handle deep emotions well. They scared the hell out of her. She had closed herself off when she'd lost her mother and even though she might let people matter to her, she still kept them at a careful distance. *That* was why she was marrying David. She wouldn't have to worry about completely falling in love with him.

That was why she'd run from him—she didn't want to let Logan in. She loved him just as much as he loved her. Knowing how badly she handled any kind of serious commitment, he knew love terrified her. "You want to know why I think you ran?" he murmured against her ear. "I'll tell you."

Bo simply closed her eyes and dropped her head. Logan laughed and slid his arms around her waist. He nuzzled her neck and said, "I'm starting to figure it out but why don't you tell me?"

She muttered softly, "This whole mess is insane, Logan, you know that?"

"Answer me, Bo. Tell me why you ran."

Bo lifted her head a little and glared at him from under her lashes. He kissed her nose and continued trying to cajole it out of her.

Logan didn't do playful much and it was a good thing. That charming smile, his whispered demands were just a little too endearing. She was trying to remember what he'd done—kidnapped her, hauled her off to some cabin by a lake—and she still wasn't sure she completely understood the reasons.

Liar. She remembered the look in his eyes when she had put her ring on. Fury. Possession. Jealousy. Yeah, possessiveness was definitely one of the reasons he'd done this but not because of some weird competition thing. He really did love her. Suddenly, her throat went tight and she had to struggle to get air in.

Love. The real thing. It was something Bo had avoided most of her life, even if she didn't like to admit it. His hand pressed against her cheek and he eased her face back up to his. "Look at me, Bo. Don't be afraid."

Afraid? She wheezed out a harsh breath of air and blinked, trying to focus on his face. *Afraid* didn't really cover it. Terrified did. Yeah, terrified was good.

"You and me, we can do this. Hell, we've been handling it most of our lives. Doing it together can't be any harder than doing it apart."

His lips touched hers and she mumbled against his mouth, "Wanna bet?"

Logan laughed. His other arm wrapped around her waist and he pulled her tight against him. He'd managed to slip his hand inside her shirt so his arm was pressed against her naked back and her breasts were crushed against his chest. "Yeah, why not? I've been going without you for years, Bo, and it's hell. I don't want to do it anymore." He bit her earlobe gently and then muttered, "Come on, Bo. Tell me."

She turned her head and murmured into his ear, so softly, so quietly, she wasn't sure he could even hear her. But by the look on his face when he looked down at her, he'd heard her.

He bent his head and whispered against her lips, "That will work for now. But sooner or later, I'm going to make you scream it."

Epilogue

O uch."

David looked up from the ring in his hand to find Dusty staring at him from the doorway. Outside, he could hear a car door slam. From the window, he could see the drive and he couldn't resist moving to watch as Logan held the door open for Bo.

His right hand was throbbing and his knuckles looked a little swollen. That pain was nothing to what he felt inside though, as he watched Logan drive away with Bo at his side. As much as it hurt, David couldn't say he was too surprised.

"You eavesdrop too much," he said tiredly to his cousin as Dusty walked into the room and joined David at the window.

Dusty just shrugged. "Bad habit." They watched until neither of them could see the car anymore. Dusty was the first to move. He turned and braced his back against the wall next to the window, staring at David with sympathetic eyes.

"Neither of them wanted to hurt you," Dusty said softly. "Logan's always loved her, though."

David cocked a brow. "So have I."

"But she doesn't love you. Not like she loves him." He glanced back out the window and sighed, a deep, hard sigh that made his shoulders rise and fall. "Got to admit, though, you're handling it better than I would have. I would have done more than punch him."

Flexing his fingers, David said, "He's still got a jaw like a rock."

"Goes well with his head." Dusty pushed off the wall and shifted back and forth on his feet. "You okay with this?"

Now David laughed. "Okay?" he repeated. He smiled bitterly and shook his head. "No. I'm not okay with it. But what can I do?" Now his smile turned sad. He went back to contemplating the ring in his hand. "Like you said, she doesn't love me. And I guess I always knew that. Doesn't mean I'm okay with it. Or that I have to like it."

"This love crap totally bites, if you ask me," Dusty said.

David just smiled. "I'll drink to that."

Suddenly Dusty grinned. "Hey, why don't we do just that? Logan's got a bottle of scotch stashed away that he's been saving. Why don't we drink to the happy couple?"

David started to say no. Then he stopped and thought about what he'd just lost to Logan. The least Logan owed him was a good stiff drink. He tucked the ring away in his pocket and said, "Yeah, let's do that."

Miss October

MADISON HAYES

For Tina and Jaid.

One

Y eah, tell me about it," Tavia muttered. She made a face at the small video screen on the Hummer's center console. Shifting the vehicle into overdrive, she continued down the long, straight stretch of highway.

The talk show's opening topic was *The Dilemma of Being Beautiful* and Tavia was having a hard time scraping up much sympathy. A former beauty queen took the microphone to complain about the pitfalls of being gorgeous. "How's a girl like me supposed to find true love?" she lilted. "In the last three years, ten different guys have proposed to me. But when a man asks me to marry him, I don't know if he cares about me—about who I am—or if it's just the face and the figure that has him coming on."

"You're breakin' my heart," Tavia grumbled as she frowned at her reflection in the rearview mirror. Brown eyes glowered back at her as she dragged a hand impatiently through her long mass of curly chestnut hair. "You think you got problems? Look at me. In my case, the face and figure ain't exactly the issue." She snorted as she glared again at her reflection. "In my case, it's the

face value and *figures* that have me questioning a man's intentions. Five million can really tip the scales in your favor when
you're dating a guy."

The truth of the matter was that Tavia was too heavy to win
any beauty contest. Despite this fact, she didn't think of herself
as unattractive and had never lacked for male companionship—
even before she had money. Although she was a big woman, she
couldn't remember a single man who'd complained about her
large breasts. Her bottom was large too. But then, so was her
bottom line.

She was Octavia Smith, better known as Octavia October in
the publishing industry. She authored three or four books a year
with print runs of 500,000. Simply put, Tavia was worth five million dollars. And every single man she'd dated in the last three
years knew it.

Scowling at the small screen, Tavia swerved suddenly when
she realized her SUV was drifting to the side. She tugged on the
steering wheel just in time to avoid hitting a car lodged on the
side of the road. The old junker was pale blue, bleached dull and
lifeless by at least forty years of arid, sunny, high altitude weather.
Tilted off the shoulder of the road, the car sat with its hood
raised—a brief explanation for its presence on the highway's sloping shoulder.

I'm dead. Sorry.

How the decrepit old piece of junk had survived all those
years to expire on the side of the road between Fort Garland and
Taos was beyond her. It looked as though it should have died
years ago. Tavia shook her head in disgust. Highway 159 was a
notoriously long, hot, deserted stretch of blacktop. What kind of

lug nut would be stupid enough to try to run the gantlet between Fort Garland and Taos in an old wreck like that?

A mile beyond the abandoned car, Tavia got her answer when she caught up with the lug nut stupid enough.

His back was turned as he scuffed down the long, dry road, his thumb out at his side. It was a broad back—with the sort of sloping shoulders that spoke of massive strength while the narrow hips and long legs hinted at agility and speed. From the back, the guy was an animal. Pure testosterone with a dash of Wrestlemania. Without even thinking, Tavia took her foot off the gas pedal, slowing the car as she approached the hitchhiker.

She felt sorry for the guy even if he *was* stupid enough. The sun was out and baking the highway. Transparent lines wiggled up off the tarry surface of the asphalt, making it look as though the world was melting. Out in the high desert midafternoon sun, it was hot enough to steam lizards. There wasn't much traffic on the empty road. The hitchhiker would be lucky if another car passed him in the next half hour. And Tavia had driven this stretch of road often enough to know that his cell phone wasn't going to work out here any better than hers did—if he even had a cell phone. Absently, she flipped her phone open and glanced at the "no service" message.

As Tavia pulled to within a hundred feet of the hitchhiker, he turned to face her, walking backward with his thumb extended.

She hesitated.

From the front, the big man with the huge shoulders looked no less like an animal. His features were rough and masculine. Not pretty. Not handsome. Just incredibly male with a brutally hard edge. The guy was all male. All Commando. No suggestion of sensitivity whatsoever. His hair was a brush cut gone wild, if you could imagine a brush cut about three inches too long. Lots of thick, stiff hair—mostly brown but bleached gold here and there. The cold surface of his slick, blue-mirrored sunglasses made him a blank, unreadable entity.

Reluctantly, Tavia depressed the gas pedal as she sped past him.

Watching her rearview mirror, she saw him turn and toss up his hands as he threw back his head. She was close enough to see the ugly word on his mouth. She didn't need sound to read those rugged lips. That particular word was a pretty easy one to decipher when blasted out with vehemence.

Watching him grow small in her rearview mirror, Tavia swiftly forgot about him when she felt a tug on her steering wheel. The road surface suddenly got very bumpy and the car swerved on the blacktop to a steady pace.

She had a flat.

Well, shit. That was typical.

Slowing down, Tavia pulled off onto the side of the highway. Scowling at the driver's-side rear flat, she opened the rear gate of her vehicle and retrieved the tire iron as well as the hydraulic jack. Her father had shown her how to fix a flat when she was sixteen. Loosen the nuts first then raise the car.

Jeez, it was hot out. Dragging a wrist over her upper lip, she fitted the tire iron onto one of the wheel's lug nuts then went to work. She was still trying to budge the first stubborn nut when a shadow fell across her shoulder.

Crouched against the hot, black asphalt, Tavia froze as a pair of heavy black boots scuffed into view. Reflexively, her fingers tightened on the heavy tire iron. Slowly, she lifted her eyes up a long pair of legs clad in faded blue jeans.

The jeans were incredibly worn and threadbare, pale, pale blue—almost white in places—torn across one knee, stained across the other. Other than that, they fit really well. Really well. They weren't tight across the hips. Just nice and snug. There was a hefty bulge beneath the worn, button-down fly—not like the man was hard, just like there was a lot of male equipment on call inside his jeans. And those thighs were really packed into that thin denim with *nothing* to spare.

The hitchhiker slouched with his shoulder against the rear panel of her vehicle. "Hot day," he drawled.

Squinting up at him, Tavia watched him drag the ragged hem of his white T-shirt over his damp upper lip. He had deliciously mean lips. The meanest lips she'd ever seen on a man. Set in a permanent scowl. Sweat gleamed on the flat, brown surface of his stomach where bronze hair swirled down into his jeans.

"Yeah," Octavia clipped out, dragging her eyes from his pan-flat stomach. "I noticed. I'm quick that way."

He nodded slowly as he angled those expressionless sunglasses down at her. "Yeah? Well, you didn't seem to notice when you passed me ten minutes ago."

"I don't pick up hitchhikers," Tavia grunted as she strained against the tire iron.

"There's a difference between a hitchhiker and a stranded motorist," he growled down on her.

"That your piece of junk back there on the road?"

The corner of his mouth pulled back—tight. "That's my Charger, yeah."

"I don't pick up hitchhikers," she repeated.

He hooked a thumb into the top of his jeans. "That's your bad luck. If you'd picked me up, I might have changed that flat for you."

"I can change a flat."

He snorted. "I can see that."

"I can *change* a flat."

"Maybe you could, if you could get the lug nuts off."

"I can change a flat!"

His muscles rippled across his chest and his shoulders rolled as he shrugged. "Hey," he said, "I'm convinced. But *I* can get the lug nuts off."

"Listen, Sir Galahad. If you're not going to offer to help, why don't you just head on up the road?"

He shifted his hip on the car and the next time she looked up at him, she saw her own cleavage reflected in his shining blue sunglasses. "I like the view right here," he murmured in a low, husky drawl. One bronze eyebrow arched over the edge of his glasses as he smiled down into her gaping blouse. At the periphery of her vision, Tavia saw the mound in his groin stir like a huge, uncoiling monster.

Dropping onto her knees, Tavia glared up at him as she very pointedly fastened the top button of her yellow cotton blouse. As she secured the button, a gruff sound of male amusement rumbled up from his chest.

"You got a cell phone that works out here?"

Tavia grimaced. "No."

"You drive a rig like this but you don't have satellite service for your phone?"

He was right. She should have invested in a better phone. But she'd been busy and just hadn't gotten around to it.

"Tell you what, lady. I'll change that flat for you if you'll give me a ride to Albuquerque in return."

"I'm not going to Albuquerque," she answered. "I live in Santa Fe. I have an appointment there at six o'clock."

The hitchhiker slouched against the Hummer's rear panel, all muscle and damp, sweaty male. "I'm in no rush."

"What does that mean?"

He shrugged again. "You can take me to Albuquerque after your appointment."

"It's not that kind of appointment," she told him acidly. "It's the kind of appointment that lasts all night."

She watched his eyebrows lift. His gaze slid down the length of the Hummer as he tilted his head thoughtfully. She knew what he was thinking. He was wondering what an ordinary-looking girl like her was doing, driving a Hummer and hurrying home for an all-night appointment.

Arrogant son of a bitch. She wished he could see her with Alex. It wasn't every woman who dated a male cover model.

"This is a nice piece of equipment," he finally said. "I'd like to own a Hummer."

"Yes, well, we can't all have everything, can we?"

"Nope," he answered. "What else do you have at home?"

"What, other vehicles?"

"Yeah, okay." He grinned. "You can tell me about your other vehicles, if you like."

"You going to change this tire while I'm telling you?"

"You going to drive me to Albuquerque?"

Tavia thought about this as she gazed down the long empty highway. Without cell phone service, she was now as stranded as he was. And those lug nuts weren't coming off for *her*. It was going to take a whole lot more muscle than *she* had to get those nuts loosened and get that wheel off. Tavia had no choice but to enlist the guy's help and give him his ride in payment.

But she was damned if she was going to cancel her date with Alex. For that matter, she wouldn't mind showing this guy what kind of men she went out with before she was shut of him. "It will have to be in the morning."

"You got a place I can stay until then?"

Tavia hesitated. Did she dare do this? It wasn't like she'd be alone in her house with the guy. Alex would be there.

Tavia nodded.

"Thought so." The large man didn't quite smile, but a hard little curl of arrogance appeared at the corner of his masculine mouth. "Give me that tire iron."

She cut a glance up at him. The heavy cross of metal was her last line of defense and she was loath to give it up to a man she didn't know. She slid her gaze down over his body. His jeans hung low on his hips. He didn't seem to have anything concealed in his pockets or his jeans—at least, nothing that could be considered a weapon. Of course, with hands like that, he probably didn't need a frickin' weapon. Jeez, the guy was a mauler.

His mouth kicked up into a sly smile as he tracked her gaze. "What are you looking at?"

"Just making sure you don't have a gun," she muttered.

He nodded, pulling his hands away from his sides and turning slowly so she could check out the pockets hanging off his backside. "Of course," he pointed out, "if I had a weapon, I'd probably have gotten it out by now. But I'll be glad to strip if it makes you feel better."

A hot bead of sweat leaked down into the crease between her breasts. It tickled and she resisted the urge to swipe it away with her fingers. Jesus. Could it get any hotter? "That won't be necessary," she told him.

That won't be necessary, she told herself firmly, *regardless of the fact that it would probably make me feel a whole lot better.*

"You're about to lose your cell phone," she advised him, jerking her chin to indicate his back pocket.

Reaching behind him, the hitchhiker eased his thin, silver phone from the wide hole at the bottom of his jeans' pocket. With a flick of his thick wrist, he redeposited the folding telephone into one of his front pockets. She watched his big fingers as he patted his hand over the rectangular bulge.

When he reached down for the tire iron, Tavia hesitated again. Of course, if the guy wanted to hurt her, he could probably rip the tool from her fingers and get on with it with nothing more than his bare hands. The road was deserted. It wasn't like there'd be anyone to stop him. She considered his large hand, outstretched and turned palm up. It hovered patiently between them as he waited for her to surrender the tool. She checked his face. When he smiled encouragingly, she handed him the tire iron.

She'd never seen a tire changed so quickly and neatly before in her life. While she fumbled to free the spare, he got the lug nuts loosened, the car raised and the wheel off.

"I'll get that," he told her as he joined her behind the car then brushed her aside to pull the spare tire free of its mounting. She glowered at him, feeling uselessly female. How did men do those things so fast? She slid a glance toward his large hands and his thick, strong fingers. Those hands would be a definite advantage when it came to working on a car—or a woman for that matter. Those strength-hardened arms wouldn't hurt either. Wide shoulders. Muscle-ripped chest. The whole package was just made for getting the job done.

As Tavia watched, he shouldered the spare onto the axle and hand-tightened the nuts. Releasing the hydraulic jack, he let the wheel settle back onto the ground then used the tire iron to tighten the nuts a final time.

As he stood, he dusted off his jeans. "Want me to drive?"

Her face twisted with incredulity. How chauvinistic could you get? "No!"

He shrugged his huge shoulders as he opened the driver's door for her. "Just thought it would be polite to offer." He smiled as he closed her inside the Hummer then made his way to the back of the car where he stowed the tire iron and jack.

When he was settled in the seat beside her, he slipped off his sunglasses. Although the Hummer was the biggest car Tavia had ever been in, her passenger made it feel packed, somehow.

"I'm Bolt," he announced, turning his head to smile at her. "Bolt Hardin."

"Bolt," she blurted before she could stop herself. "Your name is Bolt?"

"Short for Bolton," he explained. "My grandmother's maiden name."

Were . . . those eyes gold? Truly gold. Oh my God. Not

brown, not yellowish brown, not brown with gold flecks. Gold. Realizing that she'd be staring if she gave those eyes one more second of her goggle-eyed attention, Tavia jerked her head in a nod.

"Do *you* have a name?" he prompted her. "Or should I just continue calling you lady?"

"Yes." She turned the key in the ignition. "I have two names, actually. My real name and the name I write under." She eased the car out onto the road.

"You're a writer?" Reaching backward, he pulled the seat belt over his shoulder and stretched it across his hips.

She tried not to stare into his lap as she rubbed her lips together. "Mm-hmm. My real name's Octavia Smith—"

"Octavia! Who saddled you with a name like that?"

"—and I write under the name of Octavia October."

"October," he murmured. "Never heard of you. So, Miss October, what do you write?"

"Romance."

He yawned as he stretched in the soft, calfskin seat. "That explains why I've never heard of you. So, are you going to make me call you Miss October or do you have something else I can use besides Octavia?"

"You could call me Tavia if you want to."

"Sounds good," he said with a nod. "What does your husband do for a living, Tavia?"

"Why would you assume I have a husband?"

"Why would you assume I was assuming anything? Maybe I'm just fishing to find out if you're married."

She scowled through the windshield at the road ahead.

"So I take it you're not married," he said into the silence. "Divorced?"

"Why do you insist on assuming this *must be* or *must have been* my husband's car?"

"This is a man's car," he stated, rolling his shoulders. "So I'm a male chauvinist pig. So shoot me."

"If I had a gun, I would," she growled back at him. "This is *my* car," she informed him. "I'm not married and I never have been."

He shifted in his seat as he rumbled out a deep murmuring laugh. "So you do pretty well, then—writing?" He glanced around the Hummer's interior.

She gave him a curt nod. "I do okay. And what do you do for a living, Mr. Male Chauvinist Pig?"

He chuckled—a deep, rich sound of pleasure. "I work on cars."

"You work on cars?"

"Why do you sound so surprised?"

She flicked her gaze at him. *"Maybe* because your own car is presently broken down on the side of the road?"

"Oh that?" He shrugged the wide, sloping line of his shoulders. "I just bought the Charger. It needs some work. I have to order some parts before I can fix it."

Tavia pursed her lips. No car. No money for parts. The guy had no potential whatsoever. But, oh my God, was he hot! The air conditioner was on, circulating the air inside the car, filling her nose with the intoxicating scent of hot, golden-eyed male. She resisted the urge to take a deep breath and fill her lungs with the warm, sun-bronzed aroma of the man sitting beside her.

Tavia broke the silence several miles later. "Are you a marine or something?"

"Me? No. Why do you ask?"

"Just wondering where you got that scar."

With the tip of one rough, calloused finger, he stroked the corner of his mouth. "This one?"

"Yeah."

"Car accident."

Right. "What about the one on your arm? Was that an accident too?" she put to him snidely.

"Nope. That one I got in a fight."

She shot a mean grin at him. "Looks like you lost."

He shook his head. "I won." The grin he returned was positively evil. "If you think this is bad, you should have seen the other guy."

"What did he do?"

"He lived."

Despite herself, a snort of laughter escaped Tavia's lips. "No, I mean what did he do to make you so mad?"

Bolt shrugged. "I wasn't mad. *He* threw the first punch."

"Oh. Then what did *you* do to make *him* mad?"

His mouth settled into a wicked smile. "Stole his date."

Tavia flicked her gaze to the right. "You stole the man's date?"

"I can be a bit of an asshole when it comes to something I want. I fight dirty," he translated. His eyes crinkled at the corners as an expression of pleased reminiscence fell over his face. "She was hot. She was wearing these spiked heels with . . . ankle straps. You know the kind I mean? I've always had a thing for those shoes with ankle straps."

Tavia's eyes widened as she realized his gaze had drifted over her black capris, down her calves, to her plain brown loafers. She jerked her chin. "Yeah, I know the kind you mean," she answered.

Jeez. The guy was checking out her feet. Tavia shook her head. But she couldn't help the smile that crept into the corners of her mouth.

Two

The sun was low on the horizon when Tavia pulled up the long, winding driveway that led to her mountain home. The large, flat space in front of her house was packed with an army of cars and trucks that had been blocking her garage doors for the past week. She was surprised when her passenger had the car door open before she'd pulled the key out of the ignition. Tavia watched as his long legs took him quickly across the concrete in front of her home.

Four men were struggling to raise a long wall on the new addition to her house. Bolt strode toward them. Joining a thick, burly man at the corner, Bolt stooped, caught the top of the wall with one large hand then heaved upward. With Bolt's help, the wooden framework of two-by-fours angled upward then settled onto the bolts spearing up through the sill plate. Someone shouted and he reached for a hammer lying on the plywood floor in front of him. The worker next to Bolt offered him a handful of nails. Shoving three of them into his mouth, he tacked the walls together at the corner.

When Tavia realized her mouth was hanging open, she pressed

her lips together. For a complete loser with no potential, the man seemed incredibly . . . capable.

He turned and smiled at her as she joined him at the corner of the new construction.

Tavia gave him a grudging smile. "Don't you dare chew on those," she growled. "I don't want my new addition put together with bent nails."

He lifted his chin in answer then spat the remaining nails onto his palm and shoved them into his back pocket—the one that was still intact. His eyes focused behind her as he let out a long wolf whistle. "Is that your appointment?" he murmured with a supercilious grin. "Your *all-night* appointment?"

Tavia scowled at him then turned to watch Alex step out of his yellow convertible. The tall, lanky blond wore a dark blazer and gray slacks. His long froth of yellow hair was loose and hung all the way down to the middle of his back. Turning a cold shoulder on Bolt, Tavia left the cocky bastard behind her as she hurried across the concrete drive to greet Alex.

"Tavia!" Alex started a smile that faltered a bit as he stared over her left shoulder.

"I'm Bolt," she heard a deep voice announce from behind her. Then Bolt's long, tanned arm was between her and Alex as he gripped the smaller man's hand. Alex winced and Tavia actually heard the bones in his hand crunching inside the mallet of Bolt's fist. "Bolt Hardin," he introduced himself. In his free hand, Bolt hefted the heavy, claw-head hammer he'd picked up moments earlier.

Alex grimaced a smile up at him. "I'm Alex," he offered when a stunned Tavia failed to introduce him. "Bolt," Alex repeated vaguely, his eyes switching from Tavia to the hunk of sculpted steel standing at her side.

Tavia gritted her teeth. "He's just a hitchhiker I picked up this afternoon." When she threw her elbow into Bolt's ironclad side, she almost chipped a piece of bone off her joint.

"A hitchhiker?" Alex frowned up at the man beside her.

"I helped Tavia change a flat," Bolt said easily, all smooth, unruffled confidence. He reached back and shoved the hammer's wooden grip to hook through the ragged hole in his back pocket. "She offered me a ride to Albuquerque in return," he reminded her in a cutting voice.

"Which I'll be doing at the very *earliest* possible opportunity," Tavia countered through clenched teeth.

"I'll be spending the night," Bolt translated with a lazy smile.

Alex's eyes widened as Bolt nodded down at him.

"So, what's for dinner?" Bolt asked as he locked his hands behind his head and stretched. His rugged mouth curved into a hard grin and his eyes glinted with a predatory gleam as he regarded Alex like some huge tawny mountain lion eyeing a fluffy yellow house cat.

Tavia just stared at Bolt. God he was magnificent. In a horrible way, of course. Magnificently awful. Mouthwateringly, magnificently awful. "I think Maria's planning on steaks," she answered through flattened lips as she stepped away from the men and led the way to the front door.

Leaving Alex standing in her living room, Tavia hurried Bolt down the hall, glancing at the watch on her wrist. "I'll ask Maria to put on an extra steak. Dinner will be ready in twenty minutes. This is my room," she told him as she breezed through a set of double doors that opened out into the wide hall. "You can take

one of the rooms at the end of the hall. Help yourself," she threw
over her shoulder as she kicked off her loafers and hurried across
the thick, cream-colored carpet into the tiled bathroom.

She almost screamed when he appeared in the mirror beside
her. "Jesus, Bolt!"

"I need a shower," he told her.

"There's a bathroom in every bedroom," she told him with exasperation. "Take your pick."

He propped his shoulder against the bathroom doorjamb. "You
got anything I can put on afterward? These jeans are a bit . . ."

"Not unless you're willing to wear pink sweatpants."

"Hey," he drawled. "I look good in pink."

Pushing past him, Tavia yanked open a drawer and dragged
out the first pair of sweats she found. They were gray.

He shook the sweatpants out and held them up against his
legs then adjusted them lower. "Hmm," he murmured. His deep-
toned drawl sounded outrageously seductive within the walls of
her bedroom. "They're either going to be low on the hips or short
in the ankles. Do you have a preference?"

Despite her annoyance, Tavia snorted back a sharp bark of
laughter.

He grinned back at her, his golden gaze full of mischief. "So
what is it? Hips or ankles?"

"I'll leave that for *you* to decide," she told him. "Now get out
of here, will you?"

But her guest was staring into the long expanse of her walk-in
closet. "Jesus! How many pairs of shoes do you *have*?"

She shook her head. "I don't know. Fifty. Eighty, maybe. Would
you get out of here so I can have a shower?"

"Yeah?" he said, as though he hadn't heard her. "Do you happen to have a pair with those . . . straps around the ankles?"

"I don't know. Maybe. Probably. Why?"

"I just like them. They're sexy."

"Okay. If I can find a black pair, I'll wear them. *Okay?*"

He stood solidly in the middle of the room. "They don't have to be black."

"If I can find a pair, I'll wear them," she almost shouted. "Now would you please get out of here?"

"Promise?"

"I promise!" Flattening her hands on his chest, Tavia gave him a shove.

The big man didn't budge. Instead his arms moved quickly to cage her there against his damp, male-scented T-shirt. *"Don't,"* he said in a sharp, quiet voice. "Don't touch. Unless you mean business."

With a rough jerk, he had her tight against his hard frame. The man might have been made of iron for all the give there was to him. She could feel every bulging plane of his muscle-stacked chest as it pressed against hers. His large, flat palms slid down her back, molding her body against his, slipping over her backside where his hands clamped around the full, round globes of her bottom. "Do you know what I mean by business?" he rasped out in a growl. Although his voice was deep, the words were cut with an unexpected edge of urgency that took Tavia by surprise.

His hips moved and she felt the long, angled ridge of his erection scrape across the soft fullness of her belly. Staring up into the molten, gold heat of his eyes, Tavia swallowed hard. "I know what you mean," she forced out on a stutter. "But you and I *have* no business, Bolton. Your room is down the hall," she reminded him.

❦

"Cabernet or Merlot?" Alex offered a little later as Tavia joined the two men in the dining room. She'd taken a shower and had slipped into a long, swishy blue dress that buttoned down the front. Her hair was still wet but it looked good that way—a tangled mass of wet curls.

Her emotions were in a bit of a tangle as well. She had a date with Alex. She'd been looking forward to this date for several days. And now that she had him there in her dining room, all she could think about was the man she'd picked up on the side of the road a few hours earlier. What was up with that? She should have been repulsed by a guy who grabbed her ass and ground his hard-on into her belly.

She *should* have been.

She wasn't.

There was something so . . . primitive and male about the way he'd staked his claim on her, following her into her bedroom and snaring her in his arms while her date dallied in the living room, his hands in his pockets. The guy was all male with a keen predatory streak that set him apart from the more civilized breeds she was used to.

She tried not to stare at Bolt. He looked good wet too. His gold-brown hair was clumped together in thick spikes, adding a splash of wild animal to an already outrageously masculine appearance. He'd opted for low on the hips. The sweatpants. And those sweatpants were slung so far south she could see where his pubic hair climbed out of his groin to join the hair that swirled beneath the dent of his belly button.

"Merlot," Tavia answered.

"Bolt?"

"I'll have a beer if there's one to be had."

"There's a case of Miller in the fridge," Tavia told him. "Ask Maria in the kitchen." With a small wave of her hand, she indicated a swinging door leading out of the dining room.

As Alex poured the red wine into the crystal glasses set out on the table, Bolt disappeared through the door to the kitchen. Tavia smiled tensely at Alex while Bolt's deep murmuring bass rumbled from the kitchen. Her cook responded in her Spanish accent. Picking up a wineglass, Tavia emptied it in a few swallows then reached for the dark bottle and refilled the glass.

When Bolt sauntered back into the dining room, brown bottle in hand, Tavia took her seat at the rectangular table. She sat where she always sat, facing the windows, plunk in the middle of the table's long side. Normally this assured her lots of light as well as room to spread out with whatever she was reading—or writing—at the time.

After a brief instant of hesitation, Alex took the seat on her right, placing himself at the head of the table. She assumed Bolt would then take the seat on her left, at the other end of the table. She was surprised when he took the seat opposite her. Briefly. Then she realized that he'd be incredibly hard for her to ignore, seated directly in front of her. If he'd sat on her left, her attention would have been divided between the two men.

The evening was shaping up like a game of X's and O's. Appropriately, the Irish linen tablecloth was divided into a square pattern of white openwork. Tavia considered the men who shared her table.

The two men were certainly a contrast. Alex in his pricey

Italian blazer and crisp pressed slacks. Bolt in nothing but a pair of low-slung sweatpants, his bare chest glowing with a splash of sun-bronzed hair, his bulging arms wrapped in a wiry network of veins. When it came to sex appeal, it was no contest. Before today, she'd thought Alex was one of the sexiest men alive. Bolt put him in his place. And that place was somewhere far, far below the predatory breed that sat across from her.

He was talking to her, she realized. "I found your laundry room in the hall," he was saying. "Threw my clothes in. Hope you don't mind."

"Of course not," she murmured.

When Maria put a salad in front of her broad-shouldered guest, Bolt looked up to thank her. Oh man. That smile of his really melted a lot of the hard edges on his exterior. Tavia had to tear her eyes from the gleaming white that parted his sexy lips. With her fingers wrapped tightly around the stem of her wine-glass, she swigged down several more gulps of wine. The Merlot was smooth. It went down easy.

Tavia had a feeling that the wine was the *only* thing that would go down easy tonight. Without having said anything, the two men were emitting so much static toward each other, you could almost see the tension crackling in the air.

Not surprisingly, the first volley came from Alex. No doubt the attractive blond felt a mite threatened.

When Bolt asked Alex whom he favored in Sunday's game, Alex smiled. It wasn't a very nice smile either. "England," he answered. When Bolt hesitated, Alex followed those words with a very patronizing, "I'm sorry. You were probably talking about American football, weren't you?"

Bolt shrugged. "Yeah," he shot back in an easy drawl. "I'd forgotten about the rugby game this weekend. But I think the All Blacks look good this year."

Touché. The guy followed international sports.

After that, the men settled down and behaved themselves for a while as they compared the Colts and the Patriots—American football. Both men wanted to see the Colts in the Super Bowl so the conversation was amicable and proceeded in an orderly manner. Which meant Tavia didn't have to referee.

Alex's next question was a loaded one, fired point blank just after Maria set the steaks out. "So, Bolt," he asked, slipping a glance in Tavia's direction, "where do you think the market is headed next?"

Tavia almost choked on her Merlot. What the hell would a guy like Bolt know about—

As Tavia forced the gulp of wine down her throat, Bolt's gaze narrowed on her date. His nostrils flared and his eyes glinted with a metallic sheen. The big man knew he was being baited. "Right now," Bolt answered slowly, "I think just about everything's headed downhill for a while. At least, that's what my analysis program indicates."

"Analysis program?" Alex lifted his eyebrows. "I was thinking the same thing. Even the technology sector?" he asked sharply.

Bolt inclined his head. "Especially technology."

"What program are you using?" Alex asked with sudden interest.

Bolt shrugged but his eyes smoldered. "It's just something I wrote myself, based on integrals. I'll get a copy to you if you'd like."

"Integrals? Why integrals?"

"To smooth out the market variations so you can pick out the trends more clearly."

Tavia pressed her lips together while Alex looked stunned. The big man had to be faking it—throwing out words and phrases he'd picked up from some financial news television program. Still, she fought the urge to laugh at Alex's expression.

"What . . . what are you investing in then?" Alex finally coughed out.

"Nothing right now," Bolt returned. "I bought a lot of gold three years ago and I'm just holding."

"Gold? The price of gold has tripled over the past two years."

"I didn't buy it because I was smart," Bolt drawled. "Just lucky. My best friend suggested I pick some up. She's a mining engineer."

Tavia rolled her eyes at this false display of humility. If the guy sitting across from her owned any gold, it was all in his teeth! And it would be easy to know that precious metals had skyrocketed during the last few years. So the guy had a smattering of knowledge where investment was concerned—big deal!

Alex's disgruntled expression fixed on the wall behind Bolt where a new piece of artwork hung. The blond's face relaxed as he focused on the canvas. "Is that a Dalton?" he asked Tavia. His golden eyebrow arched upward with more than a hint of superiority.

She smiled as she nodded. "My publisher has contracted him to do my next three covers. He sent that small one as a gift."

"I like his work," Alex told Bolt.

Bolt nodded. Then without even turning to look at the canvas on the wall, he added, "That's not surprising. He draws beautiful women then adds a lot of color. Since most men are a bit color-blind, they find his oil pastels refreshingly bright while women find them stunning and bold."

Okay. Now Tavia was staring. So was Alex.

Again Bolt shrugged in his lazy, self-diminishing way. "At least, that's what Dalton says."

Okay. So he'd read a magazine article about the popular pastel artist while waiting somewhere for a haircut. But. Jeez.

"But enough about art." Bolt fixed his malicious gaze on Tavia's elegantly groomed date as one bronze eyebrow winged upward in challenge. "How much can you bench-press?"

Tavia laughed out loud as Bolt followed this with a cat-like grin in her direction and Alex's mouth flattened into a thin line.

When Alex steered the conversation toward politics, Bolt was carefully quiet as he finished his steak and worked his way through a large serving of apple pie and ice cream. Evidently, Alex had hit on a subject that Bolt couldn't fake—either that or the big man preferred to keep his political opinions to himself. While Bolt demolished dessert, Tavia and Alex discussed America's foreign policy.

She was arguing with Alex when the door to the kitchen cracked open behind him. Bolt's gaze flickered that way as Tavia's Spanish-speaking cook stepped into the dining room. Unaware of Maria's presence, Alex continued, "I'm just saying that the current policy toward immi—"

The next thing Tavia knew, Bolt was nudging his beer bottle up against Alex's full glass of red wine. The glass tipped over with a sharp crack and Alex's chair scraped backward as he jumped to his feet, cursing.

Bolt stood up with him, apologizing all over the place while gracing little Maria with the sweetest smile Tavia had ever seen on such a patently mean mouth.

"I'm sorry," the small woman faltered. "I was getting ready to leave but I couldn't get my car started. Could somebody perchance give me a jump?"

"Let me take a look at that," Bolt offered immediately, striding across the room and holding the kitchen door open for Tavia's cook. From beneath the thick fringe of his eyelashes, he shot a smiling glance back at Tavia.

Tavia stared at the door as it swung closed. *Was that what she thought it was?* In spilling the wine all over Alex, Bolt had stopped her date from making a potentially embarrassing comment in front of her Spanish-speaking cook. Had Bolt been trying to save Alex's ass or had he been acting on behalf of Maria's feelings? It had to be Maria, Tavia thought wryly. Her little cook from south of the border—while perhaps five years older than her dinner guests—was both petite and darkly attractive.

Distracted by those thoughts, Tavia herded Alex into the kitchen. The door leading outside to the driveway was open. She heard the heavy, metal creak of a car hood moving upward. "I'll get some club soda for that stain," she told Alex as she headed for the fridge, passing the large granite-topped island in the center of the kitchen.

When Bolt stepped back into the kitchen a few minutes later, Alex was grumbling about Maria while pouring club soda over the front of the pleated gray slacks he wore. "This isn't the first time she's needed a jump start," Alex complained in a tight voice.

As Bolt made his way to the kitchen sink, he frowned at the

blond. "Maria's Honda should be good from here on out," he growled quietly as he soaped up his hands. "The battery posts were corroded. I cleaned them off."

Alex grunted as he surveyed the damage to his slacks. "I'm going to have to take these off long enough to run them under the tap." He cut a glaring glance in Bolt's direction as he strode from the kitchen, ostensibly making his way to one of the bathrooms down the hall.

Wiping his hands on a dishtowel, Bolt glowered at the swinging door as Tavia watched him. "I take it you don't much care for my boyfriend," she stated carefully.

"Boyfriend?" Bolt snorted as he wadded the towel into a ball and slung it at the counter. "That guy isn't interested in you."

Tavia couldn't have been more surprised if he'd slapped her. She probably couldn't have been more hurt either. It felt like somebody had punched her right in the heart.

Bastard.

"Oh yeah?" she returned icily. "I guess that's why he proposed to me last week then."

Bolt's eyes snapped to lock on hers. "He *what?* What did you tell him?"

"I told him I'd think about it."

Impatiently, Bolt rolled his eyes. "Give me a break, Tavia. That guy's more interested in me than he is in you."

"Then why'd he ask me to marry him?"

"I don't know," he cut at her. "How much are you worth?"

She felt the pain tighten around her heart. Tighten cruelly. *"Fuck you,"* she snapped back at him, fighting an unexpected surge of tears. "So you think Alex is only interested in my money.

Thanks a lot, Bolt. But just because *you* think I have no sex appeal whatsoever—"

"*What?* Don't you go putting words in my mouth, Tavia. There's nothing wrong with your sex appeal—believe me. But that guy wouldn't know sex appeal from apple peel."

"What?"

"And I can prove it," he told her in a rich, deep rumble of sound.

"You can prove it?" she demanded with as much scorn as she could muster while blinking back hot, angry tears. "How?"

For about two seconds he glowered at her. Then he took a step toward her. His thick-lashed gaze fixed on her mouth as he lingered in front of her. Dark heat rolled off his body in waves, wrapping her in his provocative male scent. "Because this is the way a man acts when he's interested in a woman," he growled, pushing her up against the edge of the island anchored in the center of the kitchen. His body was hard and hot as he forced hers to yield beneath his. "This is the way he looks at her," he rasped out. His eyes were half closed as he looked down on her, his keen gaze locked on her lips as he studied her mouth with intense interest. "This is the way he touches her," he murmured as he caught her chin in his palm. "And this is the way he kisses her."

Three

Tavia held her breath as Bolt angled his golden gaze down over her lips. His fingertips trapped her face in an iron cage as his thumbs stroked into the corners of her mouth. Her lips responded to the tender stimulus, swelling with anticipation, parting to give him entrance as a longing wisp of sound escaped her lips.

With her face caught in the uncompromising steel of his calloused hands, Bolt handled her with surprising gentleness. Tavia had never felt so fragile, so treasured, so . . . feminine. She felt his other hand slide around to the back of her neck as he cupped her nape. Slowly, he lowered his mouth across hers.

He rubbed his wet mouth across hers in a slow, teasing pass. She felt his breath against her lips, warm and enticing. For an instant she caught a taste of his rough, masculine flavor. Words couldn't come close to describing what happened next. Bolt's lips crushed down on hers like an avalanche and Tavia just hung on for dear life as his mouth dominated hers with a mixture of soft and wet and overpoweringly insistent male.

His tongue took her mouth immediately, forging between

her teeth and sliding in a hot, sensuous scrape against her own. Stunned beneath the dominance of his kiss, Tavia held her breath for a very long time before she finally heard him gasp and reposition his mouth over hers. She sucked in a breath at the same time. The dark heat of his mouth moved against hers in a slide of wet lips and thrusting tongue as a deep growl of hunger vibrated within his chest. His body moved against hers in a hard surging wave—slow, sensuous, suggestive and very, very demanding. She melted against him, riding a heady wave of arousal, feeling soft and pliable.

Ready.

I-want-a-man-and-I-want-him-now ready.

His open palms brushed down her arms on the way to her waist. With his hands gripping her middle, he hitched her backside up onto the edge of the island, forcing her legs to open for his hips, pressing between her legs—all without breaking the branding kiss that dominated her mouth. His blunt fingers dug into the cushion of her bottom as he held her into his groin and ground the long, thick line of his erection into the fleshy seam between her legs. She could feel his cock stiffen and grow as he shoved his sex against the pout of her parted pussy. Her sex warmed for him—softened and moistened and thrummed with a dark, eager hunger.

He broke from her suddenly, panting roughly. "Shall I go on?" His eyes narrowed on her swollen lips. As if he couldn't resist, he leaned forward again, his lips crowding briefly against hers as he bit at her lower lip. "Shall I?" he demanded.

Dazed, she stared up at him. Without thinking, she nodded.

He growled a rough burst of laughter against her neck. His

hands slid beneath her skirt and up her thighs, working the flimsy fabric up her legs. "You sure? Do you want me to show you how a man fucks a woman when he's interested in her, Tavia? Because that's what comes next, baby doll. Are you ready? Just let me know," he murmured in a wash of damp heat against her ear. "Because I can get my cock out of these sweatpants before you can say 'fuck me now.'"

Tavia heard the kitchen door creak on its hinges then stared, alarmed, into Bolt's eyes. He focused his malicious, golden gaze on the door behind her. Beneath the thin material of her skirt, his hands tightened on her backside—a clear message that he didn't intend to give up a single inch to the man who stood behind her.

Alex.

Bolt cleared his throat. "Sorry about the slacks, Alex. Let me know if you need help getting your car started."

Alex's voice was cold behind her. "Are you trying to tell me something, Hardin?"

"Yeah, I am." Bolt laughed, low and wicked. "I don't know what you had planned for tonight, but you might find it a bit crowded in Tavia's bed."

"*Fuck* you." Sweeping across the stone-tiled floor, Alex jerked the exterior door open. He shot a look of vehemence back at Tavia as he stood with his hand wrapped around the doorknob. "Tavia," he ground out between clenched teeth, "you don't even *know* this guy."

She stared at him blankly.

Alex stalked through the door then slammed it behind him.

As the door banged closed, Bolt's cock pulsed against Tavia's pussy—a virile, male declaration of victory, claiming the right to the space between her legs.

She burrowed her face against his shoulder as she stifled a moan of anguish. Her cheeks were burning up in shame.

Bolt's gaze was slanted toward the exterior door. "Don't go away mad," he muttered in a pleased, dark murmur.

"I can't believe you did that," Tavia moaned. "I've been going out with Alex for months."

"You wasted months on that guy?"

"I've only known *you* . . . Jesus. I can't believe I'm doing this."

He nuzzled his mouth against her neck, initiating a sharp shimmer of desire. The wanton sensation flashed over the surface of her skin, wrapping around her aching nipples and scraping at the nerve endings enclosed within the wet heat of her pussy.

"Come on, Tavia. You knew you were going to do this. You knew it back on the highway when you decided I could spend the night in your home."

"What?" she said slowly as Bolt dragged his teeth around the shell of her ear. "What?" she repeated in a cold, incisive word. She felt him stiffen.

He stopped mouthing her ear as he regarded her warily.

"So you just figured a girl like me would be glad to have sex with a guy like you."

"Most women are," he argued with an arrogant roll of his shoulders.

"But you figured a girl like *me* would *jump* at the chance."

Like a thin beam of molten fire, his eyes narrowed on her. "Exactly what are you getting at, Tavia?"

"You figured that because I'm big, I'd jump at the chance to have sex with you."

For several seconds he regarded her quietly. "Oh hell," he finally drawled, "you're not that big. I've laid bigger women than you."

"You have?" she blurted out.

"Yeah. I like big women. They're great to fuck. The more the cushion, the better the—' "

Her mouth gaped open. "You're such a *pig*."

"No kidding," he murmured against her ear.

She tried to ignore the dazzling warmth of his breath on her skin. "So you don't mind having sex with a woman my size."

His lips nipped at the flesh beneath her ear. "Nope."

"But you'd never consider marrying a woman like that. A woman like me!"

"I've got news for you, baby doll. I wouldn't consider marrying anyone."

"And I've got news for you! Alex would!"

He shoved himself away from her. "Fine!" he shouted. "So marry the guy if you can't do any better. It's no skin off my dick."

"*Can't do any better?* You are *the* most conceited, most *arrogant* man I have ever met in my lifetime."

He settled against the counter opposite her, folding his thick arms over his wide chest as he directed a lazy smile between her legs. "Get used to it."

Tavia snapped her knees together. "You're wrong," she told him point-blank. "I had *no* intention of sleeping with you tonight. I had *planned* on sleeping with *Alex* tonight!"

He lifted one shoulder. "Sorry I ruined your plans," he drawled, sounding not the least bit sorry. His eyes drifted down her legs and fixed on her feet. "You going to wear those shoes for me now?"

"What?"

"You promised you'd wear the ankle-straps for me."

She shook her head in disbelief as she followed his gaze down her legs to the plain navy pumps on her feet.

He lifted his gaze slowly to connect with hers. "Are you the sort of woman who breaks her promises?"

"No, of course not, but—"

Grasping her wrist in his iron fist, he dragged her off the counter, through the kitchen door, across the dining room, living room and down the hall.

"Bolt!" she cried. "You're hurting me!"

He loosed her wrist as though he'd been stung. While he was stunned, Tavia collected the open doors of her bedroom, slipped through the doorway and slammed them shut behind her.

"Tavia! I'm sorry, Tavia. Are you all right?"

On the other side of the doors, Tavia slumped against the red-painted surface that separated her from Bolt. "I'm all right," she sighed, feeling as guilty as Bolt sounded. Although he had held her wrist firmly, he hadn't come close to hurting her. Which meant the big lug nut had probably taken special care *not* to hurt her.

His muffled voice was deep and troubled. "Did I hurt you?"

She shook her head. "No, Bolt. I just. It's just that . . . you're wrong. I didn't bring you home with me so I could sleep with you."

There was a lengthy silence on the other side of the door. "I'm sorry," he repeated in a contrite rumble. The antique glass door-knobs rattled. "I didn't mean to hurt your feelings."

Leaning against the door, Tavia's lips drooped as she watched the beveled glass doorknobs. She felt so damn sad. She *hadn't* brought Bolt home to get him into bed, despite the fact that she wasn't exactly opposed to the idea after that kiss in the kitchen. But the man's arrogant assumption was so damn annoying. What a conceited ass. *Most women are*, she mimicked his response in her mind. *Most women are just crawling all over me begging me to fuck them.* Why did he have to rub her face in it? Why were men such pricks? Why the hell was she stuck on the wrong side of these doors?

A rumble of humor sounded on the other side of the door. "You locked the doors? I can't believe you locked the doors, Tavia. What did you hope to accomplish by that?" He laughed. "Don't you realize that a guy like me could have them down with one kick?"

"You wouldn't dare!" Tavia backed away from the glossy red doors as her eyes narrowed in apprehension.

"Of course I wouldn't," he soothed in a gruff voice. Then it got quiet.

With her head cocked to one side and her ears scanning for any sound, she held her breath as she listened to Bolt's long stride taking him down the hall. Silence followed. Enough silence that she finally decided she was safe. Slowly, she expelled a careful breath as she sank onto the white bedspread quilted with red stitches.

Seconds later, she was holding her breath again as she heard a series of faint tapping sounds. Then a few soft thumping sounds. The next thing she saw was Bolt, standing in the frame of her doorway, lifting the double doors aside. He smiled at her. "The doors open outward," he told her smugly.

He set the wide, double doors against the wall behind him. When he turned, he was swinging a hammer in one hand. He'd used the hammer and a nail to tap out the pins on the doors' brass fittings. Strolling into the room, he slid the tools onto her shabby-chic white-painted dresser that stood against the wall just inside the doorway. Then he folded his arms over his wide chest as he regarded her quietly.

With a curse of exasperation, Tavia made for the bathroom.

"That door opens outward too," he warned her as she slammed the door behind her.

Tavia pressed her shoulder against the bathroom door. "Please, Bolt. Just . . . just leave me alone, okay?"

"Where are the shoes?" he asked from the bedroom.

"*Shoes?*"

"You promised you'd wear them. Aren't you going to keep your promise?"

"Yes," she moaned. "Of course."

"Good," he answered. "Where are they?"

"I'm not sure. In the closet. Try the green and silver box. Listen, Bolt. If I wear the shoes will you let me go?"

As Tavia frowned at her troubled reflection in the bathroom mirror, she heard a single, heavy thunk. She froze, listening. Two seconds later she heard another muffled crash. Grabbing the door open, she rushed out of the bathroom to find Bolt on his knees at the end of the bed.

"Are you all right?" she asked breathlessly, trying to decide if a man falling to his knees would make that much noise. "Did you fall?"

He gave her a slow, sensuous smile. "I found the shoes."

She returned his smile warily.

"Let me help you get them on," he told her. "Come here," he commanded her firmly. "Sit down."

Tavia clenched her teeth. "Bolt," she gritted, "if I wear the shoes—"

"*Come here*," he repeated in iron tones.

Tavia left her navy pumps beside the bathroom door and crept toward him in her bare feet. Squeezing between the kneeling man and the hand-stitched bedspread, she sat down on the end of the bed and slipped her right foot into one of the black, patent leather high heels. As she watched, Bolt pulled the wide strap around her ankle, fumbling to close the buckle with his thick fingers. When Tavia reached out her toe for the other shoe, she felt Bolt's big hand wrap around her ankle as he guided her foot to the pump three feet distant. When he'd finished buckling her left foot into the black ankle-straps, Tavia automatically moved to pull her legs together.

That's when she realized the shoes were nailed to the floor.

Four

Bolt knelt between her spread knees. The smile that curved his rugged mouth was just about as sinfully evil as a smugly horrible man could reasonably pull off.

"Bolt!" she yelled. "What the hell! What do you think you're doing?"

There was a supercilious glint behind the golden fire in his eyes. "I'm just giving you permission, baby doll."

"*Permission?* Permission to *what?*"

"Permission to spread your legs a bit," he told her in a low, intimate murmur. Catching the side of her neck with his big hand, he nudged his lips against her cheek. "Permission to be a bit of a slut. Every woman needs permission," he explained.

"Are you crazy? I don't need your permission to . . ."

His eyebrow arched upward. "To what?"

"I'm not a slut," she told him flat out.

He gave her a warm, sultry smile. "Of course you're not. That's why you're nailed to the floor."

"I'm nailed to the floor," she whispered, as the full extent of his actions finally hit her. "You nailed my shoes to the floor! Bolt! These shoes cost five hundred dollars!"

"Five hundred dollars? Really? Are you impressed?"

"Impressed with what?"

"Impressed by the fact that I have such good taste." The hard, silken texture of his lips glided along her jawline. "If you can reach them, you can take them off. 'Course I have no intention of letting you reach them, baby doll."

Tavia moaned as her back arched and her neck stretched for the touch of his lips. His mouth left a frisson of heated, crackling awareness in its wake. "Why on *earth* do you insist on calling me baby doll?"

"Why not?" he countered. "You're all . . . dimples. And when you're six-six," he went on, "even a tall woman's a baby doll." He put a hand in the middle of her chest. "Now lie down like a good little slut while I check out your pussy." With those words he pushed her onto her back. Immediately, Tavia struggled to sit up again but his large hand pinned her to the bed. "I'll tie you down if I have to," he warned her with a whispering growl.

Tavia was ready to scream with frustration. She'd never come across a more patently aggravating man. He was sneaky, manipulative and as crafty as demon spawn. Using illogical arguments and dirty tricks, he'd managed to get her spread open at the end of her bed with her feet pinned to the floor. She opened her mouth to darken his name with curses—but stilled when his hands curled around her ankles.

She *wanted* it and *he* knew it. She wanted him, even if he *was* the most maddening man on the face of the earth. It sounded cliché, but her chest was heaving—heaving before her eyes, rising and falling in eager waves as she watched Bolt kneeling between her legs.

She felt his hands travel slowly from her ankles to her knees. Felt the cool air on her calves and knew the skirt of her filmy dress was surfing up her legs under the glide of those large, masculine hands. With lowered eyes, she watched the frothing folds of her dress travel slowly up her hips at the same time she felt his hands sweep to the outside of her thighs.

"Tavia!" he murmured. "You're . . . wearing underpants." He began to chuckle. "Oh, you are *so* screwed," he advised her in a deep, provocative growl.

"What do you mean?" she asked him breathlessly.

"I mean—that the next time I ask you to wear these shoes, you'd better get rid of your panties first."

"The *next* time you—*Why?*"

He leaned over and pressed a kiss into the fabric that stretched across her belly. "Because your feet are nailed to the floor, sweetheart. And that means this underwear *isn't* coming off any time soon."

"But couldn't we just—"

"Sorry, Tavia. It's too late now. We're just going to have to work around the situation."

Still kneeling between her legs, Bolt settled his large hands on her inner thighs and urged her legs apart. She held her breath as his palms pressured her already stretched thighs even wider while his rough, calloused fingers moved slowly toward the apex of her legs. Before they reached the warm crease at the top of her thighs, she saw his head dip and felt his breath warming her mound. Her back arched and her eyes rolled back in her head as waves of humid heat washed over her pussy. Anticipation had her riding a razor-edge of passionate need as every muscle in her body tightened. When he finally graced her with the smooth touch of his mouth—full, soft and heated against the silk stretched over her pussy—Tavia choked back a tiny, telling, little sob.

Bolt breathed out a low, masculine sound of pleasure. He clucked his tongue and it smacked between her legs gently. "Red," he muttered against the heated silk. "Bright red panties with a blue dress. Who'd you wear the panties for, Tavia?"

The room was silent except for Tavia's soughing breath.

Bolt nudged his hot mouth against her pouting labia, bathing her silk-clad pussy with his warm breath. "Who'd you wear the panties for, Tavia? And you'd better not tell me Alex."

Tavia swallowed hard. "I didn't . . . wear them for anybody."

"Aw, now you're just hurting my feelings." His mouth opened along her slot and when he closed it, he nipped at her plump labia. He pressed the flesh firmly between his blunt teeth then opened his mouth and stroked his lips across the damp silk of her panties. The tip of his tongue crept through the seam of her sex, intruding between her hungry lips as far as her filmy underwear would allow. "Tell me who you wore the panties for, Tavia."

When she didn't answer again, she saw his head tilt between her legs. She almost jumped when his tongue slid inside the elastic leg of her panties, lapping gently but insistently at the naked flesh of her outer labia, tugging at her thickened lips, encouraging them to part a breathless half inch. As his tongue slid out of her panties, her flesh closed again over the folds of her sex. Then she felt the firm press of his thumbs in the crease between her legs, stretching her open on either side of her long slit. With both thumbs pulling her sex wide, Bolt drew his flattened tongue up the hot silk stretched over her open pussy.

The fine fabric of her underwear was wet and steamy as he opened his mouth over the red silk and settled his tongue over her clitoris. He gave her hungry clit a long, leisurely lick. "Tell me who you wore the panties for."

She blew out a frustrated breath. "You," she said in a short, quiet word.

"What was that?"

"You," she shouted. "I wore the red panties for you!"

"Thought so," he drawled. "Too bad I don't like underwear on a woman."

She snorted. The sound was a little bit of amusement mixed up with a lot of frustration.

"I'll let it go this time," he advised her. "Just don't let it happen again."

"*Again?*"

Leaning over her, he reached for the buttons of her dress, smiling into her wide-eyed gaze as his long fingers fumbled the buttons open—all the way from the scooping neckline right down to the rumpled hem. Then he spread the dress apart. Like a lick of liquid flame, his gaze traveled down her exposed body then returned to the heaving mounds of her breasts, crammed into the full cups of her red lace bra. His hands smoothed up her midriff until he held the sides of her breasts in the cradle of his large palms. Automatically Tavia arched on the bed, pressing her lips together as Bolt handled her tits with murmuring appreciation. His voice was rough-soft as he expressed his devotion in quiet, rumbling bursts of sound. His thumbs brushed across the cups, the calloused pads catching on the fancy lace of the brassiere. When he leaned forward, his bared abdomen came into warm contact with her open pussy. His skin pressed against the slick silk. "More underwear," he complained in a taunting grumble. "Are the snaps in the back?"

"Bolt?"

"The snaps to your bra. Are they in the back?"

"I think so," she breathed.

"That's inconvenient." Delving with his fingers into the large cups of her bra, he tugged her breasts out of the red lace.

From beneath her half-closed eyelids, Tavia watched him expose her nipples as he shoved the frilly fabric under the heavy mounds of her breasts. Her bra was still fastened in the back and the wadded material was tight beneath her chest, lifting her breasts while squeezing them together.

With his thumbs riding over her nipples, his hands collected the heavy sides of her breasts into his palms. "Fuck," Bolt whispered. "These are perfect. I'd like to get my dick between these beauties on a hot day."

"On a hot day?"

"On a hot day." His voice was gravelly with lust. "When it's all damp and sweaty between your breasts. I'd like to fuck your tits and watch my cum wash into your cleavage. I'd like to use my dick to spread it over your nipples."

Tavia choked back a moaning expression of need. She ached at the thought of him thrusting between her breasts, his cum spitting from his cock head in hot surges, spattering onto her skin, coating her breasts as he rubbed his heavy, wet shaft over her needy nipples. Jeez, she wanted him. Her pussy was primed, burning with wet heat, aching to have him wrapped up inside her, banging into her and flogging the back of her cervix with the punishing knot of his cock head.

As his thumbs rubbed over the rough, pebbled surface of her nipples, Tavia whimpered out a shivering murmur of arousal. Between her legs, the ridge of his cloth-covered shaft slid against the plump cushion of her labia. As Bolt rocked against her pussy, the thick girth of his erection slowly worked a groove between her soft, slick lips. Tavia twisted on the bed. So close—he was so close, but not goddamn close enough.

Planting his hands on either side of her chest, Bolt levered himself upward, continuing to thrust between her legs while he lowered his mouth to her nipples. His mouth was hot as he drew the hard silk of his lips over the puffy tips of her breasts. Then he turned his face and dragged the stubbled steel of his jaw over the same eager flesh. With a rough, wet tongue, he circled her areola languidly then sucked her in suddenly, drawing the whole of her full, pink areola deeply into his mouth. When the heat and suction finally diminished, her nipple was caught in the firm grip of his teeth. He held the small bud in the blunt clamp of his incisors as he lashed the captured tip with his tongue.

The sensation was utterly, deliciously evocative and a hot line of desire burned from the tips of her breasts to the deepest place in her cunt where she longed for him with a dark, insistent hunger unlike anything she'd ever experienced. She wanted him. She needed his breath, hot between her legs, pelting her wet flesh as he pulled her labia open with his fingers. She wanted him to touch her with rough intimacy. She wanted the abrasive pad of his fingertip brushing across her clit. She wanted him to play with her sex, to tease her and taunt her and take her to the edge of madness. Then she wanted him to fuck her.

She wanted him to rise over her, his weight pinning her to the bed, his skin rubbing in a hot, male slide against hers, the light hair on his chest teasing her nipples into tight knots of anguish. She wanted him to fuck her hard. Break her open with ecstasy as he plowed into her, stretching the delicate pink of her vulva and slamming into the back of her cunt.

But those damn red panties were stretched between her legs, standing in the way of everything she wanted. With another small whimper, Tavia wondered if it was too soon to start pleading. She'd never begged for a man before. She'd never begged a man to fuck her. But then, she'd never felt like this, swamped in an aching need that lashed her body with sexual urgency and urged her to spread her thighs for the man between her legs. Spread her sex and open her pussy for the rapine touch of his fingers and the brutal caress of his cock.

Rising to his feet, Bolt hooked his thumbs in the top of the sweatpants and pushed them down his muscular thighs. His erection swung free like a huge, hungry beast, long and heavy and dark. The wide girth of his shaft was flattened along the top, giving his cock a sinfully serpentine appearance. The thin skin was stretched smooth and tight over dark veins that wrapped his length. The top of his shaft was capped by the heavy slug of his cock head, healthy and fat, engorged with lusty blood. Enthralled, Tavia watched a glimmering pearl of moisture ooze from the small creased opening in his cock head.

She licked her lips as Bolt curled his fingers around the broad root of his shaft, his eyes narrowed on the space between her legs. Falling over her, he rested his weight on his elbows.

She felt the thick, fat width of his cock head pressing against her silk-covered opening. Like a huge, blundering animal, his blunt tip surged against her barred entrance as his hips flexed and he thrust his sex at her again and again.

"Damn panties," he growled between harsh breaths. "They're always getting in the way. I don't know why women wear them."

Tavia moaned as he pounded the rounded head of his cock into the silk of her underpants. Each harsh, feral rip of his hips took him a little deeper into her vagina, but not far enough. Never far enough. It was never going to be far enough. She needed more. More of him. More of that thickly veined cock deep inside her.

"Bolt," she finally wailed. "Don't you think those panties would come off if you gave them a good tug?"

He grunted in response. "I don't want to ruin a perfectly good pair of red panties that you *wore for me*."

She blew out a tight scream of frustration. "The panties cost seventeen-fifty. You didn't mind nailing my five-hundred-dollar shoes to the floor! Do me a favor, Bolt, and rip the damn panties."

The mean, thick head of his cock pounded temptingly at her entrance. "Sorry," he panted with an evil smile. "I don't do underpants. If a woman wants my cock, I reckon the least she can do is bare her pussy for me."

"Bolt," she tried hesitantly, "what if I told you I didn't wear these panties for you?"

He stilled. "You don't want to get me mad, Tavia."

She knew she was whining. "But if you got mad, maybe you'd tear them off."

He shook his head. "You *don't* want to get me mad, Tavia."

"Bolt," she shouted. "This isn't working."

"It's working for me," he told her. "A few more strokes and

I'm going to come all over the front of these underpants you're wearing."

"Well, it isn't going to work for me!"

"You should have thought of that sooner. What are you doing?"

With her thumbs hooked into the tops of her panties, Tavia worked the sweat-dampened silk down her sides as far as she could reach. With a certain amount of desperate wriggling, she managed to get the damn things over her hips and under her bottom. But the panties refused to go farther. The elastic waistband bit into the flesh of her open thighs and would go *no* farther. The scarlet barrier was now a thin, tight, highly annoying roadblock, caught just below her sex, wrenching into the flesh of her thighs.

"Please, Bolt," she begged shamelessly. "Please help me!"

As she watched, Bolt tilted his head and frowned. With his massive shaft straining in his hand, he touched the huge knot of his cock head against her pouting cleft. When he pushed his shaft down against the red barrier, the silk cut more deeply into her thighs.

"I don't think this is going to work," he drawled.

"Bolt!" she screamed.

Laughing darkly, he put a knee on the bed. "I'm sorry, baby doll, but I can't get to you with my cock. You're just going to have to settle for my tongue. Are you ready for some give and take?"

"Give and take?" she whimpered helplessly.

He nodded. "That's where I give it out and you take it. All of it."

"Give it?" She sobbed as her head tossed on the bed. "Give what?"

"Whatever I want to force on you, baby doll. You're the one with her legs spread and her feet nailed to the floor. I'm the one with his face in your pussy," he chuckled.

As Bolt stretched out beside her, his tongue slipped into her cleft and rode down the entire length of her slot in a bold stroke. A hoarse cry escaped her lips at the sheer explosive pleasure of that wet tongue sliding against her hot flesh. Tavia pressed her knees wide as she strained within the restricting bonds of those wicked shoes as well as the panties lashed around her hips.

"Do you like that?" he murmured as she tried to rock her sex into his mouth. "Let's see if I can get these panties out of my way enough to reach your cunt with my tongue."

As he pushed down on the front of her panties, the tautly stretched silk cut a cruel line across the tops of Tavia's thighs. She didn't complain. Instead, she waited with breathless anticipation for the delicious gift of his mouth, low on her sex. She moaned with gratitude as the rough tip of his tongue slid through her folds and played around her entrance before returning to her clit.

"You want to return the favor?" Bolt put a knee over her shoulders and straddled her face. "Wrap your lips around my cock, Tavia."

Tavia swallowed hard. The intimidating length of his cock hung before her eyes, mouthwateringly male, cunt-dampeningly attractive—wide, dark and ridden with heavy veins that pulsed with raging virility. Tavia groaned as she chewed on her bottom lip. While his penis was long, it wasn't the length, per se, that concerned her. It was the massive girth. "Bolt," she started apologetically, "I'm not going to be able to get much of this in my mouth."

"Just take as much as you can, sweetheart. Just lock your lips around my cock head and suck hard. I'll do the rest." His hips undulated slowly as he lowered his groin to drag his shaft over her face. In a silken slide of hot, male flesh it traveled across her cheek. Reaching back with one hand, he levered his shaft downward and nudged the damp, moist head against her lips.

Tavia opened her mouth as he fed the crown into her mouth. A deep rumble of pleasure vibrated down his body as she pulled the plum-shaped head between her lips and hooked her tongue under the rim of its mushrooming hood. He froze. His wet mouth was suddenly still on her pussy as she sharpened her tongue to a point and drove it against the sensitive wrinkle of flesh caught beneath the hood of his cock head. His huge diameter gave a mighty, threatening pulse that stretched her lips wide as he groaned into her pussy flesh. Quickly, he retracted his hips, dragging his cock from her mouth. She watched his shaft stretching heavily before her face. Her saliva glimmered in a shining veil around the top of his cock and a thick drop of pre-cum welled from its tip before it dripped onto her chin. Tavia gasped in a hungry breath, full of the rich, potent scent of aroused male.

"Play fair," he growled.

Feeling more confident, Tavia smiled as she reached for him, hooking her fingers around his shaft and drawing his cock back into her mouth. His hips moved in a rapid, brutal slide as he forced his cock to the back of her throat, embedding his shaft deep in her mouth before she had a chance to work her evil with her tongue. With small nudges, he pressed his tip against the back of her throat. Her mouth was so full of cock that she gagged an instant.

Bolt withdrew a few inches. "Take me, Tavia. Take all of me," he urged as he surged into her mouth again. She tried to shake her head but Bolt wasn't having it. "Open your throat and swallow," he commanded. "Take a breath then swallow me on my next thrust."

Tavia took a breath and swallowed as he shoved into her. Seconds later he pulled back and she drew in a sharp gasp of air then swallowed him again as he rode into her with a series of long thrusts and short retreats.

Between her legs, his wicked tongue was slashing down through her folds again. Viciously, purposefully, pitilessly, he attacked her clitoris with the wet lash of his tongue, pausing only occasionally to push a soft kiss over her tortured clit before he savaged it once more. Her legs relaxed, her knees fell wider and her hips started to jerk as her throat worked to take his cock deeper. The pressure built inside her mouth as his expanding shaft flexed in her throat and his warm, rough testicles brushed against her nose.

His tongue stabbed through her folds again in a long, delicious drive that set every pink pussy nerve ending at the edge of bliss, screaming in the searing, mind-bending pleasure that comes just before climax. Straining her hips upward, Tavia held her breath, waiting on the sharp edge of orgasm. Knowing that the next rough touch of his tongue would be the one to do it.

She was coming. She was coming right into his dark, hot, manipulative mouth.

As though he knew exactly that, Bolt dallied, the tip of his tongue prodding lightly into the nick of her cleft, warm and tempting and unbearably wet, promising everything but halting just short of delivering the satisfaction her body now screamed for. Gently, he lapped at her clitoris while he pulled his hips back an inch, allowing her to grab a quick breath before he forged back in to fill her throat.

With his cock filling her mouth, Tavia growled as she writhed in the tight spread of the shoes fixed to the floor. Deep inside her vagina she ached for the hammer of his cock head pounding against her cervix. She longed for his wide diameter, stretching the rim of her vulva. She didn't want his tongue anymore. She wanted his cock. His huge, powerful, punishing cock seated deep inside her wet sex as he fucked her with an animal intensity that would leave the stamp of his cock head imprinted on her womb forever.

Beneath his damp mouth, she thrashed to escape him and his wicked tongue. She twisted her head, trying to expel his giant length from her mouth, but his hips shifted as he forced her to accept the presence of the shaft stretching her throat.

"Hold still," he commanded, his lips moving against the full softness of her labia. He wrapped his arms around her upper legs and his hands tightened on the sweat-dampened flesh beneath her thighs. He warned her with the hot, hard press of his tongue at the top of her cleft. Breathlessly, she stilled. Waiting for deliverance.

When it came, she shouted around his cock as his tongue drove down through her ready sex. Jerking into his mouth, she spilled over the edge of tight need into unraveling bliss, her cunt clenching on air in a long series of tight, shuddering spasms as a wet surge of heat spilled from her vagina and slid into her crease.

As she came, Bolt dragged his cock from her mouth. She felt his fine skin catch on her teeth as he retracted his long length.

It hung above her, wet and pulsing, dripping a thin wash of pre-cum onto her neck. As she twisted in voluptuous need, she tasted his musky release wetting her lips. Collecting it with the sweep of her tongue, she closed her eyes and swallowed his potent discharge. "Oh my God," she murmured and praised and whispered, lifting her head to pull her worshipping tongue along the dark veins that twisted around his wet shaft, seeking out more of his unique, male flavor.

"You're not done yet," he told her in a raw voice. She felt the panties bite into her flesh more deeply as he made himself a little more room to operate between her legs. Touching his lips to the top of her labia, he kissed her gently, pushing his rugged mouth against her sex as he sucked her clit between his lips. Gently but persistently he continued to suck the little knot of flesh in the hold of his warm lips. This time there was no hint of roughness in the wet kiss he lavished between her legs. Just the warm enveloping heat of his mouth, making love to her stunned clit.

Turning her head, Tavia tried to reseat his shaft in her mouth, but he pulled away, allowing her nothing more than the occasional, languishing lick up his long, ridged length. Her folds felt thick and used. Her clit felt swollen—increasingly unsettled and unsatisfied, despite the shattering climax she'd just experienced. Slowly, she felt the tight knot of satisfaction loosen inside her vagina as her muscles relaxed and opened again—interested, eager and voraciously greedy. Hungry for a man. Ready to be filled with the huge girth of vein-rich flesh that hung before her face.

But again, the sadist denied her the gift of his brutal length. As she approached a fast meltdown, he locked the tops of three fingers into her streaming cunt. With the same three fingers spreading her labia, he pressed his middle one firmly against the whole length of her slot. With her clit crushed beneath that hard finger, Bolt's hand vibrated ruthlessly and his fingers stretched her vulva wide as she came again. Gritting her teeth, she came and she came and she came in a shockingly long sequence of contractions that continued in an endless stream of disturbing ecstasy. Every time she thought it was over, he tightened his grip along her slot and spread his fingers in her vulva, coaxing another surge of anguished delight from her cunt. She thought the pleasure would never end.

Several body-wracking convulsions later, Tavia was drenched in sweat as the moisture that crept through her crease dripped from her bottom onto the hand-stitched bedspread. She felt wrung out and wrenched, strung out on pleasure. Her cunt was totally closed. Locked up for the night. Locked up forever. Soft and achy and gloriously sated.

Then, with his finger pressed over her clit, Bolt forced her to come again. Under his merciless manipulation, her cunt opened for a brief, surprised instant as she experienced a short, tight wave of deep, searing pleasure.

"No," she sobbed, as he pushed his fingers down through her pussy to her opening and rimmed her streaming entrance with the rough, calloused pad of his fingertips. "No. Not again. Please."

"You give up?" he murmured with a tight laugh.

"I give up," she moaned.

"Learned your lesson?"

She nodded.

"No more underpants?"

Again she nodded. "Not when you're around," she surrendered

with a grating moan. "Are you going to let me out of these shoes now?"

"In a minute." Turning, he straddled her hips and leaned forward. With his weight on his hands and his knees stretched wide, Bolt fed his cock between her slick, sweat-dusted breasts that were packed tightly together within the confining framework of her bra. Dragging his cock through the tight hug of her breasts, he jerked his hips as he fucked her tits. She watched his hard abdomen surge above her as he drove his hips at her time and again.

Reaching between his spread legs, Tavia wrapped her fingers gently around his balls, handling his rough testicles as she felt them harden, felt him still and felt him spill onto her chest in hot, liquid surges of spewing ejaculate that poured onto her breasts and rolled in thick rivulets toward her shoulders. With one hand wrapped around his root, Bolt grunted as he rubbed his shaft into the shining puddle between her breasts then painted Tavia's tight nipples with his slippery cum.

When Bolt finally rolled off her, he gathered Tavia's head in the cradle of his big hand and pressed her face into his damp groin. The sharp, tangy smell of Bolt's cum filled her lungs as she fell asleep with her legs spread, her feet nailed to the floor and his semen drying to a thin skin on her chest.

Five

When Tavia woke, the dark house was quiet. The light that grayed her bedroom window suggested dawn's approach. Bolt had rolled away from her in the night. He lay on his back, sprawled across the bed with the fingers of one hand tangled in her hair. Rousing herself enough to unfasten the buckles on her shoes, Tavia tucked her breasts back into the cups of her bra and pulled her dress around her.

Her stirrings had roused the animal stretched out beside her and he reached for her with one arm, snaring her into his hold, pulling her into the warmth of his chest. His lips brushed across her forehead before he fell asleep again. His breathing was long and even as she twisted in his arms. When her back was against his chest, his arms shifted to twine around her. One hand came under her arm to wrap around a lace-cupped breast, the other splayed out to claim the soft curve of her belly.

Tavia sighed. She could get used to this. Everything Bolt did seemed sexy. Even the way he cradled her belly in his large hand.

For the next hour or so, she lay quietly within the strong cage

of his arms, savoring his sexy, male presence as she waited for the
sky to lighten. When she figured it was close to six o'clock, she
worked her way out of Bolt's embrace and headed for the bathroom where she showered. Wrapped up in a fluffy white robe, she
snagged a cup of coffee in the kitchen and headed for her office
where she went to work on her current story.

Although Tavia tried to concentrate on resolving her plotline,
the thick heat that pooled between her legs distracted her. Her
throbbing sex felt swollen and used, her clit bruised as her pulse
threaded through it in a thick reminder of how she'd spent the
night. Impatiently, she crossed her legs then quickly uncrossed
them. When she looked up, Bolt was in the doorway, his shoulder
propped against the jamb. The gray sweatpants were gone, replaced by his faded jeans hanging low on his hips. Like a lovesick
pup, her clit responded to his presence with an aching pulse of
desire.

Jeez. How could she be thinking of sex? Her poor abused
pussy was so battered and mauled, it probably needed a week to
recover. Bolt gave her a tentative smile and her clit twinged while
her vulva gulped in anticipation. She returned him a watery smile
of her own.

"How do you feel this morning?" he asked in a soft, rough burr
that sounded so damn . . . affectionate.

"Great," she answered quickly. "Great." She tugged her eyes
from him and fixed them on the computer screen, feigning the
utmost interest in whatever the hell it was in front of her face.

She heard the scuff of his bare feet as he sauntered into the
room. He stopped when he reached her, wrapped his hand
around her nape and squatted beside her rolling chair. "Hey," he

murmured, "don't get all shy on me now. I'm the guy who ate you out last night."

And that didn't help. Her swollen pussy ached at the reminder then throbbed with a heavy wave of new arousal. She shook her head as the thick pad of his thumb caressed the corner of her mouth.

"I got hit with an unexpected deadline this morning. My manuscript has to be in by noon," she mumbled, averting her eyes as she wondered why she was lying to him.

Her story wasn't due for another month. She didn't know why she'd just lied. She just knew she didn't want to drive him to Albuquerque. She couldn't tell if she was reluctant to spend an hour alone with him in the car or whether she was trying to delay his departure.

He nodded.

"I . . . won't be able to give you that ride to Albuquerque." The hard curve of his lips kicked back into a smile. "Maybe one of the carpenters will be heading in that direction at the end of the day," she suggested falteringly.

In a long, delicious stretch of hard, male muscle, he rose to his feet. "I'll check with them," he told her. "What time does Maria get here?"

"Maria doesn't work on Thursdays."

"I'll head for the kitchen then and see what I can find for breakfast."

As soon as he was out the door, Tavia buried her face in her hands. There was a hungry, pounding ache in her vagina and an obstinate pulsing interest in her poor, ravaged clit that was beyond belief. Her traitorous body parts apparently didn't know what was good for them. Exactly how much did they think a girl could take?

For the next half hour, Tavia stared at the computer monitor, trying to focus. She had accomplished exactly nothing when Bolt reappeared carrying two plates, one of which he slid onto the desk beside her mouse pad.

"What's this?" she asked hesitantly.

"Bacon and mushroom sandwich." He pulled up a chair on the other side of her desk. He dropped into the chair then returned to his feet with a start. Reaching for his back pocket, he pulled out his hammer and laid it on the desk beside his plate.

"You can cook?"

"Don't act so surprised," he chided her.

Suddenly, she remembered her manners. "Thanks," she murmured.

"I'm the oldest of four kids," he said without looking at her. "My mother went to work full-time after the divorce." He shrugged. "I learned to cook."

Tavia nodded and took a dainty bite of the warm sandwich. Almost immediately, she closed her eyes. "This is good!" she exclaimed.

"Thought you'd like it." He grinned, baring a wicked glimpse of gleaming white teeth. "We gotta keep your strength up so you can continue writing those best sellers."

"Who said I wrote best sellers?"

Gnawing off a huge chunk of crusty bread wrapped around crisp bacon and fried mushrooms, Bolt shrugged as he threw a glance around the room. "This house. Your car. The new addition."

"My boyfriend?" she said with a wry laugh.

His eyes shifted with a guilty gold slide of color. He shrugged. "Well, I don't trust Alex. But you're an attractive woman, Tavia."

She took another bite. "Yeah?" she said with a smile, inviting him to continue.

"Yeah." He considered the idea thoughtfully as he tore another piece out of his sandwich. Slowly, he chewed then swallowed. "I didn't notice at first," he admitted. "Although I liked your tits right off." He shrugged. "Then later on, I noticed that you were . . . kind of sexy. Very sexy," he corrected himself as his gaze smoldered on her.

"Later on? How much later on? You mean later on . . . when you discovered I had money?"

He nodded before he took another bite. His expression was deeply contemplative as he chewed. "I think that's part of it. Not just the fact that you *have* money, but that you were smart and ambitious enough to go out and make it."

This reply wasn't exactly what she'd anticipated. She had expected some sort of denial out of the big man. His response was surprisingly honest. "What on earth do you mean?"

A deep ridge formed between his tawny brows. "I mean that . . . your money wouldn't be as attractive if you'd inherited it, for instance." When she stared at him, he grinned. "But it wasn't just the money. When we got in the car and you started giving me shit, that's when I noticed you. When you're built like me, there aren't many people who sass you like that. There sure as hell aren't many women. I have a few friends who don't feel like they have to watch what they say. But most people are careful." Again, he shrugged. "It gets old."

Tavia nodded as she stared at him. Several seconds passed before she noticed the change in his expression.

His eyes glinted with a fierce, purely predatory gleam. "Are you naked inside that robe?" he asked in an unexpectedly husky voice.

Reacting instinctively, her hands flew to the neckline of her robe where she clutched it closed above her breasts. Unfortunately, that left her hands in the wrong place to fend off his attack when he rose from his chair, circled the desk and slid to his knees in front of her. His big hands were under the robe, sliding the soft fabric up over her knees as she protested. When the white terry cloth was puddled in her lap, he pushed her legs wide and dropped back onto his heels.

Tavia squirmed in the ensuing silence, her eyes squeezed shut.

"Oh God, yes," he rasped. "Pussy paradise."

Squeaking one eye open, Tavia caught his hungry gaze burning into the curling thatch between her legs. The man looked like a kid who'd just discovered Christmas.

When she squirmed again self-consciously, his big hands moved soothingly along her inner thighs. "Don't be shy," he whispered. "I've got you, Tavia. I've got you. I won't hurt you. I just want to watch you get wet."

A breathless moan escaped her lips as she felt her insides melt and relax and settle with a deep, ravenous hunger. "Bolt," she argued breathlessly.

"Look at this," he murmured as he tugged her forward to the edge of the chair. "Your lips are so swollen and rosy. Your bud is so ripe and full. It looks like it's ready to burst. You're either horny or hurting," he told her. "Which is it?"

"A bit of both," she confessed.

His rough hands caressed the sensitive flesh of her inner thighs, back and forth, approaching and retreating as each questing foray brought his fingers inexorably closer to the crease between her legs and her sex. Finally, his thumbs ran into the crease, pulling slightly at the thick flesh of her labia. Pulling more. Pulling until she felt her lips part and felt the slightly cool touch of air on her damp folds. His thumbs settled on either side of her pussy. Then his lips were against her labia, wet and hot, soft and sliding as he kissed her sex and his thumbs stroked, stretching her vulva open then allowing it to relax while all the time his mouth moved over her sex in the most tender of kisses. "That doesn't hurt, does it?" he murmured against her open pussy.

She let loose a light moan. "Not quite. Or at least if it does, I don't care."

"That's my girl," he soothed. "This is one pretty little piece of cunt. So fragile and pink. So fuckable. Move your legs apart a bit more. That's it. Now relax. I'm just going to play with you a bit and watch you cream. I'll be careful."

He settled his mouth against her sex again and his thumbs pulled her wide as he sucked rhythmically, rolling her clit beneath his tongue, gently at first then more aggressively, scraping it beneath his teeth, sucking hungrily, fiercely. He pulled away suddenly, breathing hard and just watching her sex, open and exposed beneath his thumbs. "That's it, baby. Spill for me." Slowly he leaned forward. Softly he touched his lips to her spread sex.

As her opening shuddered beneath his mouth, Tavia fought back a moan of pleasure. The strangled sound came out somewhere between a sob and a choking whimper. Pressing her knees wide, she pushed her streaming sex into his mouth. His hands moved around to clutch her ass as he mauled her slot with his mouth, his lips everywhere, working her fragile pink folds and suckling her clitoris. Then his tongue swept low, rimming her vulva, slipping on the moisture that spilled from her cunt. He stopped with a deep, male rumble of warning. "Are you ready?" he rasped in a voice raw with lust.

When she whimpered in response, he ate into her again.

"Are you close?" he growled.

"Yes," she sobbed. "Yes, I'm ready."

"Then ask for it," he whispered against her sex. He pulled away. Then touched her. Pulled away again. His tongue nudged against her clitoris and she cried out in anguish. "You don't get it until you ask for it, baby doll."

She twisted in the chair. "Please. Please. I'm ready," she cried and moaned and whimpered.

He laughed and touched her again, taunting her clitoris with the feathering stroke of his tongue.

"Bolt!"

"I'm waiting, Tavia. Say the magic word."

"Please, Bolt."

"That's not the magic word I was looking for, Tavia."

"Bolt. Please. Please . . . fuck me."

"That's more like it," he growled out in a low rasp. "How do you want it, sweetheart?"

"I don't care," she whimpered.

He stilled. *"You don't care?"*

Tavia stopped breathing. She knew she was in trouble. Bolt's tone was both insulted and incredulous. She froze under the narrow heat of his gaze. "I just meant . . ."

He pushed away from her. "Well, hell, Tavia. If you don't care," he drawled, "I'll be damned if I'm gonna bother getting my cock out for you."

She snatched at his shoulders before he could get away. "What!" she screamed. "Oh God, Bolt, please. I'm so hot. I'm burning alive. Don't just . . . don't you *dare* just leave me like this."

"*Are* you hot?" he taunted her in a murmuring whisper. "Really hot?"

"Bolt!" she cried.

"Show me where you're hot, Tavia. Spread your sex for me with your fingers. Put your finger on your clit and show me where you're hot."

With a sobbing whimper of defeat, Tavia leaned back in the chair.

Bolt helped her widen her legs as his feral gaze strafed into her pussy. "Show me," he coaxed in a voice heavy with dark undertones.

"You're a bastard," she sobbed.

"Show me," he growled.

Her fingers hovered a moment over the thick lips of her sex. Slowly, she fingered her labia apart and exposed her small, rosy nub. Bolt sucked in a hissing breath of pleasure as she stroked her fingertip over her clit. She was so close that she shivered at the contact of her own finger. Her head dropped back on the chair and she closed her eyes as her finger slid down through her heated slot then up to her clitoris again. God, she was hot! She could feel the heat pulsing out of her pussy and wafting against her hands as she breathed.

"That's enough," he ordered abruptly. His voice was tight and strained.

She screamed when something blissfully cold pressed against her clitoris. Her eyes flew open. "Bolt. What the—"

"Does that feel good?"

"*Yes*, but."

"It's just the hammer, Tavia. Just the cool, smooth, metal head of the hammer. I'll stop if you ask me to."

The hammer's wide head covered her clit completely as he pressed firmly and massaged her clitoris in a circular motion. "Hold on, baby doll. Hold on. Can you get your legs a bit wider?"

"Bolt," she whimpered as she moved her legs apart—shamelessly wide, obscenely wide.

Bolt pressed the hammerhead against her clit as he watched her pussy with avaricious greed.

"Bolt," she moaned. "I'm so . . . close."

"Hold on," he whispered. "Hold on, Tavia. I'll tell you when."

"I don't think I can wait," she warned between panting breaths that seared her lungs.

When the hammer stopped its cool circular motion, her gaze swung wildly to his face. Waiting until he had her attention, Bolt turned the head of the hammer and drew his tongue over the flat surface of the metal, drawing her taste into his mouth and hollowing his cheeks around her flavor, obviously savoring the essence of her arousal.

"Now watch the hammer," he commanded as he returned the metal head between her legs and pressed hard on her pulse. As

Tavia watched him press the hammer between the pouting lips of her sex, her vagina tightened a long instant in pleasure. When the hammer moved again, he tapped the metal head quickly and gently against the fleshy head of her clitoris. He stopped suddenly and she glanced at his face. His expression was dark and feral as he grasped first one of her ankles then the other, hurrying her feet onto the desk's edge behind him.

Kneeling between her splayed legs, he pressed the hammerhead hard again. Again, her sex clenched for him. Slowly, he rotated the hammer around her clitoris. Pressure built at the apex of her sex, deep inside her clutching vagina. Every time she thought climax was imminent, he changed the position of the cool hammerhead, sliding it down to her vulva and penetrating the rim of her wet entrance, returning it to tap maddeningly at her clit, pressing hard over the entire top of the clitoris, rotating slowly.

"Fuck," he rasped, "you're spilling all over the chair. Hold on," he whispered in a hoarse voice. "Hold on and I'll make it worth your while, Tavia. Just a little bit more and I promise I'll shaft you. I'll fill you so full of cock, you'll scream. I promise, sweetheart. Just hold on and I'll ride you so hard and so long you won't remember your name."

In the end she was begging for it. Begging for the bright relief of climax, her feet braced on either side of his shoulders on the desk behind him, her knees falling wide as she twisted in the chair, one very small inch away from orgasm.

"Now," she gasped as she watched his eyes burning into her spread pussy. "Now, Bolt."

He pushed out a breathless laugh. "You are *so* easy," he stated in a voice saturated with smug, male satisfaction. "I love a woman who isn't too proud to beg for it." Leaving the hammer on the floor, he rose between her damp legs as she trembled beneath him, trembled and shivered, her sex poised at the anguished edge of need. Slowly, cruelly, he plucked at the buttons of his fly until she couldn't take any more. Reaching for the metal buttons, she tore at his fly and yanked at the waist of his jeans, helping him to loose his erection. It sprang free—hot and hard—jutting toward her face as he angled it down to her mouth, watching her worship the hooded crown with her tongue.

"Are you protected?" he asked in a rough burr.

She looked up at him as she nodded, letting her tongue slide up and down his shaft.

When he met her gaze, he lifted his chin in acknowledgment, watching her hungrily, indecision burning in the bright, liquid gold of his eyes.

"There are some condoms in the top drawer of my dresser." She ran her tongue up his length again. "In the bedroom."

He was silent a moment as his jaw tightened into a slab of hardened bronze. "And who did you buy those for?"

"What do you mean?"

"I'm not using a goddamn rubber you bought for Alex."

She stopped licking his cock to give him an angry glare. "I didn't buy them for Alex. I just bought them . . . to have them."

"For who?"

"For whoever!"

"Forget it!" he exploded with sudden violence. "I don't want to use a fucking condom anyhow. I want to fuck you naked. I want to fuck you with my bare skin sliding inside your tight, hot pussy.

I want to feel your cunt—wet and burning—sucking at my dick."
He pulled in a breath heavy with tension, rough with desire. "For
once in my life, I want to fuck a woman without a goddamn condom," he snarled.

"For once in your life?" Tavia hesitated. "What do you mean?
Are you telling me you've never skipped using one before?"

He inclined his chin a hard fraction. His mean, curving lips were
set in a determined line. His jaw was like a jutting piece of steel. But
the man was holding his breath, waiting for her decision.

She gave him a tiny tilt of her chin. "I guess that would be all
right then. I'm protected and . . . safe."

"Thought so." Some of the tension left his body in a long,
rough breath. "How many times do you want to come?"

"What . . . do you mean?"

"How many times do you want to come?" he repeated. "I don't
want to miss anything but I don't want to wear you out either."

"I don't know," she answered. "Nobody ever asked me that before."

"How many times do you usually come?"

"Usually? Once."

"Once when you're with a man?"

She gritted her teeth. "That's right."

"How many times *can* you come?"

She thought about this, hating to answer the question with all
of its dirty little implications. Finally she countered with, "I came
three times last night."

He grunted as though he was dissatisfied with this response.
"That was different. I didn't have you on my cock," he growled.
"Do you need time to build up again after the first orgasm?"

"No. After the first, the next ones are easy."

"Three it is, then."

Lowering himself, he locked his hands around the arms of her chair. His long, hard body shimmered in tension as a vibration of hunger traveled his frame. His muscles tensed, hard and defined as he hovered on the sharp edge of passion. Tavia felt his wide cock head probe through the long, silky slot of her pussy and she canted her hips to meet his thrust. The thick head pressed against her notch for an instant.

"Get those knees apart," he grunted. "Spread them wide." When she pressed her knees wide, he heaved his hips at her and penetrated her in one long, savage sweep.

He was huge but she was ready for him. Her cunt was burning with slippery, wet heat as he shoved into her. Her vagina closed around him as he drove to the back of her sheath where he smashed up against her sweet spot and held. For several seconds she was lost in perfect ecstasy as he shafted her, his cock head crushed into the back of her cervix as he ground his hips. His teeth were bared in a feral snarl and his eyes blazed with primal lust as he watched her orgasm, her mouth open, her eyes fixed on his. The color in his eyes shifted, glazed to hard gold as he lowered his panting mouth to hers, raping her mouth with his tongue while the walls of her vagina contracted around the hard cock that filled it.

When her sex finally settled and was quiet again, Bolt half closed his eyes. He pushed out a small, tense laugh. "Oh God, I love that," he rasped. "I love the feel of a woman's cunt rippling down my length, tightening and closing and loosening again. There's nothing like it in the world," he said. "Well," he added, "except for this."

With a methodical patience bordering on obsession, Bolt began to work himself over her, pulling his hips as he slid from her heated channel then thrusting forward to fill her again. He was merciless and thorough, spearing her on the end of his cock with the long vicious sweep of his hips as he shoved into her, slowly at first but with increasing velocity and growing violence. Sweat glimmered on the golden stubble of his beard and across his broad chest as he hammered his cock between her legs. The chair rocked on its rollers as he grasped the arms and dug in with his feet to deliver blow after blow to the back of her vagina. He grimaced as he watched her face. "You're ready to come again, aren't you?"

She nodded her head.

"When?"

She jerked against him in answer and his hips quickened as he pounded through her orgasm, the savage pummel of his hips accelerating as she sat, spread in the chair, pinned beneath his weight, his cock stretching her vulva brutally wide as he thrust against her with steady strength and mad, vicious intensity.

"Okay," he gritted as her vagina closed around his cock in small finishing surges. "One more time, Tavia. Meet me one more time and we'll both get fucked this time."

With sudden urgency, he slipped his arms under her legs, lifting her knees so he could take her at a more direct angle, so that he could stretch into her more deeply, more completely. His strokes were shorter, faster, as he plastered his groin against the cushioned mound of her sex and ground into her in hot, gritty surges. This one was for him, Tavia realized as he slammed into her. This time he was going to fuck her, pure and simple, noth-

ing fancy. There'd be no reserve on his part, no careful tim-
ing involved. Just a man in the satisfying act of dominating a
woman, claiming her for his pleasure and fucking her like an
animal.

A fresh sheen of sweat burst out over his skin, gleaming on his
chest as his lungs heaved. His breath roaring against her ear was
a harsh testament to his need.

"Fuck," he grunted. "You're so wet and hot and soft. Take me,
Tavia. Open up your tight little cunt and let me fuck you all the
way. Come on me now, and my cock is yours, sweetheart."

Tavia hurried to join him in climax, winding herself up tight
then letting herself loose as he expanded inside her, stretching
the walls of her channel as he burst inside her cunt and filled her
with his hot, steamy cum.

"Fuck!" he shouted as he came. His voice was a hoarse scrape of
sound as he grunted out his stunned pleasure. "Fuck," he groaned
again quietly as he pulsed and emptied inside her. His damp forehead rested against her temple.

Dragging his heated lips down the side of her cheek, he buried
his face in the warm hollow of her neck as his hips continued to
surge gently, milking the experience for everything he could take
from it. "Tavia," he breathed in a heavily sated growl, "now . . .
aren't you glad you weren't wearing underpants?"

Tavia's heartfelt giggle was her only response.

"They should make more women like you," he mumbled into
her neck.

With her fingers caressing his hot, rough cheeks, Tavia pulled
his face out of her neck and smiled softly. "And why is that?"

"Because," he told her with a deep, exhausted rumble of contentment, "if they made more women like you, I'd order myself a dozen and stay fucked all the time."

Tavia chuckled. "A dozen?"

He nodded as he pushed himself away from the chair and onto his feet. He tucked his cock inside his jeans, did up a few buttons then rubbed his palm down the faded line of his button-down fly. "A dozen. That way I wouldn't wear you out."

She cocked an accusing eyebrow at him. "You didn't hear me complaining."

He gave her a warm smile and a lazy nod. Leaning over, he stooped to nudge two fingers between her thick labia. Slowly, he drew his fingers through her hot, swollen folds. "Wait until this afternoon," he told her ominously. "By the time I'm finished with this tight little piece of pussy, you'll be screaming for backup."

When she smiled at him, he pressed a lingering kiss to her lips.

"I should let you get back to work." Slipping his plate over hers, he smiled down at her. "Guess I'll go talk to the carpenters."

"I imagine you're anxious to get away." Her voice came out lower then she'd planned.

There was a pregnant pause. "I wouldn't mind spending another night."

When Tavia lifted her eyes, he was grinning at her. Damn, he was a smug, cocky bastard.

"But right now you've got a deadline to meet and I'm not much good at doing nothing." Sweeping the hammer off the floor, he hooked it through the hole in his back pocket. "So I'll keep busy outside until . . . later. I saw a flatbed pull up with a load of trusses while I was in the kitchen."

"Trusses?"

He nodded. "For the roof on your new addition," he told her. "I'll see if the carpenters need any help."

"You could do the dishes," she pointed out as he sauntered toward the door.

"Don't do dishes," he threw back at her. "Don't do dishes and don't do panties."

"Chauvinist," she yelled at him.

"Get used to it," he called back.

Six

Tavia went back to work with a smile and a warm feeling of contentment. Forcing herself to concentrate on her current project, her fingers tapped on the keyboard amid the dull thump and pound of distant hammers. Eventually, she left her office to shower again and dress. Dallying in front of the huge floor-to-ceiling mirrors in the bathroom, Tavia pulled her hair back and turned her head, lifting her chin as she surveyed the smooth flesh of her neck. The soft skin was mottled with warm, scratchy pools of pink—blotches of color where Bolt had left his mark on her, the masculine evidence of his rough beard and male passion etched on her pale, feminine skin.

Humming in the closet, she selected another calf-length dress with a thin gauzy overlay of chiffon splashed with muted colors of soft peach and warm pink. After slipping on a comfortable pair of flat sandals, Tavia headed down the hall and into the kitchen to refill her coffee cup. On her way back, she made a sly detour to the living room window where she could spy on the new construction through the shielding veil of a sheer white curtain.

Bolt had made himself at home on her roof, standing on the

narrow wooden wall, guiding trusses into place, toe-nailing them down then ducking through the open framework as the next truss swung up to meet his outstretched hand. Every movement he made was carried out with a leonine grace, his muscles rippling in his shoulders and across his back as he balanced on the narrow wall. Tavia was so focused on the pleasant view of Bolt working that she jumped a bit when the doorbell sounded from a few feet distant. Just before she dragged her eyes from Bolt, she saw his gaze swing into the driveway. He glared at the white van parked on the concrete in front of her house.

Tavia answered the front door.

A young man in a crisp gray uniform stood on the other side of the door, a large bouquet of yellow roses in his arm. Really large. There must have been forty blooms in the bundle. She thanked him and signed for the flowers but he stopped her before she could close the door. "There's more, ma'am," he warned her. "Lots more."

"Oh!" She glanced around the small entryway that opened into the living room. "Shall I just leave the door open then?"

"I think that would be best, ma'am."

By the time the deliveryman had emptied the van and Tavia had finally closed the door behind him, she had a dozen huge bouquets spilling across her living room into the dining area. Each bundle of color had a little white card attached. All of the flowers were from Alex. The handwritten notes varied in content but not in purpose. "We need to talk" was the main thrust of the messages. "You're making a mistake" was another recurrent theme. Tavia sank into a turn-of-the-century, straight-backed chair just inside the living room.

The front door opened soon afterward. Bolt filled the opening just before the door slammed behind him. Tavia lifted her gaze to him, a handful of fancy, ragged-edged cards in her fingers as she sat in the richly upholstered chair.

Bolt's thin, worn scrap of a T-shirt was clutched in his fist and he lifted it to press above the sweating curve of his chin. Moisture dampened the gold stubble on his jaw and more sweat gleamed across the muscles of his chest. When he rubbed the T-shirt across the broad expanse of his bronze-flecked chest, she stared at his flat, brown nipples. Jeez, he looked good in nothing but skin and nipples.

Bolt glowered as he took in the roomful of flowers. "Let me guess," he growled. "Alex?"

She nodded without speaking, returning her attention to the handful of cards.

"What the fuck is his problem?" Bolt grumbled. "Can't the man take no for an answer?"

She lifted one shoulder. "I haven't actually told him no."

"You didn't have to. I told him *for* you—last night."

She lifted her head. "His family has been asking him when they should reserve the country club . . . for the rehearsal dinner."

"Did you tell him two weeks after hell freezes over?"

"No," she said quietly.

A long silence ensued as his eyes narrowed into a thin line of gold. "No," he said finally. "No. You're not marrying that princess."

"Why not?"

"Why not? Because . . . because I forbid it!"

"You forbid it?"

"Yeah, I forbid it. Jesus. He—he drives a Fiat for chrissakes." He scowled at her as though that were sufficient argument.

She folded her arms over her chest and stared back. "What do you have against Fiats?"

"Fiats are for girls."

"That's your argument?"

"Yeah."

"Well, I don't like it. I don't like arrogant, male chauvinistic pigs who feel threatened by women, girls or any man who happens to have the least bit of sensitivity."

"Threatened?" Bolt bellowed. "Do I look threatened?"

"At least his Fiat runs!" Tavia sniped at him. "Unlike your vehicle, Alex's car runs! And despite what you think, Bolt, Alex is *not* gay!"

"How would you know?"

"He told me."

"How would *he* know?"

"Stop it," she yelled. "Just stop it, Bolt!"

He pulled a hand back through his hair. "If you have to get married," he yelled suddenly, "at least pick somebody worthy of you!"

"Worthy? Of me? Alex was last year's Mr. Dream World Fantasy at the Romance Lovers Convention."

"Yeah, he's a fantasy all right," Bolt muttered. "And you're living in a dream world if you think he's anything else."

"Okay!" she shouted. "Okay, Bolt. Just who would you suggest in his place?"

"In his place?"

She waited.

"How about someone like me?"

Not me, but someone *like* me. What a complete dick!

"How *about* someone like you?" she tossed back at him with a sneer. "How *about* a guy who works in a garage and apparently isn't even very good at that! A guy who can't even keep his own vehicle running. A guy who can't afford the *parts* to keep it running! A guy *I* found hitchhiking down the road wearing a ratty old *threadbare* T-shirt with his ass hanging out of a pair of jeans that were at least as old as his car?"

Bolt looked startled for a moment then his expression went blank as his eyebrows lifted in surprise. His eyes focused on the T-shirt fisted in his hand and he frowned at the thin scrap of material as though he'd never seen it before.

"Well," he announced in slow revelation, "I guess when you put it *that* way, I don't sound like much of a prize, do I?" His eyes narrowed on her with a cold, metallic sheen. "I didn't realize you put so much store by money, Miss October. Personally, I *don't!*"

"That's *obvious!*" she screamed in frustration.

He continued to regard her coldly. "I would have thought you had enough money for both of us."

"And *I'm* not exactly surprised you *feel* that way! Believe it or not, Bolt Hardin, I've met plenty of men like you. There are *plenty* of men out there who think that *I* make enough money for two to live off."

He nodded. "Well, fuck me," he murmured, then cut a glance at her. "I was speaking figuratively."

She rolled her eyes. "Do you even know what that means?"

He looked stung, his normally arrogant expression finally reduced to something less. It didn't look right on him. Bolt didn't look good hurt. Immediately Tavia regretted the cheap shot.

"Yeah," he said quietly. "Yeah. I *figure* I have a rough idea. I *figure* it means I've wasted enough time here. *Literally* as well as *figuratively*." He turned, grasping the doorknob as she shouted at him.

"Don't try to make me the bad guy, Bolt! *You* like an ambitious woman! Maybe I feel the same way. Maybe I'm looking for a guy with an education and a career and a future!"

He turned back to face her, pointing a shaking finger at her. "You are such a fucking snob! For your information, I have a career! And I could have gone to college if I'd wanted to."

"I am *not* a snob, Bolt! But I do have standards. I *do* expect a little intelligent conversation out of a man."

He threw his hands in the air. "Fine," he bellowed. "What do you want to talk about?"

"I don't know," she returned hotly. "Literature, maybe!"

Crossing his sun-bronzed arms over his chest, he leaned back against the door. "Fine. Fire away."

"Well . . ." Tavia licked her lips nervously, suddenly feeling like a bit of an ass. "What's the last book you read?"

"*Conan.*"

"That's *exactly* what I mean."

"Have you ever read Robert E. Howard?"

"No, but . . ."

"Then how can you judge?"

"Okay." Tavia took a deep breath, convinced at this point that he *was*, in fact, the ass, rather than she. "What was the *best* book you ever read?"

"Best ever?"

"Yes."

"*Catcher in the Rye*," he clipped out without hesitation.

"Really?" she faltered. "That's one of my favorites too. What did you like about it?"

"Everything," he cut at her. "It was . . . full of true things. It was real. Most books are full of crap."

She nodded.

"Like romance," he went on. "That's all crap. There isn't an honest word in a romance novel." He stopped abruptly. "Jesus, I'm sorry, Tavia. I forgot—"

"Have you ever read a romance?" she asked frostily.

"Well, I . . ."

"Then how can you judge?" Standing, she threw the handful of cards at the chair and stalked out of the room then down the hall.

He levered himself away from the door. "Fuck," he muttered. "Tavia. I'm sorry." He followed her into the bedroom. "I'm sorry, but men just aren't like that. The way they act in romance novels."

"Yeah?" She spun to face him. "Well, enlighten me, Mr. Bolt Hardin. What are men really like?"

"More like me."

"Really, Bolt? Because of all the men I've ever met, I've never met anyone *remotely* like you!"

"That's just because most men are careful. Most men act . . . civilized."

She snorted. "So you're telling me that Alex is just pretending to be civilized."

"Hell, no! Alex is pretending to be a man!"

Her jaw dropped as she stared at him. "You're a prick, Bolt. A goddamn bigoted prick."

"Me? Bigoted? I'm not a bigot, Tavia. I don't mind guys like Alex. I think they're fucking adorable. The only problem I have with Alex is that he's a gold digger."

"And you aren't!"

His expression was stunned. "Don't be ridiculous! I didn't ask you to marry me!"

"Arrgh!" she screamed. "You're driving me crazy."

"Yeah?" he muttered, dragging the heel of his palm over his button-down fly. A wry smile fell over his features. "Well, if it helps to know, you do the same thing to me." He blew out a sigh as they stared at each other.

"You know," she told him with a tired huff, "Alex isn't exactly a poor man."

"Maybe not. But I bet you'd make him rich."

Exhausted and exasperated, she nodded as she stared at the floor. Then she lifted her head. "How rich would I make you, Bolt?"

"That's not the issue, Tavia."

"No," she agreed quietly. "That's not the issue, is it?" She slumped down to sit on edge of the bed.

"We got all the trusses up," Bolt announced into the lengthy silence.

She nodded at the floor.

"I guess I'll take a shower."

This didn't seem to require any comment.

"So. Are you going to fuck me or not?"

Amazed, she lifted her head to stare at him. "You are *such* a pig."

His defensive gaze flicked across the room then returned to hers. "Is that a yes or a no? Because I want to know before I take my shower. I don't want to waste it in the shower if there's any chance—"

"There's *no* chance," she cut in.

He stared at her a few more seconds, his eyes burning with a strange gold fire. Then he spoke. "Well, Tavia. I was hoping I wouldn't have to resort to this but you leave me no choice."

As Tavia watched, he reached back and palmed his hammer out of his back pocket. When he took a few steps toward the bed, she stood and backed away from him just to be safe. But he leaned over when he reached the end of the bed and used the clawed end of the hammer to pry the long nails from the black ankle-straps spiked into the carpet. With the shoes swinging from his long fingers, he stalked from the room.

Tavia shook her head as she watched the empty doorway. Seconds later, she heard two slamming bangs. Horrified, she rushed from the room. "Damn it, Bolt! Those are hardwood *floors!*"

Screeching to a hasty halt in the middle of the living room, Tavia stared, aghast. The shoes were spaced about three feet apart in the dining room—nailed to the polished hardwood floor. The toes were tucked beneath the edge of the dining room table, which meant that she'd be facing the table . . . once they were buckled around her ankles. And she didn't imagine it would be long after that before Bolt had her facedown, with her cheek pressed against the curly maple veneer of the tabletop.

"No," she said in a tiny, awestruck voice as she backed away from the table, the dining room, him. She turned to run but he caught her by the hips and dragged her ass backward across the room

"You promised to wear the shoes," he told her firmly.

"I already delivered on that promise!" she yelped as she fought to free herself.

He wrestled her around to face the table. "Are you trying to renege on our agreement?" he grunted.

"I already wore the shoes!" she screamed.

She fought him every inch of the way, first pounding her fists on his chest then kicking back with her heels after he'd turned her. But with an iron-like fist manacling her ankle, he got her sandals off and got her right foot buckled into the ankle-straps. The next time she kicked out, he caught her foot and held it tightly.

"You know," he said lightly, "if I were you, I'd stop worrying about the shoes at this point and start worrying about those underpants you're wearing."

She went suddenly still. "What?" she queried in a small voice.

In answer, he guided her left foot to the shoe anchored on the floor.

"No," she screamed suddenly, tearing her dress up her legs and yanking her panties down. "No!" she screamed again.

The vicious sadist laughed as her heel caught him full in the chest.

Somehow, drawing her knee up into her chest, Tavia managed to wrestle the silk bikinis over her left foot before he grabbed her ankle again, turned her and strapped her in.

Panting, she braced her hands on the table. Her hair hung before her face in long streaming ringlets of bright chestnut. Her discarded panties were puddled around her right foot. Tavia blew out a sigh of relief then pulled in a slow breath of longing as she felt Bolt's hands pushing her dress up over her bare ass. There was a rush of cool air on her skin followed by the rough contact of his denim jeans against her bottom.

She resisted the urge to snuggle her derriere into his warm, thick groin. The arrogant bastard didn't deserve that kind of validation. It was bad enough that he'd forced her to bare herself for him. She felt his hands stroke up the back of her thighs and over her bottom. When he shifted his hips backward, she felt his large, rough palm stroke over the full, sodden lips of her sex.

"Tavia," he murmured accusingly, "you're wet!"

She moaned in answer.

"How can you be wet again?"

"I don't know, Bolt. How can you be hard again? I see you and I just start . . . leaking. I'm sore as hell, my pussy's as sore as hell, and every time I see you I . . . just *ache* for you."

"Poor Tavia," he murmured, leaning over her and bracing his hands on the table beside hers.

For a long time he just leaned against her with his chest warm across her back, rocking his denim-covered crotch against her pussy, his fingers playing with hers as his mouth hovered at her ear, pelting her cheek with his humid breath. When he put his damp lips against her cheek, she turned her face and found his mouth with hers. He returned her kiss stroke for stroke, using the hard, flat surface of his teeth like a weapon, bruising her lips, using his tongue to probe the slick inner recesses of her mouth, twisting his stubble-edged lips into her kiss.

When he finally broke away and straightened behind her, his breath was rough and harsh. There was a pause while he unbuttoned his jeans and guided his cock out of his pants. The next thing Tavia felt was the wide head of his penis riding through her sex from the top of her vulva, through the fragile, swollen folds of pink, over the tender bud of her clitoris to settle at the top of her cleft. Drawing back again, he loitered at her entrance for several moments, rimming her opening with his crown, collecting her moisture before sliding through her folds again and prodding at her sensitive clit.

Her clit was so damn hypersensitive that any more contact would have been painful. But his velvet-skinned cock head was unbearably gentle as he played its tip over the swollen knot of her clitoris. Her belly filled with heat while her vagina filled with want. Warmth and wet slid from her opening. She felt it trickle down through her folds until his cock head was sliding over her slippery flesh and heightening every wicked sensation he laid on between her spread legs.

Her body relaxed as her breath came in rushing pants and she resituated her bottom, shifting and wiggling until she'd guided her open vulva to the fat, cushioned head of his penis.

Bolt chuckled softly. "You ready, baby doll?"

"I'm ready," she breathed.

"Are you going to beg for it?"

She gritted her teeth. "Only if you make me, you fucking sadist."

Bolt pushed out a tense laugh. "Okay," he murmured. "This one's on me."

She felt his huge cock head pressing against her oh-so-tender entrance and she held her breath.

"Brace yourself," he warned her with a grunt. With those words, he grasped her hips tightly and shafted her.

Her sudden intake of breath was a whistling squeak. His massive cock stretched and scraped at the raw, used flesh of her swollen vagina. She whimpered, wanting to cry out, wanting him to stop, wanting him to go on. Sliding down onto the table, she laid her hot cheek against the cool surface of the polished maple, reaching for the table's edges and holding on for dear life while sweat popped to bead on every pore of her body. A wide ellipse of fog pooled on the table beside her mouth.

"Bolt," she whimpered, "Bolt . . . I . . . go easy, Bolt. Please."

She felt his big hands on her derriere, pulling apart the cheeks of her ass as he ground his way deeper. She sucked in a painful breath.

"You sore, baby doll?"

"A little. I . . . do you think we could do this without . . . without moving?"

He chuckled. "That would be hard."

She groaned. "I was afraid you'd say that."

"But not impossible," he added, reaching around in front of her leg and settling his fingertips over the top of her labia. "I won't spread you," he told her. "So you tell me when I'm in the right place."

When he moved his hand in a small circle, she moaned. "That's the right place."

"Thought so," he grunted.

His shaft was buried deep between her cheeks, thickly enclosed within the flesh cushioning his groin. His thick wrist slid down between their bodies and she felt his left hand moving against her skin, stroking his balls as he rocked gently against her backside, barely moving inside her, nudging the full tip of his

cock head against the back of her vagina, delivering deep, dark
ecstasy with each thumping blow.

Moments later, his right hand was slipping as he massaged the
full, wet lips that sheltered her clit. The deep pounding delivery
at her sweet spot moved her slowly toward climax as he bucked
against her in short surges. At some point the pleasure and need for
deliverance overwhelmed any discomfort Tavia was aware of. She
gripped the table's edges, braced her legs and lifted her ass to him.

"Jesus," he complained as his hands gripped the flesh of her
cheeks. "You shouldn't have done that, Tavia. Hold on, sweetheart. You're about to get fucked."

With these words he pulled his hips and slammed into her,
groaning as he drove into her with violent urgency, stretching
her channel impossibly wide as his cock expanded in his own approach to climax.

Tavia didn't hear the doorbell ring. She was orgasming when it
opened several minutes later, pressing the side of her open mouth
into the table's smooth surface. Behind her, Bolt pounded against
her backside, flaying her with the slap of his hips, flogging her
with his cock, too close to climax to stop for anything less than
the end of the world.

The stunned deliveryman stared a startled instant as a bouquet
of red roses slipped from his fingers and dropped to rattle against
the floor. Abruptly, he backed out of the house as Bolt threw his
hips at Tavia's ass three more times then stilled, coming in blister-
ingly hot surges, pumping his cum into her sheath, choking back
obscene phrases mixed with hard words of devotion.

Afterward, Tavia groaned. "Oh man," she panted against the
table, "poor guy. I bet we gave him a scare."

Bolt's shaft pulsed inside her as he ground his groin against the cushion of her ass. He jerked his chin upward. "Either that or a hard-on," he murmured.

Tavia's breath fogged on the table as she gave a weak giggle.

Bolt drew his cock out of her hold in a long, sore slide of thick flesh. "Did you get your story finished?" he asked as he pulled her dress down to cover her exposed backside.

"Story?" she mumbled vaguely.

"You had a noon deadline," he reminded her, tucking his cock inside his pants and buttoning up.

"Yes," she lied primly as he fell to one knee and released her from first one shoe, then the other.

"What about you? Did you get a ride to Albuquerque?" she asked, holding her breath.

Bolt was a moment answering. "Not tonight," he said softly. His gaze probed hers from behind thick lashes and for several seconds Tavia gave up on breathing altogether. His expression told her that he was staying the night. That he wanted to stay the night. And that she didn't have much choice in the matter.

Once Tavia was free of the shoes, she and Bolt crept across the entry to the front door. They found more flowers on the porch. Another dozen bouquets.

Tavia didn't open the notes.

Bolt spent the night.

Seven

Tavia overslept. She'd had a busy night. She smiled, stretching in the large king-sized bed as she reminisced. She particularly liked the memory of Bolt stretched over her, lying between her spread legs, his weight on his elbows as his cock pulsed inside her and he dipped his face to kiss her mouth. *That* was a good one. Turning on the bed, she snuggled her face into the pillow beside her and drew in a breath full of the rich, masculine scent of Bolt Hardin.

It was about then that she realized he was absent from the bed. Rising swiftly, Tavia wrapped her soft white robe around her and went looking for him.

She found him in the kitchen. And immediately wished she hadn't. She knew it was unreasonable, but what she saw in the kitchen turned her around in a hot firestorm of jealousy. She was out of the kitchen in a flash, striding through the dining room and down the hall, trying to distance herself from Bolt before she cursed him to hell and back.

Why were men such pricks?

Shaking her head, Tavia tried to dislodge that image from her head. When she'd opened the swinging door to the kitchen, she'd found Bolt Hardin—biggest prick on the face of the earth—with an arm around her cook. The curvy, dark-haired little woman was tucked into his side and his lips were on her neck, behind her ear. *Behind her ear!*

"Tavia!"

Tavia heard Bolt shout behind her as she spun into her bedroom, spinning again as she realized she had no fucking doors to slam in his face—and no weapon that would separate his head from his shoulders.

"Tavia," Bolt called again just before he appeared in her doorway.

"Get out of my house," she screeched at him in a whisper, her hair flying around her face, her cheeks burning up in anger. Stabbing him with her eyes, she gave him a look that guaranteed death and danger. "Get out of my house, you *fucking* prick!"

His eyes were narrowed in awe. "Tavia, you're overreacting."

"Am I?" she shouted. "*Am I?* What did I see back there in my kitchen?"

Slowly, he edged his way toward her. "You saw me kissing Maria."

She exploded. "That's what I thought I saw!"

He inclined his chin slightly, sliding another foot toward her. "Why the fuck were you kissing my employee?"

Bolt's gaze hugged the floor. "Cookies."

"Cookies?" Tavia echoed, stunned.

Again Bolt nodded as he crept a few more inches in her direction. "Give me a break, Tavia," he muttered. "The woman had a plateful of warm cookies. I'd have kissed Alex if he'd had a plate of warm cookies."

Tavia tilted her head in disbelief as her eyes narrowed suspiciously on his face. The man was contrite. *Way* too contrite. She wasn't buying it.

In the next instant it didn't matter whether she was buying it or not because, in a flash of gliding movement, Bolt had her plastered up against the wall, his knee between her legs and his hands inside her robe, groping her breasts.

In a mad froth of rage, Tavia twisted beneath him. Her struggles had no effect whatsoever on Bolt except to roughen the breath that rushed from his lips and pelted her hair. With a groan of defeat, she glared down at the hands that had captured her breasts. The pale mounds of flesh spilled out around the edges of his huge hands. His palms were beneath her nipples, lifting her breasts into his splayed fingers. With frustration bordering on angst she watched her nipples, traitorous little sluts that they were, peaking for him. Her mind might still be her own—raging against him. But her body was his—lock, stock and nipple. She glowered at her breasts as his fingers moved together, squeezing her erect nipples between the scissoring vise of his thick digits.

She was on fire. From the full, hungry lips of her pussy to the tips of her hardened nipples, she was on fire for him. She was angry and taut and tense, and on fire for a man with *no* potential who would never be *anything* more than a womanizing, lying cheat.

Wanting to cry and scream and sever his balls all at the same time, Tavia watched Bolt's gaze on her misbehaving nipples as a rough, male growl rumbled from his throat. His chest expanded as he sucked up air in lusty bursts. His gold eyes glowed with carnal heat as his lips slanted over hers and his mouth crushed into hers.

He forced the kiss on her. He forced it.

And she took it. Ate it up. Drank it down. All of it—hook, line and the long, lead sinker he had pressed up against her belly. When he was done imposing his carnal will between her lips, his mouth made a wet path to her ear. "Tavia," he whispered between the huge expansions of his lungs. "I'm only going to tell you this once, so pay attention. I'm not interested in Maria."

"Then why," she ground out between her own gasping attempts to breathe, "if you're not interested in Maria, do you have such a huge, fucking *hard-on?*"

He laughed and groaned at the same time. "Don't you know, baby doll? You are so fucking hot when you're mad. Look at you." Dragging her from the wall, he turned her to face the mirror above her painted dresser. He stood behind her as she stared at her reflection. Her hair was wild, two spots of bright color burned high on her cheeks and her eyes were just about emitting sparks above her angry pouting lips.

"If you want me to kiss you the way I kissed Maria, make me a plateful of warm cookies. But if you want me to fuck you up against the wall," he murmured into her neck, "just look at me like that."

His hands crossed beneath her chest and he lifted her breasts, one in each hand as he kneaded them in his fingers and pressed his iron-hard erection into the cleft of her ass. The scorching flame of her anger was just beginning to dampen when the spell was broken by the tinny sound of annoyingly cheery music. Bolt cursed as he reached for the cell phone in his pocket.

"Hardin," he barked into the phone. "What? Say again. You're breaking up. What? Listen. *Listen.* I'll try to call you back."

Snapping his phone closed, Bolt frowned at it for a few seconds. "I'd better make this call from a landline," he told Tavia. "Be back in a minute." He headed through her open doorway and down the hall. "We'll finish making up then."

As Tavia glared at the opening, she heard his footsteps returning. "You might want to talk to Maria," he suggested. "Make sure she knows she still has a job. She . . . seemed worried. Tell her it was my fault." He headed down the hall again.

This time Tavia's eyes narrowed on the empty opening. So Bolt would like her in the kitchen, would he? *Way* down the hall, across the living room, through the dining room and *in* the kitchen where she couldn't possibly overhear any of the conversation he'd be having on the phone in the other bedroom.

Tavia stalled. Angry. Suspicious. She eyed the telephone in her room. She could talk to Maria later. Despite Bolt's purported concern, Tavia wasn't about to fire her cook because of *his* bad behavior.

She heard Bolt laughing from the bedroom down the hall.

You *know* . . . it was funny, but that didn't sound like the sort of laugh two men shared. It sounded like the sort of laugh a man shared with a woman. Warm and deep, teasing and almost sultry. Slowly, Tavia made her way over to the bedside table and the ivory-colored phone sitting beside the lamp.

Okay. She was jumpy. She was on edge. She'd just seen Bolt pressing a kiss behind Maria's ear. Damn Bolt! Why did he have to be so sexy? Everything he did was just cut thick with sex appeal. He walked across the room and it was sexy! He stretched his arms behind his head and it was sexy! He kissed her cook and—*Jesus*.

Tavia snatched the telephone receiver out of the cradle and

pressed it to her ear. She was so frustrated and angry and suspicious she didn't even *begin* to feel guilty about listening in on Bolt's conversation. Immediately, her lips twisted into a tight knot and her eyes narrowed on her reflection in the mirror across the room as she heard a female's voice.

"When are you going to be home, Bolt?"

"Soon, sweetheart."

"How soon?"

"You're not my mother, Mindy."

"Thank god," Mindy laughed. "If I were your mother, I'd have to feed you."

Bolt laughed while Tavia burned—scorched in fact—blackened around the edges to be quite honest.

"I have a surprise for you," Bolt taunted the woman on the other end of the line.

"Will I like it?"

"Oh yeah. You'll like it. It's something really big. Bigger than what I usually bring back."

"Bolt," Mindy giggled, "you're such a tease."

Tavia jumped away from the phone like it was a snake. Glaring at the receiver she'd flung on the bed, she backed away from the hateful thing.

Okay. That's it. That was flirting. That was the sound of Bolt flirting with another woman. His girlfriend. His fiancé. His wife for all she knew! *When are you going to be home, Bolt?* Tavia stared at her burning reflection. She'd cry if she wasn't so goddamn mad.

Bolt Hardin wasn't any more interested in her than he was in Maria or . . . or Mindy—whoever *she* was. So why the hell was he hanging around? It couldn't be sex. Evidently he could get that anywhere and everywhere.

That left money.

And he'd had the nerve to call Alex a gold digger!

Well, the good thing about being rich was . . . it wasn't hard to get rid of a gold digger boyfriend if you wanted to.

Stumbling out of her bedroom, Tavia crossed the hall to her office and placed herself behind the large, shielding mass of her desk. When she dropped into her chair, it finally hit her. She covered her face, fighting tooth and nail to hold back a crushing wave of tears. Somehow in the last few days she'd fallen for the great, huge, stupid enough lug nut. Despite everything. Despite the fact that she'd known from the start he was a man without drive, ambition or potential. Despite the fact that he didn't even have the wherewithal to keep his car running.

With nothing more than a sexy saunter and a low-slung pair of faded jeans, he'd wormed his way right into her unhappy heart.

Bolt's voice startled her. "You're still mad at me."

"No," she responded sharply, willing her voice not to crack as she pulled her face out of her hands. She even managed the sem-blance of a brave smile for the man who stood in the doorway. "It's something else. I've just received some bad news."

"Bad news?" Bolt's eyebrows crushed together in an expression of concern.

Tavia ignored his expression as she forged on. "My accountant cleaned out my bank account ten days ago," she informed him. "I've had the police on him. They just called to tell me he left the country a week ago."

Bolt just continued to frown.

"I'm broke," she told him flatly.

"You have another phone line? I didn't hear the phone ring."

"The call came in on my cell," she told him.

He nodded stiffly as though holding back a rage of emotions. "You should have told me," he finally said, tightly. "I'm sorry."

She nodded without looking at him. "It was really none of your business."

"But you can keep writing." His voice was surprisingly gentle. "It won't take long before you're back on top again."

She pushed out a bitter laugh. The guy was tenacious. Why hadn't she seen this in him before?

"Anything I make for the next several years will go to pay off the debt my accountant ran up in my name. I'll have to stop work on the house and put it on the market."

Tavia watched as his fists bunched and his eyes narrowed to frigid slits. His mean mouth settled into a stubbornly vicious line. Tavia shook her head. You'd have thought it was his money that had been lost.

Abruptly, he shook out his hands though he still glowered. "I'm sorry." He scraped a hand back through his stiff, rowdy hair. "But I was getting tired of this place anyhow."

Tavia clasped her hands together and locked them against her chin to stop it from trembling. She might have expected this from the almighty prick.

He nodded grimly. "I think you'll like my place. It's smaller and cozier." He lifted one shoulder as he forced an apologetic smile onto his mouth. "I'd like to kill the guy who did this to you, Tavia. But . . . it's just money. I'm sorry. I'm not a multimillionaire but you won't starve as long as I'm around."

At this point, Tavia had to remind herself to breathe. Her heart felt like it was about to explode. The rest of her felt like she was melting. Maybe that's why all that liquid was running out of her eyes. She was melting. That was the only explanation.

"Tavia!"

The next thing she knew, Bolt was on his knees beside her. Reaching out with one hand, he cupped the side of her face as she tried to hide her tears in his hand. "Tavia, don't cry, baby doll. It's only money! You'll like my place. And . . . and I can't wait to introduce you to Mindy, my next-door neighbor—the mining engineer! She's been trying to get me hooked up for years." He glanced back at the door. "I was just on the phone, teasing her about you."

Tavia squeezed her eyes closed and hid her face in his hand, pressing her lips together as tears flooded her eyes. She had been ready to cry. But not like this. She had been ready to cry in anger. She had been ready to shed tears of pain. But she hadn't planned on crying because the male animal kneeling beside her was the most incredibly wonderful man on the face of the earth.

It wasn't the money. He didn't care about the money.

And Mindy was his best friend.

Tavia might have been the happiest woman on the planet, except for one thing.

She'd just lied to him.

And that just made her cry harder.

"Tavia," he murmured, drawing her into his arms and rocking her in his big strong embrace. "Tavia. Don't cry. Don't cry, baby doll."

"You're . . . you're just so sweet," she sobbed.

He looked both shocked and affronted as he leaned back and held her face. His wide thumbs smoothed over her tear-streaked cheeks. "Hey, hey, hey," he argued softly. "Don't get all sentimental on me now. You're scaring me. Remember me? I'm Bolt. I'm the fucking prick who kissed Maria."

Tavia laughed. And she cried. And she buried her head in his shoulder.

∽∾

"Are you mad at me?" Tavia asked Bolt after she'd confessed her lie.

"Hell yes, I'm mad at you. You thought I was only interested in your money. I'm not that kind of guy. You should *know* I'm not that kind of guy. It was never the money," he growled.

Her lips twisted in regret. "I'm sorry, but what was I supposed to think?"

He stared at her. "Did it never occur to you that maybe it was just the sex?"

"*Oh,*" she said in a small voice. "Yes. No. Not really because . . . I reckoned you could get that anywhere."

He smiled.

Damn, he was an arrogant, smug bastard. "*Was* it just sex?"

"Nah," he drawled. "I told you before. I like you. I like everything you are. Ambitious, hardworking, successful. Your sense of humor. The way you don't take shit from anyone."

She took a small breath of relief. "So you're not mad at me for lying to you?"

He averted his eyes but she caught a glint of guilt in the floating gold of his gaze.

She frowned. "Bolt?"

His mouth twitched in a small, wry gesture of apology.

"Bolt?"

He kept his gaze carefully focused across the room. "Tavia," he said finally, "the fact is . . . that *I've* been less than honest with *you*."

"No," she said, her heart in her throat. "No. You're not going to tell me you're married. Please, Bolt. My emotions have been on a roller coaster since I rolled off the track this morning. *Please* don't tell me Mindy's your wife."

He turned his shocked expression on her. "Don't be ridiculous. It wasn't that big a lie."

"You lied to me?" she wailed. "You *lied* to me?"

He shrugged one shoulder, obviously reluctant to carry on.

"What did you lie to me about?" she asked in a hurt voice.

Again he shrugged. "Alex," he muttered.

"Alex!" she blurted, somehow relieved. "Alex . . . the gold dig-ger, Alex?"

Bolt tilted his head in a guilty, sideways nod. "I might have exaggerated a bit on that score."

"On what score?"

"Alex is nuts about you."

"What?"

"He's nuts about you. Couldn't you tell?"

"But you said . . ."

"That I've been known to play dirty when it comes to some-thing I want. If you'd listened more closely, you'd know that," he muttered defensively.

For several seconds she sat there with her mouth open. Then

she gave him a slow, incredulous smile. "You *did* say that, didn't you? Bolton Hardin, you are *such* a dick."

A slow grin curled the edges of his deliciously mean mouth. "I am."

"So you're . . . so you're not going to leave me over this?"

His eyebrows winged upward. "Are you kidding?" he drawled. "You're a millionaire. Only an idiot would walk out on a woman like that!"

She punched him—hard. He deserved it.

He grinned as he pushed out a sigh. "What's today? Friday? I'd better get back to Albuquerque and get back to work."

"Why don't you just get a job here?" The words were out of her mouth before she realized what she was saying. Jeez. She was throwing herself at the big lug nut.

Bolt gave her a blank look.

"You work in a garage," she argued hesitantly. "Santa Fe has plenty of garages. Why don't you just look for a job here in Santa Fe?"

Slowly, he began to laugh. "I'm sorry, Tavia," he told her, drawing her into a hug. "I haven't explained things very well. I think you're going to have to give me that ride to Albuquerque now."

❧

When Bolt offered to drive the sixty miles to Albuquerque, Tavia turned him down. What a chauvinist! Then she smiled most of the way. The big man was just itching to get behind the wheel of her Hummer. He just wouldn't admit it.

After traveling south for an hour on I-25, Bolt pointed at a green road sign up ahead. "Turn east on I-40. My house is on the edge of town."

Nodding as she ramped onto the eastbound highway, Tavia stared ahead at the mountains. "If you live on the edge of town, that's going to put you in the foothills."

"That's right," he admitted with a grin. "I live on the *steep* edge of town."

She smiled at him, unable to decide when she'd ever been so happy, unable to remember when she'd enjoyed herself so much. Every minute with Bolt was exhilaration and laughter, passion embellished with the unexpected.

Bolt was full of surprises.

Tavia was surprised when he directed her through an older neighborhood where the streets were lined with seventies architecture. The houses were . . . quaint and homey. His own home stood separate from his neighbors', at the back of a huge lot . . . with a very large garage. Tavia stared at the long, low building as she slid from the driver's seat of her Hummer. There were ten garage bay doors punctuating the long stretch of white wall.

Bolt circled the car on his way to meet her. "This is my garage," he told her a little proudly. He pulled her into the small door at the end of the long, white building. "I built it." He flipped on a light switch and Tavia gaped at over twenty vehicles. Vintage Thunderbirds. Antique Roadsters. Sleek little sports cars. "This is where I work. I rebuild vintage vehicles from the ground up. Engine. Chassis. Interior. The works! I try to get original parts whenever possible. Otherwise I have the components machined to old specs."

"Are . . . all of these vehicles yours?"

He shook his head. "Hell, no. I couldn't afford all these. The Chargers are mine, though. I like the old muscle cars." He pointed at a faded blue car that looked very much like the one she'd last seen stalled on the side of the road. "I had just picked up that '63 in Pueblo when I ran into you on the highway. I made a call and had it towed here the next morning." He continued with almost boyish enthusiasm. "Most of the other vehicles belong to my customers. I've worked for Jay and for Clive. Do you know Clive? He writes."

"No," she said faintly. "I haven't met him."

"I did a Triumph for Dalton too."

"Dalton?"

"Yeah. The artist who's doing your covers. My sister's married to him."

"Your sister's married to Dalton, the pastel artist?"

"That's right."

Her gaze narrowed on him suspiciously. "I thought you knew something about art. You had Alex and me convinced that you knew something about art."

Bolt smiled noncommittally.

"You don't know anything about art, do you?"

"Nothing outside of what Dalton's told me," he admitted without apology.

"*Bolt* Hardin," she told him, "you are the most arrogant, obnoxious, frustrating, exasperating, irritating man I have ever met in my lifetime!

A mischief-made smile stole across his rugged features as he pulled her into his arms. "Hey," he answered into her neck. "Get used to it."

Eight

Tavia stopped outside the front door of her home. As she sorted through the mail she'd picked up from the mailbox at the bottom of the driveway, her glance traveled to the new addition, finished now for several months. In the middle of the concrete drive sat Bolt's pastel blue Charger, fairly gleaming with bright chrome, fresh glass and seven coats of rich, new paint. She opened the front door and stepped into the entry as she frowned at the long, sloping handwriting on one of the envelopes. "Jeez," she complained as she frowned at the pale yellow envelope. "Can't the man take no for an answer?"

From his seat at the dining room table, Bolt smiled at her over the financial section of his newspaper. "Alex again?"

She nodded at her . . . guest, if that's what you'd call a guy who'd spent the last ninety-odd nights with her. Every morning he drove off for Albuquerque to work in his garage. Every night he was back.

The first few weeks he had left without mentioning when she'd see him again. She hadn't pressed him. She could tell from his expression that he'd thought it might be a few days. And if he was going to say "I'll call you sometime," then Tavia didn't want to hear it. When Bolt had chased Alex off, he hadn't been offering what Alex was offering. It was obvious the man treasured his independence. But every night he had returned. Sometimes in the early afternoon, sometimes not until after midnight.

When she'd answer the door, he'd be turned toward the south, his hands jammed deep in his pockets, his huge shoulders tense. He'd turn to face her. For those first few weeks, his eyes were wild, like an unsubdued addict or an animal caged. He almost acted as though he didn't want to be there or didn't think he was *supposed* to want to be there. As though the only reason he was there was because he just couldn't help himself.

She'd kiss him in the entry and they'd fight their way to the bedroom, tearing at each other's clothing, falling over one another in their haste and their need. The moment they'd bared the necessary places, Bolt would have her on his cock one way or another—jammed into the straight-backed chair, thrusting against the dining room table, crushed together and sweating against the wall in the hall. Then they'd fall into bed together and make long, slow love.

After the first few weeks, Bolt seemed to have grown resigned to the idea that he was going to be there every night.

Lately he seemed comfortable with it.

Lately he'd been spending the weekends with her as well, dragging himself away from his work. Tavia sighed, wondering how she could have ever thought the man lacked potential— and wondering when he was going to invite her to stay overnight at his home. She could almost wish her accountant *had* left her penniless. At least then she'd be living with Bolt . . . and maybe a little more certain of where their relationship was headed.

As she ripped the envelope open and scanned the letter's contents, Bolt muttered something that sounded an awful lot like "poor bastard."

"What was that?"

Bolt shrugged. "Alex. Give the poor guy a break."

Tavia smiled wryly then strolled across the room, humming. "That guilty conscience of yours giving you a hard time?"

"I don't have a conscience," he said blandly. "And if you don't shut up," he added in a pleasant growl, "I'll give *you* a hard time."

"Is that supposed to be a threat?"

He lifted a threatening eyebrow in answer.

"Because if it is, it's not a very good one."

He lowered his paper so he could give her his full scowl. "You'd like me to give you a hard time, wouldn't you?"

With a tarted-up smile, she waggled her eyebrows and gave him her best come-hither look.

He nodded to himself. "Slut," he muttered, rattling his paper and looking entirely too pleased with himself.

"Glad you think so." She dropped a kiss on his forehead. "Pig."

Lifting his gaze, he gave her a warm smile, which she returned fondly.

"You a millionaire yet?" she asked him, watching his eyes scan stock prices.

"Close," he answered. "Getting close. What about you? You finish that story yet? The one about the hitchhiker and the rich broad?"

"Uh-huh. *And* you'll be pleased to learn that I dedicated it to you."

He made a face of distaste. "Thanks."

"You don't want the dedication?"

He rolled his shoulders. "It's okay. Just as long as none of my friends find out that I have a girl's book dedicated to me."

"You have friends?" she asked with mock surprise. "More than one?"

"I have a few," he growled.

"Well, they're not likely to find out," she groused, "since I've never met any of them other than Mindy."

"You'll meet them at the wedding," he murmured idly from behind his newspaper.

"Wedding?" she echoed. "What wedding?"

Bolt lowered his newspaper and considered her thoughtfully. "That reminds me," he told her, "I have something for you."

"Big deal," she returned abruptly, refusing to be distracted. "You always have something for me. Tell me about the wedding."

"This is a little different," he informed her haughtily. "And *this* little something comes with a question."

"A question?" she asked, suddenly very keen to learn more.

He grinned as he stood then grabbed her wrist and dragged her down the hall, stopping outside the door to her office. The doorway was blocked by her huge, heavy desk which he'd dragged right up to the doorway's opening. She peered into the room, attempting to locate her computer, which she found tucked against the wall in the room's corner.

"Bolt!" She laughed. "What the hell?"

With his hands locked around her waist, Bolt lifted her to sit on the cleared desk.

She smiled at him curiously as he reached around to his back pocket and pulled out a small, square box wrapped in silver glitter. As he bounced it in one hand, Tavia watched it go up into the air then back down to meet his palm.

"Do you know what this is?" he asked her. When she shook her head he said, "Can you guess?"

Again she shook her head, her eyes wide as she followed the glittering box he tossed in the air.

The corners of his rugged, mean mouth kicked up into a satyr's grin. "It's going to be a bit of a shock—especially when you see the size of the diamond. I think maybe you should lie down before I give it to you."

"Diamond!"

His large hand slid behind her nape, cradling her head as he eased her to lie back on the desk. Then he tossed the box at her and she grappled with the shining silver cube, juggling it in midair as she felt Bolt lifting her legs at the knees. Finally she got the box under control.

Then she saw the shoes.

The black, ankle-strap shoes were nailed to the wall she faced, about two feet higher than the desk, one on either side of the open doorway. Her jaw dropped open as she clutched the box and Bolt guided her right foot into the shoe nailed against the wall.

"Now," he drawled. "Here's the question, Miss October." He paused for effect. "What are you going to do first? Are you going to open the box with the diamond engagement ring . . . or are you going to get your panties off?"

It was no contest. The ring could wait. Tavia dropped the box and reached for her panties.